Praise for Ally Blue's *Love's Evolution*

4 ½ Hearts! "...left me both teary eyed with emotion and breathless from heart pounding sex...My only wish was that there was more to read when I was done, but that always seems to happen when I read something that grabs me and squeezes in all the right places." ~ *Larissa Hayes, The Romance Studio*

4 ½ Kisses! "...sizzling, steaming, and nearly roasting. It starts out hot and it just turns up the heat page by page...The plot themes are realistic and a great framework to hold the incredibly volcanic sensuality. **Love's Evolution** delivers exactly what the title promises: the intertwining of two lives through better and worse, ups and downs, joy and turmoil. Get this one and enjoy!" ~ *Frost, Two Lips Reviews*

"...an enjoyable book, and the chemistry between Matt and Chris is red hot...Ms. Blue is a talented writer that has penned a non-traditional story for discriminating readers of erotic romance. I highly recommend LOVE'S EVOLUTION." ~ *Nickole Yarbrough, RRT Erotic*

Love's Evolution

Ally Blue

A Samhain Publishing, Ltd. publication.

Samhain Publishing, Ltd.
2932 Ross Clark Circle, #384
Dothan, AL 36301
www.samhainpublishing.com

Love's Evolution
Copyright © 2006 by Ally Blue
Print ISBN: 1-59998-283-8
Digital ISBN: 1-59998-134-3

Editing by Sasha Knight
Cover by Vanessa Hawthorne

This book is a work of fiction. The names, characters, places, and incidents are products of the writer's imagination or have been used fictitiously and are not to be construed as real. Any resemblance to persons, living or dead, actual events, locale or organizations is entirely coincidental.

All Rights Are Reserved. No part of this book may be used or reproduced in any manner whatsoever without written permission, except in the case of brief quotations embodied in critical articles and reviews.

First Samhain Publishing, Ltd. electronic publication: August 2006
First Samhain Publishing, Ltd. print publication: November 2006

Dedication

Dedicated to the city of Asheville, which provides me with a constant source of inspiration.

A House on Chestnut Street

Chapter One

Spring Break in Asheville, Chris Tucker reflected, was a mixed blessing. He loved the cool, sunny days, fragrant with flowers and bright with color. He loved the sense of vigor and excitement. He even loved the sudden explosion of people on streets that had been too bare during the winter.

What he didn't love was the extra traffic.

"Come on, come on," he muttered as the bumper-to-bumper traffic ground to a halt around him yet again. "Not today, please not today."

Chris was in a rotten mood. He'd overslept by almost an hour, making him late for his dental appointment. On the way from the dentist's office to the restaurant where he worked, he'd gotten a flat tire. The tire iron had left streaks of grease on his shirt and pants, forcing him to detour back to his apartment to change, and now he was running late for his cooking class. His students probably wouldn't mind, but Chris did. He hated being late.

By the time he parked his BMW in the restaurant's private parking lot, it was ten minutes past the time when the class should've started. Chris shoved his wallet into the pocket of his suit jacket, locked the car door and hurried down the sidewalk.

He'd only gotten half a block when a voice came from behind him. "Hey!"

Chris ignored it, hoping the person was talking to someone else. No such luck.

"Hey, suit guy!" the man bellowed.

Chris bit back the urge to yell. He turned, expecting to be confronted by a hand held out for money. What he saw was pair of enormous eyes, the same color as the spring sky, set in a face with high cheekbones and a delicately chiseled jaw. The man's short, spiked hair was dyed a vibrant purple, making his creamy pale skin glow. Letting his gaze drift downward in the sudden still silence, Chris took in the sleek, sculpted muscles under the snug green T-shirt, the faded jeans molded to slim hips and thighs.

He'd never in his life seen anyone so beautiful.

It took him a moment to realize the man was speaking to him. "I'm sorry, what was that?" Chris asked, blushing.

The man grinned, revealing a deep dimple in his right cheek. "Dude, you dropped your wallet." He stretched out his hand. Sure enough, Chris's wallet lay in his palm.

Chris took it without looking away from the stranger's face. Their fingers brushed, sending a shock up Chris's arm. "Thank you very much," he said. His voice sounded rough.

"No problem." The man held his gaze, wide eyes not at all shy. "So. You on your way to work?"

Chris cleared his throat. "Yes. Yes, I am."

"Where do you work?"

"The Falls. Just up the street." Chris gestured toward the restaurant. "I'm head chef."

"Whoa. Fancy." The stranger's smile widened, his gaze flicking down Chris's body. "Wanna cook breakfast for me sometime?"

Oh my God, a stunned little voice whispered in Chris's head. *He's coming on to me.*

Chris's mouth acted before his brain could recover. "Would you like to go out with me? We could go for drinks after work."

The wicked gleam in those huge blue eyes made Chris's knees weak. "Hell, yeah. I get off at ten, what about you?"

"Nine-thirty," Chris answered, feeling a bit surreal. "Where do you work? I'll come get you."

"Dragon's Den. I'm a tattoo artist. You know where the place is?"

"Yes." Chris smiled, knowing he looked as giddy as he felt and not caring. "See you at ten."

The man licked his lips. "Can't wait."

Chris tucked his wallet back in his pocket, more securely this time. He couldn't stop staring at the man's so-kissable mouth. "Well. Until then."

He'd already started to walk away when the man called him again. "Hey, suit guy!"

Chris turned, trying to act casual. "Yes?"

"What's your name?"

"Chris Tucker," Chris said, feeling foolish for not having thought of introductions himself. "What's yours?"

He got a wide, sinful smile. "Matt Gallagher. See you at ten, Chris."

Chris watched Matt turn and walk away. The thought of holding that gorgeous body, kissing those plump lips, set a fire inside him. It was all he could do to make his legs carry him to The Falls, where his class waited.

He'd nearly forgotten that he was late. He whistled as he strolled down the sidewalk, his bad mood gone like a stray thought.

● ● ●

Chris floated through the rest of the day in a state akin to shock. The encounter with Matt kept replaying in his mind. He couldn't believe Matt had been so interested, or that he himself had been so bold. It didn't seem quite real.

"Chris."

He jumped at the sound of his boss's voice beside him. "Yes, Laurie?"

"Do we need more shiitake mushrooms? Dave's going to the produce market to stock up for tomorrow, so I figured I'd check." Laurie McGhee, owner and manager of The Falls, grinned at him. "What's with you, anyway? You're on another planet today."

"It's nothing," Chris said, keeping his gaze fixed on the big pot of lobster bisque he was stirring. "I had a difficult morning, that's all."

"Mm-hm. That's why you've had that goofy grin plastered on your face all day. Right."

Chris glanced at Laurie. She had that smug look that meant she knew—or *thought* she knew—all about it. "I do not have a goofy grin. And yes, tell Dave to get the mushrooms. We barely have enough for tonight."

"Mushrooms, got it. And yeah you do." She leaned closer, her voice dropping low. "Hope you realize you're gonna have to dish the dirt tomorrow."

Chris held his head high and ignored the heat in his cheeks. "I'm sure I don't know what you mean."

"Fine, be that way. But I'll get it out of you." Laurie turned to leave. "Boss-Lady demands details."

Chris waited until she was out of sight to let himself smile. Laurie and most of the female staff invariably hovered around him after one of his rare dates, asking the most shockingly direct questions. *Did he kiss you? Is he good in bed? How big is he?* No detail was too small or too personal; they wanted to know it all. As long as he lived, he'd never understand the group mind women seemed to share when it came to dating.

A sudden thought struck Chris like a brick between the eyes. He stood blinking at the wall, the spoon still because he'd forgotten to stir.

"Oh my God," he said to the neat row of spices on the shelf. "I don't have any condoms."

After a moment, he shrugged and turned his attention back to the soup. *We'll just have to go to Matt's place.* The possibility that Matt wouldn't have condoms either never crossed his mind. Neither did the possibility of going home alone.

Chapter Two

At nine-thirty, Chris tossed his chef's jacket in the laundry hamper and headed into the bathroom to change back into his suit. When he emerged, Laurie was leaning against the wall outside, grinning.

"You lucky bastard," she said. "Where'd you find that one?"

Chris raised his eyebrows at her. "Pardon me?"

"That hot piece of tail you're going out with tonight. God, he's *gorgeous!*"

Warmth bloomed in Chris's groin. "He's here?"

"Mm-hm. Waiting for you at the bar. He swing both ways?"

"I don't know yet," Chris said, smoothing a hand through his short black hair. "Why?"

"Jasmine's making a play. Better go get him before she does."

Chris hurried into the restaurant and looked over at the bar. Sure enough, Jasmine, the bartender, was flirting with impressive determination. Matt was sitting so that Chris could only see the side of his face, but his body language said he didn't mind her flirting. He perched on the edge of a barstool, leaning both elbows on the bar, gesturing as he talked. Then he turned his head and caught sight of Chris, and Chris's uneasy feeling evaporated in the heat of Matt's gaze.

"Wow," Laurie breathed as Matt hopped off the barstool and came toward them. "Never mind. I don't think you have anything to worry about."

Chris wanted to agree, but he couldn't get his mouth to work. The way Matt looked at him promised all sorts of sinful pleasures.

"Hi, Chris," Matt said, walking up and standing close enough to make Chris's knees weak. "You don't mind me coming on over, do you? My last customer canceled."

Chris swallowed. "No, of course I don't mind. Matt, this is Laurie McGhee, she owns The Falls. Laurie, Matt Gallagher."

Matt smiled and shook Laurie's hand. "Nice to meet you, Laurie."

"You too, Matt."

"Cool place you got here." Matt turned his mega-watt grin to Chris. "I like the chef."

"Yes. Well. Are you ready to go, Matt?" Chris wished his voice wouldn't shake so much.

"Sure am." Matt laid a hand on Laurie's shoulder. "Laurie, I promise not to wear him out."

Laurie raised an amused eyebrow at Chris. "I like this one."

Chris felt his cheeks going pink under two teasing gazes. He started edging toward the door. "Good night, Laurie. I'll see you tomorrow."

"'Night, guys. Have fun." Laurie waved at them as they left.

Outside, Chris took a deep breath of cool night air, trying to calm his nerves. He hadn't been on a date in several months, and he had never been with anyone who attracted him as strongly as Matt did.

"So, Chris." Matt bumped his shoulder against Chris's. "Where'd you want to go?"

"Let's see." Chris thought for a minute. "How about The Alley Kat? It's just around the corner from here, and they have some excellent live music."

"Sounds great."

They strolled along in silence. Matt's arm brushed Chris's as they walked. When they reached the corner, Matt grabbed Chris's elbow and led him into the shadow of a nearby doorway. He was so close Chris could feel the heat of his skin.

"Matt? Is anything wrong?"

Matt stared at him with fiery eyes. "There's something I have to do."

Chris frowned. "What is it?"

Instead of answering, Matt slid a hand around the back of Chris's head and kissed him. Sheer surprise held Chris frozen for a second. Matt's tongue against his lips broke his paralysis. He wound his arms around Matt's waist and pulled him close, letting the kiss deepen.

By the time they broke apart, Chris was hard enough to pound nails. Matt was clearly just as aroused as Chris, his erection pressing against Chris's thigh through jeans and dress slacks. Chris felt drunk and dazed, his head swimming. *And it was just a kiss.*

"I want you," Matt whispered, grinding his crotch against Chris's leg. "Want you to fuck me so hard I won't be able to walk straight for a week."

Chris clutched Matt closer, partly from desire and partly to keep from falling over. He felt weak with need. "I want that too." He kissed Matt again, sucking his bottom lip. "Do you want to go to bed now?"

"Yes," Matt breathed. "But let's not."

Chris blinked. "No?"

Matt grinned at him. "You asked me out for drinks. I want drinks."

Chris laughed breathlessly as Matt took a step back, one hand sliding down his arm to wind their fingers together. "Very well. Drinks it is. Talking and getting to know each other before sex, right?"

"Yeah. That's okay, isn't it?" Matt's expression was anxious.

"Of course it is." Without thinking, Chris reached out and touched his fingertips to Matt's lips. Lips he now knew to be just as soft as they looked. "I'm not in the habit of sleeping with beautiful, young men I've just met, you know."

"Me neither." Matt tilted his head to one side, staring hard into Chris's eyes. "You think I'm beautiful?"

"Yes," Chris answered without hesitation. He pulled Matt to him again, one hand holding him by the back of the neck so their mouths were inches apart. "I have to tell you, Matt, I think getting into a more public place to talk is an excellent idea, because at this moment I want nothing more than to have you right here."

Matt let out a soft little whimper. "You don't beat around the bush, do you?"

"No point." Chris brushed his lips against Matt's, relishing the way Matt's breath hitched. "We want each other, and we both know that. Why pretend it isn't happening?"

"I like the way you think, Chris."

"I like the way you taste." Chris rolled his hips against Matt's, pushing their erections together. "I like the way you feel."

"Oh God." Breathing hard, Matt sagged against Chris's chest. "If we're gonna go to The Alley Kat, we better go right now before I come in my pants."

"I couldn't agree more." Chris pulled away with an effort. "Shall we go?"

"Yeah."

Matt smiled, sweet and sexy, and they stepped back onto the sidewalk with their fingers still intertwined. Walking down the block to The Alley Kat, Chris already missed the heat of Matt's body in his arms. But he knew he'd be holding Matt again later that night, and that was enough to keep him going.

• • •

After those scorching moments in the darkened doorway, Chris had expected to have a hard time restricting himself to talking with Matt. But once they sat at one of The Alley Kat's little corner tables, Chris with a glass of red wine and Matt with a bottle of Guinness, the time flew by. Matt was easy to talk to, listening with evident fascination to Chris's stories and readily sharing the details of his own life.

Their histories couldn't have been more different. Chris had lived in Asheville his entire life, except for the time spent in culinary school, whereas

Matt had moved from Montana only three years before. Chris had come from a background of poverty and put himself through school, working full time to pay his tuition and attending classes at night. Matt and his twin sisters, Shannon and Siobhan, had grown up with wealth and privilege. The girls were in their senior year in high school, Matt said, and had plans to attend college together at Oxford after graduation.

"They're both gonna study theoretical physics." Matt shook his head, idly stirring the whiskey and soda he'd ordered after his second Guinness. "They're crazy smart."

"Obviously." Chris took a sip of wine. "What a wonderful opportunity for them to study overseas. Your parents must be so proud."

Matt's eyes clouded. "We don't have any parents. My mom took off when I was eight. Dad died last year in a skiing accident."

"Oh, Matt. I'm so sorry." Chris laid his hand over Matt's. "Who looks after your sisters?"

"They're emancipated. Dad didn't have any family willing to take them in, and of course we don't know where our mother is. I was gonna move back home and take care of them, but they wouldn't let me. Said they could look after themselves just fine. Which is true. So we talked to Dad's lawyer, and we got them legally emancipated. They turn eighteen in a couple of months." Matt's lips quirked into a sad little smile. "I miss them, you know? And my dad."

"I'm sure. It must be difficult for you."

"Losing Dad was awful. It was just so sudden. One day he was there just like always, healthy as a horse, and the next thing we knew he was dead." Matt looked down at his drink. "Makes you think about stuff. 'Bout how fast everything can change."

"Yes, I imagine it would." Chris reached out and traced a finger down Matt's cheek, unable to resist the urge to touch him. "I've always been close to my parents. The thought of losing them is unbearable. How do you stand it?"

"Wasn't easy getting through those first few months. But I managed, and I'm okay now. You do what you have to, when it comes right down to it." Matt turned his head and kissed Chris's palm. "Tell me about your parents."

"My father's a manager at Dalton's Plumbing Supply. He started as a stock clerk when I was five and worked his way up. My mother's been disabled for years with rheumatoid arthritis, but she still manages to take care of the house and my father." Chris smiled with the memory of his childhood. They'd never had much other than love, but they'd had plenty of that. "I admire them both a great deal. They're good people. And they've always given me their unconditional love and support, even when I came out, which says a lot about them."

"It does, yeah. They sound great."

"They are."

"So where did you live growing up?"

"Washington Street. It's just off of Chestnut." Chris laughed. "I used to ride my bike up and down Chestnut Street, looking at all those big old houses and pretending I lived in one or the other of them."

Matt smirked at him. "Your folks should've known you were gay then."

"Very amusing. My mother would've said that you have a smart mouth." Chris caressed the corner of that enticing mouth with his thumb, and suddenly his need returned with a vengeance. "Matt, could we—"

"Okay, folks," the bartender shouted, cutting Chris off. "Last call! You got ten minutes to order 'em and drink 'em before closing."

Matt glanced at the bar, where most of the remaining patrons were gathering, then leaned over the table with a grin. "Wanna get out of here?"

"God, yes." Chris leaned toward Matt and they kissed. "Where do you live?"

Matt chuckled against Chris's mouth. "Going to my place, huh? That's cool."

"I don't have any condoms." Chris kissed Matt again, then drew back. "Let's go now. I need you."

"You just met me today."

"I know. But I feel like I'll die if I don't make love to you soon."

Matt's eyes burned. "Me too. It's crazy."

"I don't care."

"Neither do I." Matt jumped to his feet, sending his chair scraping across the wooden floor. "C'mon. My place isn't far, we can walk."

"All right." Chris took Matt's hand in his as he stood. "Lead the way."

Chapter Three

Matt's apartment was four blocks away, an airy studio above the coffee shop two doors down from Dragon's Den. High ceilings and tall, arched windows looked out over the city streets. There were two doors side by side in the wall opposite the entry. No doubt a bathroom and closet, Chris thought. The place was bare to the point of austerity. No pictures hung on the brick walls, no rugs covered the hardwood floor. A large drafting table stood in the corner beside the windows. On the other side of the room, a small television and an impressive stereo system huddled opposite a low, overstuffed sofa. The only other pieces of furniture were a queen-size bed and a small nightstand.

"Not exactly a packrat, are you?" Chris said, smiling.

"Naw. There's lots of CDs in the cabinet over there," Matt nodded toward the simple wooden hutch housing his stereo system, "but that's about all I collect."

"It's a lovely apartment. It has a very peaceful energy, doesn't it?"

"Mm-hm." Matt flipped the deadbolt, then walked up to Chris and pressed their bodies together. "Now shut up and fuck me."

Whatever Chris was going to say was forgotten when Matt fisted both hands in his hair and kissed him hard. Moaning, Chris opened his mouth wide, letting their tongues slide together. The breathless little noises Matt made drove him wild. He was more turned on than he could ever remember being in his life.

Matt took a step backward without breaking the kiss, tugging Chris with him. They stumbled toward the bed and fell across the mattress, already working each other's clothes off with fumbling fingers. Shirts went flying in a matter of seconds. Pants were a bit more difficult, since neither was willing to untangle themselves long enough to take them off properly. "Fucking fuck," Matt grumbled when he tried to squirm out of his jeans and they caught on the purple high-tops he'd forgotten to remove first. He twisted around with Chris still on top of him in an attempt to get at the laces.

Chris would've found Matt's frantic frustration endearing if they hadn't both been so desperate. As it was, he didn't think he could wait another second to be naked and buried balls-deep inside Matt's body. Without a word, he turned to help Matt untie his sneakers and pull them off along with his jeans. He took the opportunity to slip his own shoes and socks off before moving up to kiss Matt again.

"Thanks," Matt said, fingers already working on Chris's pants.

"You're welcome."

Chris wormed his pants off and kicked them aside. Matt pulled him down, hooking one bare leg around his back, and Chris thought he might spontaneously combust from the solid heat of Matt's erection against his.

Matt let out a soft cry when Chris shoved a hand between their bodies and grasped his cock. "Oh God! Chris, can't wait, please."

Chris probed the slit at the tip of Matt's cock with his thumb, making Matt writhe helplessly beneath him. "Lube?" he asked, nipping at Matt's upper lip.

"Drawer. Hurry."

Chris, being closer, opened the drawer of the bedside table. He fumbled around for a moment and found a small bottle of liquid lube and a box of condoms. Snatching the bottle and a condom, he sat up on his knees between Matt's open legs.

The world went still as Chris stared down into Matt's eyes. He felt as if he were standing on the edge of a cliff. As if his whole life was about to change forever. He didn't understand it, but it excited him.

"Chris," Matt moaned, spreading his legs wider. "I need it, please!"

Chris blinked, shaking off the odd sensation. He opened the bottle of lube and coated his fingers with it, then leaned down to kiss Matt. As Matt's mouth opened under his, Chris reached between Matt's thighs and slipped a finger inside him.

Matt gasped into the kiss, hands digging into Chris's back. "God yes, more…"

Chris added another finger, pressing deep and twisting to search for the sweet spot. He knew he'd found it when Matt cried out, arching off the mattress.

"Oh fuck," Matt groaned. "Jesus, yes, so fucking good…"

The way Matt's insides clutched his fingers made Chris desperate to have that same velvet grip around his prick. He pulled his fingers out of Matt's ass, groped for the condom packet, ripped it open, and sheathed himself as quickly as he could. One hand around his own erection and his weight balanced on the other, Chris guided himself to Matt's slick opening and slid inside.

Matt's legs came up to wind around Chris's waist. Chris held still, trying to get himself under control. It had been years since he'd wanted to pound anyone into the mattress the way he did now. After a moment, Matt squirmed in a way that said *move* clear as day. Chris began rocking his hips, pulling partway out and pushing slowly back in, and it was wonderful. He felt himself drowning in sensation, in the cloud-soft heat of Matt's body, in the way Matt moved under him, the little pleasure noises Matt made, the smell of his arousal. Those huge sapphire eyes stayed open the whole time, locked onto Chris's.

Chris found himself watching Matt's face, just as Matt watched his. Matt's uninhibited responsiveness fascinated him. He'd had lovers who were quiet in their pleasure, lovers whose moans smacked of practiced theatrics, and a few who never let themselves go enough to respond at all. But he'd never had anyone lay themselves bare the way Matt was doing, eyes wide open and unshuttered, letting Chris see him at his most vulnerable. It excited Chris to have Matt so completely open to him, and to be able to open himself in turn without hesitation.

Chris realized, in a sudden flash of revelation, that he'd been searching for this level of intimacy his whole adult life. The knowledge that he'd found it was enough to send him to the edge. The pleasure spiraled up his spine, tighter and tighter, until he was gasping with it, shaking all over.

"Matt," he grunted. "Gonna come."

Matt's eyes went dark, pupils dilated. "Yeah. Almost there."

Shifting his weight to his left arm, Chris took Matt's cock in his right hand and started stroking fast, his grip almost punishingly tight. Matt thrashed underneath him, letting out one sharp little cry after another, legs drawing up to his chest. Chris slammed into him, holding nothing back.

"Oh, oh God, oh *God* yes," Matt moaned, his dick swelling in Chris's hand. "Fuck, yes, I'm... Oh!"

Chris stared, entranced, as Matt's orgasm hit him, bowing his back and making his ass clench around Chris's cock. Semen shot hot and slick over Chris's hand, spattering Matt's chest and belly. Those amazing eyes stayed open. Watching Matt lose himself tipped the balance and Chris came with a shudder, Matt's name on his lips.

All of Chris's strength ran out of him along with his come, and he collapsed onto Matt's chest. Pulling carefully out of Matt's ass, Chris removed the condom, tied it off, and tossed it onto the floor. Matt lay panting beneath him, one leg slung across his back.

"Wow," Matt said with a dazed grin. "You really know how to fuck a guy into next week."

Chris laughed. "Thank you. It's easy when the man you're with is so responsive."

"Mm." Matt stretched, shifting their sweaty, come-sticky fronts together in the most delightful way. His arms went around Chris, one hand playing with his hair. "You know what's funny?"

"Hopefully nothing. I'd much rather be arousing than amusing in bed." Chris tugged at the silver ring through Matt's left nipple. He hadn't noticed it before. "You have a nipple ring."

"Really?" Matt pushed up on one elbow, forcing Chris to sit up or risk being shoved onto the floor. Matt looked down at his own chest in mock surprise. "How'd that happen?"

Chris grinned and tugged harder on the little ring. He liked the way it made Matt's eyes haze over. "You were about to tell me what's funny."

"Oh yeah." Matt rolled onto his side and stared at Chris with a serious expression. "I know why you had that look on your face before."

"What look?" Chris asked, though he thought he knew.

"Like what we were about to do was more than just fucking. Like it was gonna change things, you know?" Matt traced the line of Chris's jaw with his fingers. "That was way more than a great fuck just now. We had a connection."

"Yes. I felt that too." Chris took Matt's hand, kissing his fingers one by one. His chest felt tight, his stomach fluttering. "I don't know what to make of it, Matt. It scares me, to be honest."

"Me too. But I like it." Matt moved closer, draping a leg over Chris's hips. "I know we just met each other, and we don't know if this'll work or not, but I want to try. This is too good to let it drop."

"I agree. Maybe we're moving too fast, but I don't care. I like you a great deal, and I think we both need to see where this could go." Chris pulled Matt's face to his and kissed him, soft and slow. "And it certainly doesn't hurt that we're so attracted to each other."

Matt chuckled, one hand warm on Chris's cheek. "I'd sure as hell keep you naked in bed forever if I could. You make me unbelievably horny."

Chris grinned. "Do you mean to say that you're not always like this?"

"Nope. Usually when I spread for some guy I just met, he only gets me once. You? I'm bending over for 'til you can't get it up any more."

Chris's mouth fell open in astonishment. Then he noticed the teasing glint in Matt's eyes, and burst out laughing. "Has anyone ever told you that you have a filthy mouth?"

"It can do filthy things," Matt shot back, leering. "Want me to show you?"

"Yes, indeed." Chris ran a hand down Matt's hip, curling his fingers behind the firm thigh. "It's been years since I felt this way."

"What way?" Matt's cheeks flushed pink as Chris's hand slid higher, reaching around to dip into his loosened hole.

"Insatiable," Chris whispered, his lips inches from Matt's. "Like I can never get enough of you."

"Oh." Matt whimpered as Chris probed deeper. "Chris…"

Chris ran his tongue across Matt's plump lower lip. "You were saying something about bending over for me?"

"Fuck yeah," Matt growled. His hips were moving, little barely there pulses that created a wonderful friction between Matt's half-hard cock and Chris's softer one. "Want you to fuck me from behind this time."

The mental picture went a long way toward renewing Chris's erection. Matt noticed, if the increasingly determined roll of his hips was anything to go by. Chris stared at Matt's mouth, thinking of what he had said and picturing the possibilities in his mind.

"Matt?"

"Hm?"

"Do you still want to show me the filthy things," Chris interrupted himself to bite Matt's shoulder, "that your mouth can do?"

"Mm. Yeah." Matt tilted his head back so Chris could kiss his neck. "Wanna suck your cock."

"So what you're saying," Chris said, lips brushing the pulse in Matt's throat, "is that you want to do filthy things to my cock?"

A tremor ran through Matt's body when Chris added a third finger beside the two already in his ass and started pumping hard. "Oh. Fuck, you're driving me crazy here."

"That's the idea." Chris spread his fingers, tearing a sharp cry from Matt's throat, then abruptly pulled out. He rolled onto his back and opened his legs. "Suck me."

Matt stared at him with unfocused eyes for a second before scrambling between Chris's thighs and swallowing him whole.

"Oh God," Chris sighed as the tip of his cock hit the back of Matt's throat. "Yes, Matt, so good…"

Matt hummed and sucked harder, one hand playing with Chris's balls and the other tracing random patterns on the inside of his thigh. Chris carded his fingers through Matt's hair, letting Matt set the pace. His arousal felt lazy and languorous this time, all urgency consumed in the intensity of their first union. He knew he could last a good long while, and he intended to do just that.

Chris soon discovered that Matt's stamina was a match for his own. Matt kept up a slow, steady rhythm, sucking and licking at the head of Chris's prick, tonguing the slit then deep-throating him. His hands were never still. They roamed Chris's body as far as they could reach, stroking his thighs, pinching his nipples, fondling his balls. Chris was reduced to a bundle of raw nerves, holding Matt's head still and fucking his mouth with increasing fervor. Matt took it with apparent gusto. His moans vibrated deliciously around Chris's cock and up his spine.

When he couldn't take another minute without coming, Chris pushed Matt's head away. "Stop," he panted.

Matt blinked up at him, looking dazed. "Huh? What's wrong?"

Chris smiled. Matt's cheeks were flushed, his lips red and swollen. "You look incredibly sexy right now," Chris said, caressing his cheek.

Matt gave him a loopy grin. "So do you. But why'd you stop me? I was totally getting off on that."

"I was close to coming."

"So? That would've been fine with me."

Chris sat up and kissed the end of Matt's nose. "You'd swallow on the first date?"

Matt arched an eyebrow at him. "Who said anything about swallowing?"

"I see." Chris laughed.

Matt sat back on his heels, still smiling. "So if I can't suck you dry, what do you want?"

Chris leaned forward and captured Matt's mouth in a passionate kiss. "Bend over for me, Matt. I'd like to show you the filthy things *my* mouth can do."

Matt's eyes went dark with lust. Without another word, he fell onto hands and knees and crawled to the middle of the bed. He rested his elbows on the mattress and planted his knees wide apart. Turning his head, he gave Chris a *come fuck me* look over his shoulder. The sight of him like that, delectable ass in the air and cock swinging between his legs, made Chris's skin ache.

Chris scooted forward and ran both palms up the backs of Matt's thighs, over the swell of his buttocks, and along the graceful curve of his smoothly muscled back. "Your body is so beautiful, Matt."

Matt licked his lips. He seemed about to say something, then Chris inserted two fingers into him. Chris saw the exact moment at which Matt lost the power of speech. Crooking his fingers, Chris found the sweet spot and pressed. Matt moaned, laying his chest flat on the mattress as if to open himself even more.

Chris found the sight unbearably exciting. He removed his fingers and replaced them with his tongue.

Matt keened, clenched fists bunching the sheets. "Oh, oh oh! Yeah, fuck!"

Chris expressed his agreement with a loud moan and a deep press of his tongue. Matt tasted sharp and rich, his natural flavor enhanced by a hint of clean sweat. It heightened Chris's arousal to a fever pitch. He loved the pulsing heat around his tongue, the solid weight of Matt's thick cock in his hand, the scent of sex perfuming the air. It wasn't as long as he would've liked before the need to fuck became too insistent to ignore.

Matt whimpered in protest when Chris stopped. "No, no don't, don't stop!" He twisted his upper body around to give Chris a wild, pleading stare.

"Sorry," Chris panted, "but I need to fuck you again."

Matt's eyes went hazy. "Do it."

Reaching for the drawer, Chris pulled another condom out, then spent a frantic couple of minutes searching for the little bottle of lube in the tangled sheets. By the time he found it, Matt had three fingers buried in his own ass.

"Hurry," Matt whispered. "Need you."

"God, Matt..."

Chris got the condom on and slicked himself without looking, unable to tear his gaze from Matt's wanton display. Batting Matt's hand away, he shoved his cock into Matt's open hole.

"Oh, oh God." Chris draped himself across Matt's back, hips flush with Matt's ass and his weight on his hands. He kissed Matt's neck, tongue flicking out to catch a drop of sweat. "You feel amazing."

Matt pushed up onto his hands and rubbed his cheek against Chris's, stubble rasping. "Feels good, Chris. So full."

Chris pressed a soft kiss to Matt's cheek, then began to move. Slow and gentle at first, his rhythm built gradually until every thrust rocked Matt's body forward and made him cry out. Chris peeled himself off of Matt's back, got a firm grip on his slender hips, and fucked him with short, quick strokes until the pressure inside him reached the critical point and Chris came with a hoarse cry. He held still for a minute, fully seated in Matt's body, letting the waves of pleasure roll through him. Only when they began to recede did he pull his softening cock out of Matt's ass and take the condom off.

Matt rolled onto his back, legs spread and one fist pumping his cock hard. He licked his lips. "Chris, please, I'm so close..."

Chris would've loved nothing better than to spend hours teasing Matt's cock with his mouth, taking him on a long, slow ride to an earth-shattering release. *Maybe later,* he thought, smiling. Clearly Matt wouldn't last that long right now. Chris bent and slid Matt's prick between his lips, relaxing his throat to take him in, two fingers inside him to stroke his gland.

It didn't take long. Matt was utterly outside himself at that point, babbling incoherently, his body in constant motion. Chris had to hold him down with an arm across his hips in order to keep sucking him. After a few minutes, Matt went still, gasped, and came, sobbing Chris's name. Chris swallowed without considering whether or not he should.

Letting Matt's cock slip out of his mouth, Chris laid his head on Matt's thigh. He kept his fingers inside Matt's ass, reluctant to lose that connection. He thought he might never get enough of that velvet-soft, living heat.

They lay for a while in a silence that wasn't at all uncomfortable. Eventually, Matt stirred, his thigh shifting under Chris's cheek. "Come up here, huh? My leg's going to sleep."

Chris happily complied. Matt turned onto his side and they lay chest to chest, arms and legs wound together, smiling at each other. Chris wondered if he looked as dazed and sated as Matt did.

"You swallowed," Matt said, eyes sparkling.

"Mm-hm."

"On the first date."

"So it would seem."

Matt chuckled, pulled Chris closer, and kissed him. "Slut."

"Look who's talking."

"Yep." Matt grinned. "I think you like me slutty."

"Perhaps." Chris laid a hand on Matt's cheek, thumb caressing his swollen mouth. "Whatever you want to call it, I certainly like how uninhibited you are."

Matt's expression turned serious. "I'm not usually like this. Not so soon, anyhow. You just make me feel like I can do what I want, you know? Like I can be how I really am inside and that it's safe. Does that make sense?"

"Perfect sense." Chris pressed his forehead to Matt's, holding him with an arm around his neck. "I'm glad you feel that way, because I feel the same."

"Yeah? Cool." Matt stared at Chris with a combination of determination and shy sincerity. "Chris? Will you stay?"

Chris smiled. "I'd like that."

They kissed again, and this time, it didn't end for a long, long while. Chris held Matt close and wondered just what, exactly, he'd gotten himself into.

• • •

Chris was late for work again. He rushed into The Falls at three-thirty, half an hour after he should've been there, and met Laurie's questioning look with a wide smile.

"Hello, Laurie." Chris clapped her on the shoulder. "You look lovely today."

Laurie smirked at him. "Somebody got lucky last night, huh?"

"Define lucky," Chris shot back, grinning.

"You know, lucky." Laurie leaned close as Chris took off his suit jacket and hung it on the hook beside the door. "As in had lots of hot monkey sex."

"And what," Chris said, taking a clean chef's coat from the tiny linen closet, "makes you think that Matt and I had sex?"

"You're wearing the same suit as yesterday." Laurie licked her thumb and swiped at the corner of Chris's mouth, reminding him rather disturbingly of his mother. "Plus you've got come on your face."

Chris managed to hang onto his dignity in spite of his burning cheeks and Laurie's teasing smile. "Thank you for pointing that out. Now if you'll excuse me, I'll just go wash my face."

Chris started to walk out of the kitchen. Laurie's hand on his arm stopped him. "Chris? I know I kid you a lot, but I hope you know how much I care about you."

Chris smiled. "I do, Laurie. Thank you."

Laurie squeezed his arm and turned back to her work. Chris headed into the bathroom. How he'd ended up with semen still on his face, he had no idea. Probably from kissing Matt after he'd sucked Chris off, kneeling on the bathmat at Chris's feet following a perfunctory shower. Chris hadn't opened his eyes until two forty-five that afternoon and hadn't been able to resist waking Matt up with a blowjob. Maybe he wouldn't have been late if he'd forgone either the fellatio or the shower, but he didn't have it in him to do without either.

Standing at the sink and swabbing the traces of come off his chin, his thoughts turned to the potentially thorny question of what it was he'd begun to feel for Matt.

He'd never known anyone who stimulated both his body and his mind quite the way Matt did. They'd spent hours alternately talking and making love, until they'd fallen asleep wound in each other's arms just as the eastern sky started to lighten. Sex between them was amazing, so intense it was a little frightening. But the thing that truly scared Chris was how much he liked Matt even when they weren't fucking.

Most of Chris's relationships up to that point had ultimately failed, Chris believed, because of a lack of balance. Great sex or great conversation, but never both. In Matt, he'd found for the first time someone who seemed to match him perfectly. Who could be a partner in every sense of the word. That terrified him and excited him.

"It's still early," Chris told his reflection, which looked appallingly smug and satisfied. "You don't know what might happen."

Which was true. He *didn't* know what might happen. Neither of them did. Philosophical or religious differences could emerge that were insurmountable. Kinks or secret fantasies might come up that would build a wall between them in bed, destroying the sense of absolute sexual freedom they'd shared the night before. They'd barely known each other for a day. They were still learning about one another.

Chris knew all of that and accepted it. But he'd learned long ago to trust his instincts and to trust his heart. And his entire being sang to him that Matt could be The One. All he had to do now was wait and see.

Grinning at his uncharacteristically rumpled and twinkle-eyed self in the mirror, Chris straightened his coat and left the bathroom.

• • •

Chris smiled and hummed his way through the afternoon and evening, expertly dodging all the questions about his date with Matt. In the absence of any hard data, wild rumors began to spring up, which Chris pretended not to hear. By the time the restaurant closed, Chris was amused to discover he and Matt had apparently driven to Massachusetts and gotten married.

"Awfully long drive to Massachusetts, Chris." Simon, the head waiter, arched a pale eyebrow at the group of waitstaff talking with their heads together as they counted their tips. "You must've broken a few laws to make it there and back."

Chris laughed. "I take it you heard about my wedding, then?"

"Yes." Simon grinned. "Does that mean I have to tell my wife's brother that you're off the market? He'll be devastated."

"Hm, yes. I *am* sorry to break the poor man's heart, but you know the vows are sacred."

Simon's face went dead white. "You didn't really. Did you?"

"Good lord, no." Chris smiled at Simon's obvious relief. "But I like Matt very much, and I believe he feels the same about me. I have a good feeling about this."

Simon regarded him thoughtfully. "You look happy. That has to be a good thing."

"It could be," Chris said as Simon clapped him on the back and headed out into the restaurant. "I think it could be."

Chapter Four

Matt's fingers flexed around the iron bar on the headboard of Chris's bed. The muscles in his back rippled. "Harder," he panted.

"You like that, don't you?" Chris gave a sharp thrust that made Matt arch and moan.

"Fucking love it." Matt pushed back against him. "C'mon, pound my ass hard, I can take it. Please, Chris…"

Chris smiled, holding on to his slow, lazy rhythm. He caressed the base of Matt's spine with the hand not holding his hip. After two months of almost daily sex, he knew exactly how much Matt could take, and it was a lot. He simply couldn't resist teasing Matt. He loved the way Matt begged when he was desperate to be fucked, pale skin glowing with sweat, blue eyes wild.

"God, Chris, *please!* Fuck me like you mean it!"

As always, the raw need in Matt's voice did it for Chris. He let himself go, slamming into Matt as hard as he could. Matt came first, the rhythmic undulation of his insides bringing Chris's release soon after. It always amazed Chris how Matt could come so easily just from being fucked.

Matt collapsed onto his side as soon as Chris slid out of him. Chris pulled the condom off, tossed it in the trash can, and wrapped his body around Matt's.

"Mmmmm," Matt hummed. "Damn, you're good."

Chris laughed and kissed the back of Matt's neck. "And you're easy."

"Hey, gotta go with what you feel, man."

"Meaning?"

Matt turned and gave him a lazy grin. "Meaning you make me feel horny as fuck and I like it."

"The feeling is, I assure you, entirely mutual."

Matt wriggled deeper into Chris's embrace, pressing his damp backside against Chris's groin. "Know what's even better?"

"What?"

"When we're like this."

"Like what?" Chris reached between Matt's legs to cup his balls. "Naked?"

Matt laughed. "Naked's great, yeah. But what I meant was, I like when you hold me like this after we fuck." Matt's voice dropped to a near whisper. "I can feel you all around me. It's the best thing."

Chris's chest went tight. He buried his face in the curve of Matt's neck and closed his eyes, breathing in Matt's clean, masculine scent. "I like it too, Matt."

"Wanna go out tonight?" Matt took Chris's hand and laced their fingers together. "We could check out that new place on Haywood."

"I'd love to."

"Cool."

They fell into a comfortable silence. Chris knew Matt had gone to sleep when his breathing became slow and even. Chris lay awake, holding Matt close and wondering when he'd fallen so hard.

• • •

They had their first real fight three days later.

"I just don't get it, Chris," Matt said as he paced the floor of his apartment. "What, are you ashamed of me? Is it how I look?"

"Of course I'm not ashamed of you," Chris insisted. "It's simply that...I'd just rather not deal with my family tonight. They always grill me within an inch of my life, and I'm not in the mood for that. I'd rather you and I spent time alone."

"Uh-huh. Sure." Matt came to a stop, arms crossed and eyes blazing, in front of the sofa where Chris sat. "Just admit it. You don't want your family to know you're seeing a freak like me."

Chris's parents had invited them both over for dinner and Chris had turned them down. When Matt asked why, Chris had found that he couldn't explain. Introducing Matt to his parents could be the first step down a more permanent road. To take that step without knowing how Matt felt seemed like tempting fate.

Before they took their relationship any further, Chris had to know whether Matt loved him too. And he wasn't sure he was ready to find out.

Chris stood and laid a cautious hand on Matt's arm. "Matt, you're not a freak, and I want my parents to meet you. Just...not tonight."

"Why? I don't believe it's just not wanting to deal with their questions and shit. There's something you're not telling me." Matt's expression radiated anger, but there was no hiding the hurt in his eyes.

Taking Matt in his arms, Chris held him until the stiffness melted out of his body and he relaxed against Chris's chest. When Matt's arms slipped in a loose circle around Chris's waist, he knew they would be okay.

Chris kissed Matt's hair. "I'm sorry."

"Didn't mean to start a fight," Matt said mournfully. "I just want to understand."

"I know. And I know that I haven't given you the explanation you wanted. Be patient with me, okay? Give me some time."

Matt nodded against Chris's neck. "What about you make me dinner at your place tonight? To make it up to me."

Chris laughed. "How could I possibly resist that invitation? It's a date."

"Good."

Matt raised his face, lips parted, and Chris kissed him. It felt so right, so perfectly natural. *I can't lose this,* Chris thought with an edge of desperation. What knotted his guts with dread was he had no idea if telling Matt the truth would bind them together or push them apart. But he couldn't wait forever to find out.

As desire rose sweet and scorching between them and Matt pulled him to the bed, Chris made up his mind. For better or worse, his confession would change everything, but he had to do it. He had to know.

Tonight, Chris vowed. *I'll tell him tonight.*

• • •

Matt leaned back in his chair and patted his stomach. "God, I'm stuffed. That was awesome, Chris."

"Thank you very much." Chris grinned as he stood to clear the table. "I thought you might enjoy it. Blackened fish seemed like your style to me."

"Smart man."

"I try."

Matt snagged the waistband of Chris's pants as he passed. "Kiss me, Chef Tucker."

Laughing, Chris bent and planted a quick kiss on Matt's upturned face at the corner of his mouth. "Would you like dessert?"

"Hell yeah, I would. But not food." Matt hopped to his feet and followed Chris into the tiny kitchen. "And what the fuck kind of kiss was that?"

"The kind where my hands are full of dirty dishes." Chris deposited said dishes in the sink, turned, and put his arms around Matt's waist. "Now what were you saying about dessert? I made a chocolate mousse."

Matt laughed, pressing his body against Chris's. "No plain old pudding for you."

"No indeed."

"Can I fingerpaint with it?"

"Only if you're talking about the sort of fingerpainting I think you are."

"You know it." Matt's face broke into a wide, thoroughly evil grin. "I love me some chocolate cock."

Chris chuckled. "You," he said, kissing the dimple in Matt's right cheek, "have a filthy mind."

"You like it." Matt leaned forward and licked behind Chris's ear, lingering over the spot that always made Chris shiver with pleasure. "I bet the reason you keep seeing me is the dirty sex."

Chris's mouth went dry. His heart was racing suddenly, as he remembered the promise he'd made to himself earlier that day. *It's time*, he thought, with something like panic.

Chris cleared his throat. "Matt—"

He didn't get any further than that. Matt pushed him away and stepped back, wrapping his arms around himself. "Don't say it."

Chris stared at him. Those huge blue eyes sparkled with unshed tears. "Matt, what's wrong?"

For a minute, Matt stood still and silent, staring at the floor. When he raised his gaze to meet Chris's, Chris thought the fear and hurt there might break his heart.

"Look, Chris, I know we fuck a lot, right, and it's good. *Really* fucking amazing, actually. But I..." Matt bit his trembling lip and looked away. "I don't want it to be just that. If sex is really the only reason you want me, then I don't...I don't want it."

Hope blossomed in Chris's chest. He stepped forward, reached out and laid a hand on Matt's cheek. "That's not the only reason I want to be with you, Matt."

Matt pinned him with a penetrating stare. "You mean it?"

"Yes." Chris took Matt's hand, winding their fingers together. "Do you still want to know the real reason why I didn't want to go to my parents' house tonight?"

Matt nodded.

Chris drew a deep breath. "It's because I didn't want to take that step until I knew whether or not you felt for me the way I feel for you."

Understanding dawned in Matt's eyes. "You love me?"

"Yes, I do. I have for a while now."

Matt threw both arms around Chris's neck. "Fuck, I was so scared."

Chris held him tight, cheek pressed to his hair. "May I assume that my feelings are reciprocated, then?"

"If that means do I love you too, then yeah." Matt pulled back enough to look into Chris's eyes. The sunny smile that made Chris's breath catch shone on Matt's face. "So now I can meet your folks, right?"

Chris laughed. "Most definitely. I'll call them tomorrow and set up a dinner date."

"Cool." Matt snuggled back into Chris's embrace, head tucked under his chin. "I'm s'posed to call Shannon and Siobhan tomorrow night. I'm gonna tell 'em, okay?"

"Of course. I hope I'll be able to meet them soon."

"You will. They're coming out to visit in a couple of weeks, didn't I tell you?"

"It must have slipped your mind."

"Maybe I was scared of the same thing as you."

"Quite probably, I'd say. The subconscious mind can have a powerful effect on the choices we make."

Matt raised his head and gave Chris a teasing grin. "Does it ever worry you that you sound like a talking dictionary?"

"Never." Chris kissed the end of Matt's nose. "Let's go to bed now."

"But I'm not tired." Matt blinked innocently at him.

"You will be when I get finished with you." Chris smacked Matt's ass and gave him a gentle push in the direction of the bedroom. "Go get undressed. I'll be along in a moment."

"With the chocolate mousse?"

"Oh yes."

"Cool." Matt started to walk away, then stopped and turned around again. His eyes sparkled with joy. "I'm so happy, Chris."

Chris spoke with an effort around the sudden lump in his throat. "Me too, love."

Matt smiled at him, whirled around and took off toward the bedroom, already shedding his clothes. Chris joined him after fetching the dessert and a can of whipped cream from the refrigerator.

It was months before Chris stopped getting an erection every time he made chocolate mousse.

Chapter Five

"Okay," Matt said, setting a large box down on the floor. "That's the last of it."

"Wonderful." Chris got up off the floor, where he'd been sorting through several boxes of books, and kissed Matt's cheek. "What's in this one?"

"Uh. Let's see." Matt frowned, brow furrowing in thought. "Oh okay, I remember now. Sheets and stuff."

"Excellent." Chris pulled Matt close and nuzzled at the curve of his neck. "Shall we take them upstairs and break them in?"

"Mmmmm." Matt arched his neck, practically purring. "I like the way you think."

Forcing himself away from Matt with some difficulty, Chris hefted the box Matt had just carried in. He swept an arm in the direction of the stairs. "Shall we?"

"Oh, yes, let's," Matt answered in a cringeworthy fake British accent. He started up the stairs, putting an extra sway in his walk.

Chris followed him, eyes glued to that sweet ass. In the bedroom, Chris dropped the box on the floor and spent a few wonderful minutes kissing Matt quite thoroughly. By the time the kiss ended, Chris was harder than the pine floor under his feet, and he knew Matt was too.

"Hey, Chris?"

"Yes?" Chris nudged Matt's arms up so he could pull his T-shirt off.

Matt raised his arms. "It's cool, huh? Having our own house, I mean."

"It certainly is." Chris tugged Matt's nipple ring, grinning at the lustful moan that caused. "I'm so happy you found this place, love."

Matt smiled while he unbuttoned Chris's shirt. "Me too."

They'd started talking about moving in together almost as soon as they admitted their feelings for each other. They both felt like it was meant to happen, that what they had would be permanent. Matt had found the Victorian cottage on Chestnut Street by accident soon thereafter, riding past the place on his bicycle just as the owners were putting the For Sale sign in the yard. He'd brought Chris by the next day. After being given an impromptu tour by the owner, they'd known right away that it was their new home. They'd made an offer a couple of days later, and now, three weeks after the day Matt had first spotted it, they were moving in.

Three months from their first meeting to moving into a house they'd bought together. To outside eyes, Chris knew it would seem too hasty, that they'd not given it enough thought. But they both knew the truth of it. As Matt had said when Chris's mother expressed that very doubt, *when it's right, it's right.*

"Hey." Matt gave Chris a hard pop on the butt. "You're zoning out, stop it."

Chris laughed. "Sorry. I was just thinking about the house. How buying this place seems to be a metaphor of sorts for our entire relationship."

Matt gave him a stern look. "There you go again. What?"

"Consider how we came to be standing here, about to make love in the master bedroom of our new home for the first time." Chris wormed a hand between their bodies to undo Matt's cargo shorts. "We found this house by accident. We fell in love with it right away. And we made it official in record time. Sound familiar?"

"Uh-huh," Matt breathed. The glazed look in his eyes said that what Chris's hand was doing was much more interesting than what he was saying. "But Chris?"

"Yes, my darling?"

"How the hell do I make you shut up and fuck me already?"

Chuckling, Chris lifted Matt's chin and kissed him. "Get naked and get on that bed."

"Fuck, yeah." Matt toed his sneakers off, shimmied out of his shorts, and threw himself face down on the bed. "C'mon, Chris!"

Chris watched with mingled lust and amusement as Matt humped the bare mattress, moaning like a porn star. He had, Chris thought fondly, not an ounce of shame or self-consciousness. That openness spilled over into every aspect of Matt's personality. It was one of the things about him that Chris had fallen in love with.

"Chris, *please!*" Matt begged. "Need you, baby, hurry."

Matt lifted his hips off the bed, reached back and spread himself open, and that was all Chris could take. He shed the rest of his clothes and knelt behind Matt, between his open legs.

"We forgot to put the sheets on," Chris said, leaning down to plant a kiss between Matt's shoulder blades.

"Too late now," Matt breathed as Chris slid a saliva-slick finger inside him. "God, yeah, more."

Chris added a second finger and began to work them in and out. "We haven't any lube."

"Do too. Oh *fuck* do that again…"

Chris obligingly twisted his fingers. "Where?"

"Right there, babe, that's it."

"No." Chris chuckled. "Where's the lube?"

"Oh. Um. Drawer." Matt spread his thighs wider, chest pressed to the mattress. "God, please, can't wait."

Chris removed his fingers from Matt's loosening hole and reached for the bedside table. Sure enough, the bottle of self-warming lube Matt favored lay in the otherwise empty drawer. Chris shook his head.

"Everything else we own is still in boxes," Chris said as he opened the bottle and coated his erection with the slippery liquid, "yet the lube is already where it belongs. Amazing."

"Priorities, babe." Matt wriggled his bare ass invitingly. "In. Now."

Chris laughed out loud for sheer joy as he positioned the head of his prick at Matt's entrance, pushing just the tip inside. "I love that you want me this badly."

Matt whimpered and pressed back against him in answer. Chris slid smoothly in, and they both sighed with the pleasure of it.

With that, they slipped into the age-old language of sex, where words were unnecessary. Their mutual desire was communicated in grunts and moans, in harsh panting breaths, in skin sliding against sweat-damp skin. The wet smack of bodies pounding together hard and fast, sharp cries of release. Hearts beating in tandem as they lay in each other's arms, sharing sweet languid kisses.

Matt snuggled against Chris's side afterward, head pillowed on Chris's chest, an arm tucked around his middle and a leg thrown across his thighs. "Mmmm. This is nice."

"It is." Chris kissed Matt's forehead, tracing a finger around the bar of sunlight gilding Matt's shoulder. "Welcome home, sweetheart. I love you."

Matt's arm tightened around Chris's waist. "I love you too, babe. And I love having a home with you."

Chris shifted a little to meet Matt's lips with his. When they broke apart, Matt settled back into Chris's embrace with a contented sigh. He was asleep within minutes, snuffling softly against Chris's neck. Lying there on the bare mattress in a sticky puddle of cooling semen, his lover asleep on his chest and the bed linens neglected on the floor, Chris thought he'd never been happier in his life.

The sheets could wait a while longer.

The Cooking Lesson

Chapter One

"Do you really have to go?"

"Sorry, but I do, yes."

"Can't you call in sick or something? One of the other chefs can teach the class just this once, come on."

Chris straightened his silk tie, turned and smiled at his lover, who was naked and tangled in the sheets. Matt stuck his lip out and widened his blue eyes. Chris had to admit he was tempted. He strolled over and kissed the top of Matt's tousled head.

"I'd like nothing better than to stay in bed with you," he said. "But you know I can't miss this class. It's being filmed for that special 'At Your Leisure' is doing on Asheville."

"Stupid TV show," Matt grumbled. He rolled onto his stomach and propped his chin in his hands. "What are you making today?"

"Red wine and dark chocolate fondue, with fruit and angel food cake for dipping."

"Mm. Sounds good. Can I come watch?"

Chris smiled affectionately at him. Matt was one hot piece of ass, lying there with his ankles crossed in the air and the sweet curve of his butt shining in the morning sun. He always managed to seem both innocent and sexy as hell, with his delicate features and wildly spiked hair he'd dyed cherry red two days before. Sometimes Chris wondered how on earth a cultured and proper gentleman like himself had ended up with a wildcat like Matt.

"Earth to Chris," Matt said, poking Chris in the ribs.

Laughing, Chris sat on the bed. "Sorry. I was just thinking."

"'Bout what?" Matt rose to his knees and stuck his tongue in Chris's ear.

Chris gave him a playful push. "You. Us. How in the world did we end up together?"

"I brainwashed you into thinking you were in love with me."

"Funny, I don't seem to remember that."

"You're not supposed to, stupid." Matt slid his naked self onto Chris's lap and ran his hands over the dark green silk of his suit jacket. "I like this color on you. It brings out your gorgeous green eyes."

Chris wrapped both arms around Matt's waist. "Thank you, I'm happy you noticed. Maybe you're not a complete fashion disaster after all."

"What do you mean? I dress good!"

Chris rolled his eyes. "For one of the Sex Pistols, perhaps."

"What, you don't like leather?" Matt pressed a light kiss to Chris's lips.

"It has its uses." Chris kissed him back and tugged at the silver ring in Matt's left nipple. "But pants are not, in my opinion, one of those uses. Especially not when said pants are purple."

"I like purple."

"I know." Cradling the back of Matt's head in one hand, Chris gave him a long, thorough kiss. When he pulled back again, Matt's eyes were hazed with desire.

"I have to go now," Chris said.

"Tease. Getting me all worked up then leaving." Matt snaked a hand down to grope Chris's crotch.

Chris squeezed his eyes shut and tried to think unsexy thoughts. "Matt, please. This is important to me."

"I know." Slipping off Chris's lap, Matt pushed Chris's knees apart and knelt on the floor between them. "Your first TV appearance. Pretty exciting."

Matt had Chris's trousers unbuttoned in seconds. Chris didn't try to stop him, though he knew he should. "Not to mention a huge draw for The Falls."

"You'll be a star." Matt grinned as he dragged Chris's zipper down, click by click. "I'll be your groupie."

"Hardly a stretch. You already act like one." Chris groaned when Matt reached a determined hand into the front of his pants, pulling out his half-hard cock. "Why are you doing this? I'm going to be late."

"No you're not." Matt's free hand was already tugging Chris's slacks and underwear down to give him better access to Chris's privates. "I won't let you."

"I can't do this right now," Chris complained, contradicting himself by lifting his hips so Matt could pull his pants off. "I'm too tense. All I can think of is the class, and being on television."

Matt favored him with an affronted look. "Yeah, you're nervous, and you need to relax a little. Why the hell do you think I'm doing this? For my health?"

"Well..." Chris had definite opinions as to why Matt wanted to suck him off now of all times, and none of them involved Matt suddenly developing altruistic tendencies.

With an irritated huff, Matt wrapped one hand around Chris's cock and cupped his balls in the other. "Just shut up and try not to obsess for five minutes."

Chris was on the verge of making an indignant declaration to the effect that he would no doubt last *much* longer than five minutes. Then Matt's mouth enveloped him, warm and wet and very, very determined, and Chris wasn't so sure anymore. Sighing, he let his nervousness slink into the background and gave himself up to the inevitable.

Chris had to admit, if sucking cock was considered acceptable therapy for anxiety, Matt could have a brilliant new career. Not exactly a news flash, of course. Matt's impressive oral skills had never been in question, as far as Chris was concerned. Nor his undeniable knack for distracting Chris with sex. But as he sat there half-dressed with his legs spread and his prick being enthusiastically devoured, Chris realized he'd never before appreciated the full power of a blowjob to clear the mind and relax the body.

Never too late to learn something new, Chris mused, and shot down Matt's throat with a heartfelt groan.

Matt swallowed, then sat there with Chris's shrinking cock in his mouth, stroking it with his tongue. He didn't seem to be in any hurry to let go. Truthfully, Chris wasn't either. He would've liked nothing better than to stay right there all day, with his pants off and Matt kneeling naked between his legs. But time was passing, and he had a TV show to do.

For the first time in weeks, the thought didn't make Chris's mouth go bone dry with fear.

"Matt, darling," Chris said, petting Matt's hair. "You were right, I feel much better now. Thank you."

Letting Chris's cock slip out of his mouth, Matt laid his cheek against Chris's thigh and smiled at him. "The things I do for your career."

"Oh yes. Such a sacrifice." Chris lifted Matt's chin, bent and kissed him, tasting the bitter-salt semen on his lips. "Now I really do need to go."

"You're not gonna do me?" Matt clambered to his feet, blue eyes wide, one hand in a loose fist around his stiff shaft.

Chris arched an eyebrow as he stood and pulled his pants on. "I thought you only sucked me so I would relax for my show."

"Yeah. I figured you'd be so grateful you'd give me one too." Swinging his hips in a slow circle, Matt gave Chris a filthy grin. "C'mon, don't you want it?"

Chris stared at Matt's dripping erection, and he *did* want it. He glanced at his watch. "God, yes. There's time, I think."

Laughing, Matt deflected Chris's hand. "No, I was just kidding. You don't have to."

"I want to." Chris tried again and frowned when Matt danced out of reach. "Sweetheart, you're acting very strange."

"What, because I won't let you suck my dick right now?" Matt stopped and seemed to think about what he'd just said. "Okay, I can see that."

"So let me."

"Later."

"Why not now?" Chris heard the whine in his voice and wished it wasn't there, but couldn't seem to stop it.

"I'm saving it." With that rather mysterious statement, Matt fastened the button on Chris's pants and kissed his cheek. "Now go already. You don't want to be late."

Suspicious now, Chris narrowed his eyes, but didn't say anything. He walked over to the dresser, picked up his brush and ran it through his hair.

"You never answered my question," Matt said after a moment.

Chris glanced at him in the mirror. Matt had returned to the bed, sprawled diagonally across the mattress on his stomach. "What question is that?"

"I asked if I could come watch. You know, watch your cooking class."

Chris set the brush down and turned to look at him. "I don't think so. You know what happened the last time. And this is for TV."

"Aw, come on. I'll be good, honest."

Chris had to laugh. The last time Matt had come to one of Chris's cooking classes, he'd spent the entire time "accidentally" dropping utensils on the floor so he'd have to bend over and pick them up, thus giving Chris a mouthwatering view of his perfect ass. The fact that this was calculated to drive Chris wild didn't stop it from doing just that. Chris had eventually excused himself from the class right in the middle of caramelizing the onions and fucked Matt against the wall of the pantry. He didn't think the students had believed his explanation that the noises they heard were caused by a stray cat outside, though Matt had given an excellent impression of one that day.

"Matt, my love, 'good' is a relative term to you. I won't risk a repeat of the last time while the cameras are rolling. 'At Your Leisure' is the most popular vacation report in the country, and I want us to look good. Anyway, don't you have to go to work today?"

"Yeah, but not for a while. It's only nine-thirty now, Dragon's Den doesn't open 'til two."

"I know, I just thought maybe you had some designs to finish or something. Weren't you working on the morning glory vine for that young woman you saw the other day?"

Dragon's Den was one of the most popular tattoo and piercing businesses in town, and Matt, at twenty-four, was the youngest master tattoo artist there. Each tattoo he did was a personalized design worked out between himself and the client, and he'd been working hard for the past few weeks on the vine, among others.

"I finished it up last night. She's coming in at two-thirty to have a look at it." Matt bounced out of bed and slid his arms around Chris from behind. "She's my first customer, too. I've got plenty of time." He bit the back of Chris's neck. "C'mon, babe. You owe me now."

Chris turned in Matt's arms, pulled him close and kissed his forehead. "If I actually thought you'd behave, I'd love to have you there. But I know better. And you should know better than to think you can guilt me into letting you come with me."

"You'll live to regret this," Matt promised solemnly, twirling an imaginary moustache between his fingers. His eyes glinted with mischief.

"I'm sure," Chris answered, choosing to ignore Matt's teasing threats. He did *not* want his oral-sex-induced calm to be destroyed by worry over what Matt had up his sleeve. "All right, I'm going now. Class starts in an hour and I'd like to make sure everything's set up before the TV crew gets there."

He extricated himself from Matt's embrace and headed out the bedroom door. Matt followed, padding naked down the stairs behind him. Chris grabbed his car keys and wallet off the hall table, then brushed a quick kiss across Matt's lips.

"Goodbye, darling," he said. "I love you."

"Love you too," Matt answered. "Good luck with the class."

Chris smiled. "Thanks." He touched Matt's cheek then breezed out the door.

Chapter Two

It was only a short drive to The Falls, the four-star restaurant downtown where Chris was head chef. He'd been hired there when he was twenty-seven and fresh out of a prestigious culinary program, and he'd been there for ten years. The cooking class was something he'd started four years ago. Its huge success had helped bring The Falls national recognition, thus the "At Your Leisure" segment being filmed that day.

Chris turned off the quiet street where he and Matt shared a rambling Victorian home and pulled onto the busy main road of the small North Carolina city. It was a lovely April morning, cool and breezy and bright with budding flowers. He rolled the windows down and breathed deeply of the spring-scented air. The sky, he couldn't help but notice, was the exact color of Matt's eyes.

Those eyes had hooked him the first time he saw them two years before, that fateful morning when Matt had picked up the wallet that had fallen out of Chris's pocket and run after him to return it. Chris had been smitten by Matt's dimpled smile, his slender yet well-muscled body, the bold way he flirted. And those eyes, wide and clear and bluer than a tropical sea.

Those were the things that had drawn Chris in, but what made him stay was so much deeper. Matt's quick mind. His playfulness. The way he threw himself so completely into everything he did, including loving Chris. From the moment they met, Matt had held Chris's heart in his keeping, and Chris had never regretted a single moment.

As always, thinking of Matt made Chris smile. They'd had their difficulties, like any couple, but surprisingly few for two such different people.

Outward appearances notwithstanding, they fit together like jigsaw pieces, their differences complementing rather than clashing. Each had recognized in the other the missing part of himself, and together they were complete.

A big, colorful van with the "At Your Leisure" logo on the side was parked in front of The Falls when Chris got there. He shook off the rosy glow of nostalgia and hurried inside.

"Chris, hi." Laurie hooked her arm through his elbow and ushered him toward the kitchen. "They just got here, and not all of the class is here yet. And they've set aside plenty of time for us, so no big rush. They want to interview you after class if that's okay."

"That's fine. Sorry I'm late, I..." Chris blushed, thinking of what had kept him. "I had to talk Matt out of coming with me."

Laurie raised her eyebrows, but didn't comment. "You're not late, Chris. And Matt could've come."

"Oh no, he couldn't. I'm nervous enough without him in here making silly faces and God knows what else behind the camera man's back."

"Suit yourself, you're the one who has to deal with him later. Come on, I'll introduce you to the crew."

Thirty minutes later, Chris stood before his class in his white chef's coat, sweating under a supernova of hot lights. Names and faces belonging to the "At Your Leisure" crew swirled around in his head, trying to connect with each other. The only name he remembered with certainty was that of the journalist doing the report—Troy Waters, a prissy little man with a humorless smile and a damp, lifeless handshake. According to Laurie, the regular host was unable to be there due to a family emergency, and they had not been able to reschedule.

Chris silently thanked whatever powers existed for Matt's absence. He would have found Troy Waters an irresistible target.

"Okay, people," the crew chief called, "if Mr. Tucker's ready, we'll get started. Sir?"

"Just Chris, please. And yes, I'm ready." Chris glanced around at the students. They seemed a little nervous, but eager to begin. He smiled. "Class, if you'll take your stations, please."

Chris's students took their positions at the spacious kitchen's five stoves, the cameras started rolling, and the class was underway.

Everything went like a dream. Mrs. Weyland scorched her chocolate, but that was the only setback. Chris managed to intervene in time to save her fondue. He closed the class by giving Mr. Waters a strawberry dipped in the rich sauce.

"All right, people, that's a wrap," the crew chief called. "Good job, everyone."

"You were all wonderful." Chris smiled at his class. "Please take home some of the fruit and cake, there's plenty."

Chris wandered out of the kitchen and into the restaurant proper as the students gathered jackets, purses and food and made their exit. Pulling off his white jacket, he plopped into the nearest chair.

"How'd it go?"

Startled at the sound of Matt's voice, Chris turned around. Matt sat in the shadows at the back of the room, with his feet propped up on a table. Chris walked over to him and thumped one green sneaker.

"Off," he said. "What are you doing here?"

Matt dropped his feet back to the floor. "Love you too." He crossed his arms and gave Chris a dark look.

Chris sat beside him, pulled him close, and kissed his cheek. "Sorry, I didn't mean to be so short with you. I'm happy to see you."

"Yeah, I bet. You were real anxious for me to come with you."

Matt's eyes glinted with something undefinable. For a second, Chris was seized with a terrible sense of fate catching up to him. He shook it off. Matt would never be so cruel as to sabotage Chris's interview. Not over something as small as not letting him watch the cooking class. Or even over lack of proper blowjob reciprocation.

Would he?

"Matt…"

Matt stopped Chris's words with a finger against his lips. "Let's try this again. How'd your class go?"

Chris stared hard into Matt's eyes. The evil gleam he thought he'd seen before was gone, replaced by pride and affection, and genuine curiosity. Chris smiled. "Perfectly. Barely a hitch. I'm glad it's over, though. I've never been so nervous in my life."

"Even after I relaxed you?"

"My love, if you hadn't done that for me, I suspect I would have been unable to function at all. Mere nervousness is doable."

Matt leaned forward and licked Chris's mouth. "You know, it's probably a good thing I wasn't there. I would've had to molest you."

"Oh really?"

"Mm-hm."

"Why?"

"Because," Matt answered, his voice muffled against Chris's neck, "it's such a fucking turn-on to watch you cook."

Chris's breath hitched when Matt licked the hollow behind his earlobe. That spot seemed to have a direct connection to his cock, and Matt knew it.

"Matt, please. This isn't the time." Chris grabbed Matt's shoulders and pushed him away. He stared into those bottomless eyes—they were on fire. Crushing Matt's body against his, he kissed Matt hard enough to bruise.

"Chris! You out here?"

Laurie's voice brought Chris hurtling back to earth. He forced himself to pull away from Matt. Laurie stood beside the kitchen door with Troy Waters at her side.

"Back here," Chris called.

Laurie glanced around, spotted him, and hurried over with Troy trailing in her wake. "There you are. Mr. Waters is ready to start the interview now. Hi, Matt."

"Hi, Laurie." Matt looked the prim little journalist up and down and clearly found him lacking.

"Okay," Chris said. "Well, I guess I'm ready then. Mr. Waters, this is Matt Gallagher, my partner. Matt, this is Troy Waters. He's the host for the show today."

"Mr. Gallagher." Troy offered a limp hand and Matt shook it with obvious distaste. "Mr. Tucker, I understood that Ms. McGhee owns the restaurant, isn't that right?"

"Yes, that's right."

Troy seemed puzzled. "Do you own another business, then?"

Chris frowned. "I'm not sure what you mean."

"Well, you said Mr. Gallagher here was your business partner."

An uncomfortable silence fell, broken only by the sound of Matt trying hard not to laugh.

"Matt is my life partner, Mr. Waters," Chris said finally.

Troy's eyebrows wandered up and down in evident confusion. Matt made an impatient noise.

"I'm his boyfriend, Troy ol' buddy." Matt sauntered over to Troy and slung a companionable arm around his neck. "I'm the guy who sucks his dick every night. And some mornings." He waggled his eyebrows, pinched Troy's cheek, and went back to Chris's side, leaving one very flustered journalist behind.

The tension was thick enough to cut. Chris closed his eyes. He didn't know whether to chew Matt out or applaud. He settled for ignoring the whole thing.

"Mr. Waters, where would you like to do the interview?"

Troy smoothed his hands over his tie and suit jacket. "If we could just go to that table over by the bar, that would be fine. More room for the lights and cameras over there, you know."

Chris nodded. "Okay. Go on and set up, I'll be right there."

Troy opened his mouth, then closed it again. Shooting a withering glance at Matt, he stalked over to the chosen table. Laurie followed, giving Matt a gleeful thumbs-up over her shoulder. Matt winked at her.

As soon as they were out of earshot, Chris rounded on him.

"Matt, why do you do things like that?"

"He's a prick."

"Clearly. And this excuses your behavior how?"

"Why should I have to be nice to him? Anyway, he obviously needed someone to clear things up for him."

Chris tried to keep frowning, but as usual, Matt's soulful eyes and deceptively sweet smile melted his anger. He shook his head and laughed.

"Fine. Now, do you think you can stay here and behave while I do this interview?"

"Sure," Matt answered cheerfully. "I won't say a word."

Chris narrowed his eyes. "And you'll stay right here?"

"Absolutely. Right here in this booth."

Matt sat, clasped his hands in his lap, and gave Chris his best aren't-I-adorable look.

Chris considered voicing his suspicions about Matt's sincerity, or lack thereof, but decided to leave it alone. If Matt was determined to make trouble, he'd do it no matter what. All Chris could do was hang on tight, go along for the ride, and hope Matt didn't get them both into too much hot water. He sighed and bent to kiss Matt's lips.

"I do love you," he murmured. "No matter what you do."

Matt gave him a thoroughly wicked smile. "Go on, baby. Mr. Pansy-Ass is waiting for you."

"You really shouldn't call him that." Chris leaned close, brushing his lips against Matt's ear. "But I like it. Such a turn-on when you're bad." He pulled away and headed for the table where Troy sat waiting.

"Are we ready, finally?" Troy asked as Chris sat in the chair opposite him.

Chris gave him a sugary smile. "Yes, I believe so."

A technician bustled over and clipped a tiny microphone to Chris's lapel. He smiled at the young woman. She winked at him and rolled her eyes, and Chris stifled a laugh. Apparently Mr. Waters wasn't exactly popular with the crew.

Within a few minutes, the lights and cameras were in position and the crew chief was ready to begin. Mr. Waters, however, was not.

"Byron, are you a complete idiot?" he sneered at the crew chief. "I must be filmed from the right! Always from the right! God!"

"Okay, Mr. Waters." Byron's face was blank as a slate. "Guys, move that camera to the other side."

The crew obediently lugged one of the big cameras to the other side of the table. They didn't say a word, but Chris could see by the dirty looks they gave Troy how they felt about him.

"That's better," the journalist said. "Now, perhaps we can begin."

Chris glanced toward the back of the restaurant. With the camera moved to catch Troy's relatively good side, he could see Matt's colorful form lounging in his chosen booth. Troy and the crew wouldn't notice him unless they turned around and looked for him on purpose. Chris liked having Matt there, his own private ray of sunshine. He smiled. Matt smiled back and waved at him.

"Mr. Tucker." Troy sounded more than a little put out. Chris shook himself and turned to the sour-faced man sitting across from him. "If you could tear your attention away from your...your friend over there, we have an interview to do."

"Of course." Chris forced a smile. "I'm ready."

"Okay, people," Byron called. "Ready to roll. And...go."

Troy's face broke into a bright, cheerful smile and his beady little eyes twinkled at the camera. "Hello again, and welcome back to 'At Your Leisure'. You've just witnessed one of the most popular and sought-after activities in Asheville—Chef Chris Tucker's famous cooking class. Today, we made a dark chocolate and red wine fondue, and let me tell you, it was out of this world."

Turning toward Chris, he leaned forward in a patently false attempt at casualness. Chris resisted the urge to recoil.

"Chef Tucker," Troy enthused, "that fondue was fabulous."

Chris gave him a cool smile. "Thank you very much, Mr. Waters. It's my own recipe."

"I hear that you have a most unusual secret ingredient, could you share that with our audience?"

"Certainly. I use just a bit of chili powder."

Troy pulled a surprised face so fake Chris had to bite his tongue to keep from laughing. The entire crew, of course, already knew what the "secret" ingredient was. He glanced over at the corner booth behind Troy's head. Matt shoved an invisible knife through his own heart and collapsed dramatically over the table. Chris smiled.

"Chili powder?" Troy was saying. "My goodness, that is different. Why chili powder? What does it add to the taste?"

Chris watched out of the corner of his eye as Matt, recovered from his fatal wound, shrugged out of his leather jacket and started undoing the buttons on his sheer red shirt. "Well," Chris began, "even though we use dark instead of milk chocolate, it is still chocolate, and we use a sweet red wine in the recipe, so…"

Matt, hidden in his corner and unnoticed by anyone but his lover, chose that moment to wet a finger in his mouth and rub his pierced nipple into a hard little bud. Chris stared, his train of thought momentarily derailed.

"Yes?" Troy prompted. "You were saying?"

"Oh, er…y-yes." Chris's gaze remained locked onto Matt, who was tugging at his nipple ring and enjoying it very much, judging by his flushed cheeks and parted lips. "Yes, well, the sauce can become too sweet, you see. That's why I hit on the idea of chili powder a few years ago. It adds just the right amount of spice."

Matt leaned back against the dark red leather of the booth, unzipped his pants—the purple leather ones, Chris noted without surprise—and shoved his hand down the front. Chris gulped. He was having a great deal of difficulty keeping his eyes on the man interviewing him when the man he loved more than anything in life was playing with himself in the corner.

"And why is that bit of spice important?"

Chris stared straight at Troy for a moment. "If you have nothing but sweetness, it's boring, isn't it? A little spice keeps things exciting."

Troy made a face that would most likely have to be edited out later, but Chris scarcely noticed. His attention was fixed on Matt's hand caressing his erect cock. Chris licked his lips.

"Mr. Tucker?"

Chris jumped a little and tried to focus on the interview.

"Hm? Yes?" He smiled brightly and Troy gave a barely perceptible sigh.

"I was asking," the journalist said, laying the patience on extra-thick, "what drew you to cooking as a profession?"

Matt spread his legs and thrust his hips up, pushing into his own hand. Chris pinched himself under the table to keep from getting completely lost in the sight.

"Well," he answered, "I, I've always enjoyed playing with my…with my food."

Matt dipped a finger into the pre-come dripping from his cock and slid the sticky digit into his mouth. A jolt of desire shot through Chris.

"That is to say," he stammered, "I've always enjoyed being creative with food, making up recipes and so forth, ever since I was a child. I suppose it's just something you're born with, because I don't remember ever…ever feeling…any other way… Oh dear…"

Matt was on his knees in the booth now, with his pants shoved down around his thighs, pumping his cock hard with one hand and fingering his ass with the other. His eyes were closed, his mouth slack with pleasure. Chris stared and felt his own member spring to life.

"Mr. Tucker, are you all right?"

Troy's voice was filled with polite concern every bit as fake as his smile. Chris tore his gaze from the arresting sight of Matt getting himself off and managed to appear far calmer than he felt.

"Yes, I'm fine," he said. "Just a bit…bit of a headache, that's all."

"Well, we're nearly done." The journalist reached over and patted Chris's hand. His clammy touch made Chris's erection wilt just enough to relieve some of the pressure between his legs.

"You've been with The Falls for ten years," Troy continued. "You've been head chef here for six of those ten years. Now that, I would think, is a very busy and fulfilling job. What made you decide to take on the extra duty of teaching a cooking class? You began that four years ago, yes?"

"Yes," Chris answered. "I never saw it as an extra duty. I love cooking, and I love to share what I've learned over the years with others who also love it."

He kept one eye on Matt as he talked. He could tell Matt was close to orgasm by the way he tilted his head to the side and bit his lower lip.

"And what about your partner, Mr. Tucker?" Troy asked. Chris raised his eyebrows in surprise and Mr. Waters gave him a greasy, unpleasant smile. "Does your partner cook as well?"

Chris grinned as Matt came all over the red leather seat. "Actually, he makes a delicious white sauce."

Autumn's Music

Where are the songs of Spring? Ay, where are they?
Think not of them, thou hast thy music too…
John Keats, "To Autumn"

Chapter One

There it was. Right there in front, obvious as a drag queen in a room full of nuns.

A white hair.

Chris leaned forward and frowned at his reflection in the bathroom mirror. "Two," he mumbled. "There's two of them. Dear God."

He dug through the medicine cabinet until he found the tweezers, then separated the bright strands from their dark neighbors with his left hand. Green eyes narrowed in concentration, he settled the tweezers carefully around one snowy root and gave it a sharp tug.

"Whatcha doing?"

Chris jumped at the sound of Matt's voice behind him. The tweezers dug into his scalp and he let out a yelp.

"Jesus, Matt, don't sneak up on me like that. You scared me."

Chris turned to glare at his young lover. Matt covered his mouth with one hand and tried to look contrite, but the sparkle in his large blue eyes gave him away.

Chris stifled a smile. "Go on and laugh. I know you want to."

"No, I don't," Matt protested, the amusement in his voice contradicting his words. He slipped both arms around Chris's waist and kissed his chin. "Sorry I scared you, baby. You okay?"

"Yes. Just a little scrape, that's all." Chris pulled Matt closer. He rubbed his cheek against Matt's hair, which was currently dyed bright red. It would probably be many years before any white appeared in that wildly tousled thicket.

"Did you get it?" Matt asked.

"Get what?"

"How the hell should I know? Whatever you were after in there." Matt combed his fingers through Chris's hair. "You got fleas or something?"

Chris swatted Matt's behind. "Very funny. I found two white hairs."

"So what?"

"So, I'm getting old."

"You're only thirty-seven, dumbass. That's not old."

"It is compared to you."

"Fine, have it your way. You're old. Older than dirt. Ancient, even. A real fossil."

Chris tried to look stern. It wasn't easy when Matt smiled like that, showing the tooth he'd chipped snowboarding last winter and the deep dimple in his right cheek.

"Okay, you've made your point." Chris kissed the end of Matt's nose.

Matt plowed on as if Chris hadn't spoken. "I like my men old. White hair and wrinkles turn me on. I can't wait 'til your teeth fall out, I'm gonna make you go down on me all the time."

Chris laughed. "I do that already."

"Why don't you start wearing Depends in bed? That'd be hot."

"Watch that smart mouth, young man. You're not too old for me to put you over my knee."

"Yeah, right. I know you, all talk and no action." Matt bit Chris's neck. "Now come on, we're gonna be late for my appointment."

Chris made a face. "I still don't understand why you want to get pierced…you know, there. Won't it be terribly painful?"

"Only for a second. It's gonna feel great later." He pulled back and frowned at Chris. "You're not gonna chicken out, are you? You promised you'd go with me and hold my hand."

Chris sighed. When Matt had told him the previous week, in typically blunt fashion, "I'm getting my dick pierced," Chris had been shocked. He thought he could get used to the idea of Matt having a piece of metal imbedded in his cock. Matt's nipple ring had certainly never bothered him. But the thought of watching it happen made him queasy. However, he had indeed promised he'd go, and he had no intention of breaking his promise.

"You realize, I hope, that I wouldn't be doing this if it weren't your birthday," Chris said.

"But it is. Lucky for me, I guess." Matt stuck his tongue out at Chris and turned toward the bathroom door.

Chris grinned at his back. "Okay, let's go. We wouldn't want to keep Kelly waiting."

Matt smiled as they started down the stairs hand in hand. "Kelly's not doing it. She's off to Jamaica with her husband for a couple of weeks."

"Oh, yes? Well, good for her. The girl works far too hard."

"You should talk."

Chris ignored that. "So who's doing the piercing? Does this mean that Dragon's Den has a second piercer at last and Kelly won't have to work so much overtime?"

"That's exactly what it means." Matt grabbed Chris's car keys off the hall table and tossed them to him. "Kelly hired him last month. You met him at that party she had a couple of weeks ago, don't you remember?"

Chris's brow furrowed in thought as he locked the front door and they stepped off the porch into the July heat. "Oh, yes, I remember now. Rick Gonzalez, right? That tall man with the long hair. You were working on a tribal tattoo design for him."

"Yep. Had the last sitting for that yesterday. It's good. You can see it today if you want."

They climbed into Chris's BMW and buckled up. Matt smiled at Chris, and Chris leaned over to kiss him.

"Happy birthday, sweetheart," he said. "I love you."

Matt cupped Chris's face in both hands and kissed him back. "I love you too, grandpa."

Chris laughed, but the casual remark lodged itself in his brain and made him wonder.

Chapter Two

Fifteen minutes later, they sat side by side in the waiting room at Dragon's Den, where Matt worked as a tattoo artist. Matt was even more fidgety than usual, bouncing one knee and chewing his fingernails.

"Matt, are you sure you want to do this?" Lifting Matt's hand, Chris kissed his fingers.

Matt turned a surprised face to him. "Yeah, why?"

"You seem nervous."

"Well, yeah, I am, kind of. I'm about to get a metal ring in my dick."

Chris winced. "Yes. Well. As long as you're sure."

"I am." Matt slid onto his lap. "Kiss me."

Chris did. As usual, Matt's kiss drove everything else right out of his brain. They both jumped when the door to the piercing room opened. Two girls emerged, followed by a tall, handsome man with long chestnut curls tied back in a low ponytail. One girl had her freshly pierced tongue hanging out of her mouth.

"Remember," Rick Gonzalez told her, "mouthwash twice a day. And no tongue kissing or oral sex for six weeks."

"Wa? No theth?" The pierced girl looked horrified.

"I told you that before I pierced you." Rick grinned. "She can do you, you just can't do her for a while. It's not so bad; use your imagination. Go buy some toys."

The girls glanced at each other and giggled. The one with the new piercing handed Rick a couple of crumpled bills and they headed out the door. Pocketing the money, Rick walked over to the couch where Chris sat with Matt still on his lap.

"Hi, guys." Rick smiled down at them.

Chris tried his best to maintain his dignity with Matt sucking enthusiastically on his neck. "Hello, Rick. Nice to see you again."

"You too, Chris." Rick nudged Matt's shoulder. "You ready, Matt?"

Raising his head, Matt grinned up at Rick. "Yeah. Chris is gonna come with me, okay?"

"Sure thing. C'mon."

He turned and went back into the private room. Chris watched him. His body was lean and muscular, and his low-slung jeans and black tank top left very little to the imagination.

Matt elbowed Chris's arm. "Hot, isn't he?"

Chris shrugged as they stood and followed Rick. "I suppose."

"For you, that's a rousing 'hell yeah.' He swings both ways, you know."

"Really. How fascinating. Are you going to tell me what his favorite position is too, or must I ask him myself?"

Matt laughed and squeezed Chris's hand. Rick gave them a quizzical look as they walked through the door. "What's funny?"

"Nothing," Chris said.

Rick raised an eyebrow as though he didn't believe him, but he let it drop. "Okay, Matt, go on and get in the chair. Might want to take off the jeans. You can leave your underwear on if you want."

"Naw. It's easier without." Matt stripped off his jeans and Elvis boxers, then settled himself in the paper-covered chair. He reached a hand out and Chris took it.

Rick busied himself setting up a tray of sterile instruments and supplies on a rolling table. "You want the ring, you said?"

Matt nodded. "Yeah."

"Barbell heals faster."

"I know. I want the ring."

"Ring it is. Where you want it?"

Matt picked up his cock and ran his thumb over the head. "Gimme the Prince Albert."

"You got it."

Chris frowned. "What's that exactly?"

"Through the urethra and out the underside of the head, where it joins the shaft," Rick explained as he rolled his tray of supplies closer. He grinned at the horrified expression on Chris's face. "Don't worry, it really doesn't hurt all that much. Not like some of the others. Plus it heals faster than most."

"If you say so," Chris said with a shudder. Matt laughed.

Rick sat on a rolling stool and pulled on a pair of gloves. "Okay, dude. Spread 'em."

Matt opened his legs. Scooting closer, Rick draped a sterile cloth with a hole in the middle over Matt's privates, covering everything but his cock. Chris managed to keep watching while Rick swabbed the head of Matt's penis with a cleaning solution. When he picked up something that looked like a medieval torture device, Chris decided to watch Matt's face instead.

"Ready?" Rick asked.

Matt gripped Chris's hand hard. "Let's do it."

"Okay," Rick said. "Here we go."

Matt closed his eyes and took a deep breath. After a moment, Chris heard a metallic snick and Matt gasped.

Chris kissed Matt's white knuckles. "You okay?"

Matt nodded. His face was beaded with sweat and his cheeks flushed. "Yeah. Yeah, fine. Jesus, what a fucking rush."

Chris gaped at him. "Are you saying you enjoyed that?" He glanced down and was stunned to see Matt's cock swelling. The stainless steel ring glinted in the light.

"Lots of people do," Rick said as he stood and peeled off his gloves. "It feels amazing during sex too. That's one reason so many guys get this one. You gotta be careful when you top, though, the jewelry can cause damage."

"I don't top much." Matt ran a finger over the ring. "Hey, Chris, you can get a chain to put on here, wouldn't that be wild?"

Rick's brown gaze lingered on Matt's semi-erect member. "You can get those at Krash."

Matt raised his eyebrows. "You mean that S&M shop over on Patton?"

"That's the one."

"Cool." Matt turned to Chris. "Let's go get one. I'll be your sex slave and you can lead me around by my cock."

"I think you're led around by that particular bit of your anatomy too much as it is," Chris said, giving the organ in question a little pat.

"Huh." Quirking a teasing smile at Rick, Matt gave his shaft a shake, making the new piercing vibrate. "You'd chain up my dick and make me be your sex slave, wouldn't you, Rick?"

Rick laughed. "Hey, don't give away my secret fantasy."

"So you've been perving on me all this time." Matt leered, fingers caressing his cock. "I knew it."

"What can I say?" Sighing, Rick pressed a hand to his heart. "I've got it bad."

Matt chuckled, but his eyes burned. A queasy feeling fluttered in Chris's stomach.

Chris cleared his throat. "Are you planning to sit there and play with yourself all night or shall we go?"

Matt jumped to his feet. "Let's go, I'm ready to par-tay!"

"What's the occasion?" Rick asked as he started cleaning up the piercing supplies.

"It's my birthday." Grinning, Matt pulled his boxers and jeans back on and carefully zipped up. "We're gonna go get drunk and dance 'til we fall over."

Rick laughed. "Sounds fun. So how old are you?"

"Twenty-five."

"Mmmmm," Rick purred, dark eyes smoldering. "Still young and tasty."

Matt licked his lips, and Chris frowned. This time, there was no mistaking the electricity that jumped between the two other men. Chris's stomach plummeted into his feet. Watching Matt and Rick flirt back and forth, Chris thought he knew what was happening.

He's tired of me. He wants someone younger and more exciting. In an instant, Chris's world went gray. He clamped down hard on the sorrow inside him and managed not to start crying on the spot. He looked up at Rick, who blushed and dropped his gaze to the floor.

"So...um, guess that's it then," Rick said. "Matt, you know the drill. No bodily fluids except your own on the piercing for six weeks, keep it clean, and let me know anytime if you need me to take a look."

"Sure thing." Matt reached out and grabbed Rick's arm. "Show Chris the tat I did, he wanted to see."

Rick glanced at Chris in a strangely shy way, then pulled his shirt off and turned around, slinging his hair over his shoulder and out of the way. The tattoo began at the base of Rick's neck and trailed all the way down the center of his back to disappear under the waistband of his jeans. Chris stared at the intricate network of black lines and swirls against the golden-brown skin. The stark beauty of it almost made him forget the way Rick and Matt had looked at each other. Matt's talent always had that effect on him.

"Matt, this is fantastic." Chris touched it without thinking. The healing skin felt rough under his fingers. He couldn't be sure, but he thought Rick flinched just a little. Feeling oddly rejected, he pulled his hand back.

"Thanks, baby. I figured you'd like that." Matt draped his arms around Chris's neck. "When're you gonna let me do you?"

Chris forced a smile. "Sorry, Matt. Tattoos just aren't for me. Not even one of your creations."

"I'll wear you down one day, just wait." Matt bit Chris's lip, then pulled away. "C'mon, let's go. Rick, thanks for doing me."

Matt flung himself at Rick and hugged him hard. Chris couldn't help but notice the flush coloring Rick's cheeks when he put his arms around Matt's waist and hugged him back. He wouldn't meet Chris's eyes.

"Hey, no problem," Rick said as Matt let him go again. "For this much ink, I'll pierce anything you want, just say the word."

"I'll let you know. Thanks, man, see you later." Matt grabbed Chris's hand and pulled him out the door.

Outside, Chris wrapped an arm around Matt's shoulders and kissed his forehead. He couldn't help wondering if it would be the last time he ever got to hold Matt that way. Matt leaned against him, one hand in the back pocket of Chris's jeans. They strolled along in silence for a while. The sun sinking behind the mountains west of the city painted the sky a brilliant orange, and the air was starting to turn cool.

Asheville on a summer evening always held a certain indefinable magic, but Chris wasn't feeling it like he usually did. All he could think of was the heat in Rick's eyes and the answering spark in Matt's when they looked at each other. He nuzzled Matt's hair. Matt always smelled like sunshine and clover. He wondered if he'd ever learn to live without waking up to that scent, and Matt's warm body in his arms.

"Chris!" Matt poked him in the ribs and he jerked back to the present.

"Sorry," Chris said. "I was miles away."

Matt frowned. "I'll say. I was asking if you wanted to head over to The Orange Peel and see if they have any tickets left for tonight. The Arcade Fire's playing. What the hell were you thinking so hard about?"

"It's nothing."

"Bullshit. You always zone out when you're thinking about something intense. So what was it?"

Chris tried to smile and couldn't. "Matt, let's not talk about it right now, okay? It's your birthday, let's go have fun. Whatever you want to do. We can go see The Arcade Fire if you like."

Matt pulled back enough to give Chris a sharp look. Taking both of Chris's hands, he led Chris into a nearby alley.

"Okay," Matt said, "what's wrong? And don't even try to tell me 'nothing' again, because I know better. Was it the piercing? Did it really gross you out that bad?"

"It's not that." Chris bit his lip. "Matt, you know I love you, right?"

Matt raised his eyebrows. "Yeah, I know. And you know I love you."

"I never doubted that before."

"Before? What, you mean you do now?" Matt shook his head. "You're yanking my chain, aren't you?"

Chris didn't know how to begin saying what he needed to say. He lifted a hand to caress Matt's face. Matt laid his own hand over Chris's.

"Baby, tell me what's wrong, okay?" Matt's expression was unusually serious.

Chris ran his fingers over Matt's smooth cheek and across his soft, plump lips. "Do you ever get tired of being with someone so much older than you?"

Matt's clear blue eyes widened. "Chris, it doesn't matter that you're older or I'm younger or however you want to look at it. We belong together. I knew that the first time I saw you."

Chris sighed. "I'm no innocent, Matt. I've been in other relationships, and I've had my wild single days. I've never regretted leaving those days behind. God knows you're all I've ever wanted." Clasping Matt's hands in his, Chris kissed his fingers. "But you're so young, Matt. There's so much you haven't done yet. And I've seen the way people look at you. You could have any man you wanted. Any woman too, for that matter."

"Just what the fuck are you trying to say?" Matt's eyes were huge in a face gone dead white.

"I...hell." Chris drew a deep breath and forced himself to go on. "I saw the way you and Rick looked at each other. I know you're...you're attracted to him. I don't blame you for wanting someone closer to your age, someone who can keep up with you. And, and I don't blame you if you and he have... Well, Matt, I love you more than I've ever loved anyone. More than I ever thought I could love anyone. It would kill me to let you go. But I want you to be happy. If being with someone else is what you need to be happy, then I'll…I'll…"

He couldn't finish, but he didn't need to. Matt got the point just fine. He yanked his hands away and stood staring at Chris, shaking all over. His eyes glittered with unshed tears.

"What the fuck, Chris? Is that really what you think of me? You think I'd throw away everything we have just so I could get with somebody younger? Jesus fucking Christ! We've been together two whole years, how can you think I'm that fucking shallow?"

"Matt, love, that's not what I meant…" Chris touched Matt's arm. He skittered out of reach.

"The hell it's not!" Tears spilled down Matt's cheeks. "I love you, Chris. I love you. You're everything to me. How could you think you're not? How could you just let me go like that?"

Chris felt like he'd been punched. "I just thought…"

"Well, you thought wrong."

"Darling, I'm so sorry." Chris stepped toward Matt, and Matt stumbled backward.

"Don't," he said. "Just don't."

"Matt, please…"

"Look, Chris, just go on home, okay? I need to be alone for a while."

Matt turned away without waiting for an answer, hugging himself so hard his fingers were white. Chris watched him go, feeling helpless and desperate.

"How…I mean…you're coming home, right?" *Please, please come home. Don't leave this way.*

Matt stopped, glanced over his shoulder, and started walking again. "I'll get a cab." He strode back onto the sidewalk and disappeared around the corner. Leaning against the brick wall, Chris buried his face in his hands.

Chapter Three

For the next couple of hours, Chris wandered the teeming streets, trying to pretend he wasn't looking for Matt. Every face he passed became Matt's, wide cerulean eyes full of hurt and accusation. When he couldn't stand it any more, Chris walked back to his car and drove home, half-blinded by tears.

He managed to get all the way upstairs before collapsing. He curled up on the floor in the hall and sobbed out all his pain against the wall Matt had insisted on painting purple. They'd argued over that. Chris still teased Matt about it sometimes. He pressed his cheek against the wall and swore to himself that if Matt only came home, if he'd only forgive him, he could paint the whole damn house purple if he wanted.

Several hours later, Chris woke with a start to the sound of the key in the front door. He levered himself off the floor, grimacing as he stretched out his cramped and aching muscles, and leaned across the railing overlooking the foyer.

"Matt?" he called as the door opened. He hurried to the stairs and ran down them two at a time. "God, I'm so glad you came home, I'm so sorry, I…"

When he saw Rick he skidded to a halt. The tall man had one arm around Matt's waist, and Matt leaned against his side with his eyes closed. Chris's heart stopped.

"Hi," Rick said, breaking the awkward silence.

"Hello." Chris congratulated himself for keeping his voice calm. "What's going on?"

Before Rick could say anything, Matt opened his eyes. He let go of Rick and launched himself into Chris's arms. Chris held him close, stroking his hair and drinking in the familiar warmth of his body.

"Rick brought me home." Matt pulled back and gave Chris a loopy grin. "I'm a leeeetle drunk."

Chris glanced over at Rick. Rick nodded.

"More than a little," he said. "He's completely hammered. We ran into each other at The Orange Peel, then we talked for a while after the show. I was worried about him getting home, so I got him a cab and rode over here with him. Hope that's okay?"

Rick seemed nervous, and Chris knew it must be because of him. Squaring his shoulders, he met Rick's gaze.

"Of course it is. Thank you. Rick, I don't mean to pry, but can you tell me what you and Matt talked about?"

"I told him, Chris," Matt mumbled against Chris's neck. "'Bout our fight I mean. Are you mad?"

"No, sweetheart, I'm not mad." Chris lifted Matt's face and kissed him, tasting whiskey on Matt's tongue.

"Sorry I ran off," Matt said between kisses. "Guess I over retracted. Reacted, I mean."

"You didn't. I was wrong, love. Can you forgive me?"

Matt smiled, showing dimples. "'Course I do. I love you. Dumbass."

"I love you too." Chris kissed him again. "Now I think you should go on to bed, okay? We'll talk in the morning. Or more likely the afternoon, I suppose."

Matt giggled. "Yeah."

Chris glanced at Rick, who was staring holes in the floor and shuffling from foot to foot. "Rick, could you stay for a bit? I'm just going to put the birthday boy to bed, then I think we should talk."

Rick nodded unhappily. "Yeah, I know. I told the cab driver to go on."

"Thanks. I'll be right down."

Chris managed to get Matt halfway up the stairs before his legs gave out. Matt sat down hard on the stairs, rocking with laughter. Without a word, Rick came to the rescue. Together he and Chris hauled Matt into the bedroom and laid him on the bed. Matt gazed up at Chris with unfocused eyes.

"Hey, Chris?"

"Yes?"

"I love you. And you're not old."

Chris smiled. "I love you too." He pulled Matt's shoes off, then bent and kissed his lips. "Now go on to sleep. I'll be up in a little while."

Matt's eyes were already drifting closed. "'Night, Rick. Thanks."

"No problem, man. 'Night."

Chris flipped the light off, and he and Rick trooped back downstairs. Rick followed Chris silently into the living room.

"Sit down, Rick," Chris said. "Would you like some tea?"

"No thanks." Rick sat stiffly on the edge of a chair, still staring at the floor.

Chris settled himself on the sofa. "Rick, what did Matt say to you exactly?"

Rick glanced up at him, dark eyes wide and fearful. "He, um, he said you guys got in a fight. He said you thought that he and I...that we...well, you know."

"Yes. I'm ashamed to say that I did think there was something between you. I suppose I've been a bit insecure lately. I thought Matt was tired of being with someone so much older than him, and you and he seemed to be attracted to one another, so I—"

"I know," Rick interrupted. "You don't have to say it. He told me."

Chris scanned Rick's face, trying to read his expression. "Was I imagining it, Rick? Because I don't think it was all in my head. I underestimated Matt pretty badly, but I know what I saw."

Rick hunched his shoulders like he was trying to disappear. "I don't guess you imagined it. But it's not quite like you think."

"Then tell me, please." Chris leaned forward and laid a hand on Rick's arm. The muscles under the golden skin were tight and trembling. "I'm not accusing you of anything. I know now that you and Matt haven't been together. I just want to figure this out. I made a terrible mistake tonight, and I hurt the person I love more than anything in this life. I could've lost him, Rick. I don't want to make a mistake like that again. Please help me figure out what happened."

Rick stared at him for a long time, twisting his fingers together in his lap. Chris waited.

"It's not Matt," Rick said finally. "It's you."

Chris's jaw dropped open. "What?"

"It isn't Matt I want. I mean yeah, he's a babe, plus he's a great guy. I love him a lot. But I've had kind of a crush on you since I met you at Kelly's party. I could tell you thought me and Matt had something going on today, you looked so sad. I felt terrible, but I didn't know what to say." He took Chris's hand and leaned toward him. "I'm really sorry, Chris. I didn't mean to cause trouble between you two."

Chris shook his head. "Not your fault, Rick. It's mine. I had no real reason to think that Matt wanted to leave me, and I never should have said that to him. That was just me being insecure because I'm so much older than he is, and he's young and beautiful and sometimes it's hard to believe that I'm the one he chooses to be with." He gazed into Rick's big, velvety eyes. "So you...you wanted me?"

Rick smiled. "Is that so hard to believe?"

"Well, yes, it is, to be frank. I'm almost forty. That's a bit past prime to most people your age. There's nothing special about me. Matt's the one people turn to stare at every time we go anywhere."

"Like I said, he's a babe." Rick stood and moved to sit beside Chris on the couch. "But so are you. You're just as special as he is."

"Oh, come on..."

"You are. You're one hell of a sexy man, Chris. You've got that intelligent, sophisticated, Jude Law kind of vibe going on. It's hotter than hell.

I'm not the only one who thinks so either. I've heard lots of people talking about Matt's hot boyfriend."

Rick slid closer and Chris's pulse sped up. "Well, I'm...I'm flattered."

"Know what else Matt said?"

Chris shook his head. Rick laid one big hand on his cheek. His eyes burned.

"He said," Rick continued, raking his hand through Chris's hair, "that we should get together some time."

"G-get together?" Chris's breath was coming short now. He couldn't seem to make himself stop Rick's hand from traveling down his chest.

"A threesome." Rick leaned over and brushed his lips across Chris's mouth.

Chris let out a small, surprised sound. Rick kissed him again, his lips soft and gentle, then pulled away. Shocked, Chris stared at him.

"I should probably go now," Rick said after a silent moment. "Sorry if I made you uncomfortable, Chris. But I've been wanting to do that ever since I first met you. Matt said he wouldn't mind if I kissed you."

Chris took a deep breath, trying to collect his scattered wits. "It's okay. Did Matt really say that? I mean about us, the three of us..." He trailed off, unable to finish the thought.

Rick nodded. "He did."

"And what do you...I mean, do you want to?"

"Yeah, I do. Do you?"

"I don't know. I mean, you're certainly an attractive man, and I can't pretend I didn't like it when you kissed me just now." He licked his lips and caught a trace of Rick's taste, sweat and beer and something else, something distinctly male. "I did like it. A great deal."

Rick smiled at him. "But?"

"But, I've never done anything like that before. Well, actually I have, but not while I was in a serious relationship. It changes things."

"I know." Rick stood and started toward the door. Chris followed him.

"Just think about it, okay?" Rick said as they walked out onto the porch. "Talk to Matt."

"I will."

Rick held out his hand. Chris took it and they shook.

"Hey," Chris called as Rick headed down the steps, "would you like for me to call you a taxi?"

Rick shook his head. "Naw. I only live a couple of blocks away, I can walk."

"Be careful."

Rick smiled at him, turned, and walked away. Chris watched him until he was out of sight, then went back in the house and locked the door.

Upstairs, he undressed and brushed his teeth, then stood smiling at the nearly naked form sprawled across the bed. Matt had taken his shirt off and thrown it on the floor, and his jeans were tangled around one ankle. He lay on his stomach, with the Elvis boxers halfway down his thighs. Chris pulled the crumpled jeans off Matt's leg, then crawled onto the bed, leaned down, and kissed his bare butt.

"Hm...Chris?" Matt rolled onto his side and gazed blearily at him as he worked Matt's boxers off and tossed them aside.

"Hey, sexy," Chris said.

Matt reached for him. Chris hauled Matt into his arms and they snuggled together.

"D'you talk to Rick?" Matt kissed Chris's shoulder.

"Yes, I did."

"He tell you?"

"He did."

"And?"

Chris lifted Matt's chin and stared into his eyes. "Do you really want to do that? Have a threesome with him?"

Matt shrugged. "Yeah, why not? Haven't done that in a while, could be fun. 'Sides, I think it'd be brutally hot to watch you guys together. He wants you, y'know."

"Yes, I heard." He stroked Matt's cheek. "So, you've done a threesome before?"

"Mm-hm."

"You never told me that."

"Never came up." Matt wound an arm around Chris's neck. "I've done lotsa things, Chris. I'm not giving up my chance for worldly expedience...I mean, experdi... Shit!" Matt stopped and frowned fiercely. Chris stifled a laugh. "Ex-per-i-ence," Matt said, as clearly as he was able. "M'not giving it up by being with you. Stupid."

"Good. I'm sorry I said those things to you, Matt. I truly didn't intend to underestimate you the way I did."

"'S'okay." Snaking a hand between Chris's legs, Matt grabbed his balls none too gently. "Let's fuck."

Chris extricated himself before Matt could do any damage. "I think you're too drunk."

"Am not. C'mon, I wanna have hot make-up sex." He rubbed his crotch against Chris's thigh, then yelped when the new piercing caught on Chris's leg hairs.

Chris laughed. "You're cute when you're drunk. But I think you should just sleep it off now."

"I'm cute aaaall the time, mister." Matt licked Chris's throat, then cuddled against him again. "Can we have hot make-up sex tomorrow?"

"Oh, definitely." Chris kissed Matt's forehead.

"Promise?"

"Promise."

"I love you, Chris."

"Love you too, you crazy thing." He cupped Matt's face in his hand and they shared a long, lazy kiss.

When they pulled apart, Matt gave Chris the smile that always made his heart lurch. He buried his face in Chris's neck and was asleep again almost instantly. Chris stroked his hands down Matt's soft skin, tracing every curve and plane he knew so well and loved so deeply. He felt the thud of Matt's heart, in perfect sync with his own.

Chris closed his eyes and soon drifted into sleep, with Matt's body molded to his. He dreamed of the future—retirement, a garden, holding hands on the front porch. A bond that strengthened as the years went by. It felt real and true, a vision of what lay ahead for the two of them.

In the midst of his dream, he smiled.

Degrees of Sin

Chapter One

When Chris Tucker got home Saturday afternoon from a last minute trip to the grocery store, the house was shaking.

He chuckled as he hefted a bag full of fresh vegetables on his hip. Matt did like to crank the volume up. A tangible wave of sound hit him when he opened the front door. Placebo, one of Matt's favorite bands. He shook his head.

"Matt!" he shouted. "Could you come help me get the groceries?" He walked into the sunny kitchen and set the bag on the counter.

Matt danced in from the deck out back. "Sure thing, baby." He wrapped his arms around Chris's waist and gyrated against him in time to the throbbing beat of "Spite and Malice".

Chris laughed. "Matt, you really don't want to distract me like that right now." He wound his arms around Matt's neck.

"Why not?" Matt pressed a soft kiss to Chris's lips. "We've got plenty of time. No one'll be here 'til five." He grabbed Chris's butt in both hands and squeezed. "C'mon, let's have a quickie. You can bend me over the counter."

The thought made Chris's cock twitch. He glanced at the clock and groaned. "Matt, it's after four already. And I still have to prepare the vegetables for grilling and stuff the mushrooms, among other things."

"Why don't you stuff my ass instead?"

"Matt!"

"Fine." Matt gave an exaggerated sigh. "That's what I get for falling in love with a chef. Can't even have a cookout for a few friends without getting fancy."

"Hardly fancy." Chris extricated himself from Matt's grip and they headed out the front door hand in hand. Matt switched off the CD player on the way.

"Chris," Matt said as they descended the porch steps, "you've got steaks marinating in the fridge. You spent all morning making chocolate-raspberry cheesecake. You bought five different kinds of wine, for Christ's sake." He opened the back door of Chris's dark blue BMW and picked up two bags of groceries. He peered into one and laughed. "And it looks like you're about to make that bread thing with the tomatoes. That's not fancy?"

"It's called bruschetta." Chris got the last two bags and bumped the car door shut with his hip. "And no, it's not fancy. It's very simple. Everything I'm cooking today is simple, really."

"So what's wrong with burgers and potato salad? That's what most people have for Labor Day."

"Most people can't cook like I can."

Matt laughed. "Too bad you're so unsure of yourself."

"False modesty is pointless and hypocritical." Chris balanced a bag on one knee so he could open the front door. "I know I'm an excellent cook, why should I pretend that I'm not?"

Matt gave him a dimpled grin. "You shouldn't pretend. That's what made me fall for you."

"Oh, I see," Chris said as they carried the groceries into the kitchen. "You only love me for my fabulous cooking."

"Yep. Feed me and I'm your happy whore."

"Ah."

Matt laughed and abandoned the groceries in favor of giving Chris a long, deep, sizzling kiss. "You know damn well that's not what I meant," he murmured when they pulled apart. He stroked his fingers down Chris's cheek and over his jaw. "I love how you never pretend anything. You're the only person I've ever known who can be fucking brutally honest all the time without pissing everyone off."

"That's because I know when to speak up and when to keep my mouth shut. Unlike some people." He took Matt's hand in his and kissed his palm before turning back to the groceries.

"What's that supposed to mean?"

"Nothing." Chris grinned at Matt's skeptical expression. "Would you mind cutting me some basil? For the bruschetta?"

Matt dug the kitchen scissors out of the drawer. Arching an eyebrow at Chris, he opened the screen door and went out to the herb garden on the deck. Chris watched him crouch beside the barrel planted with basil and smiled at the strip of creamy skin showing between his T-shirt and his baggy shorts. Matt turned and caught him looking.

"Hey!" he called through the screen. "You just wanted me to do this so you could see some skin, you perv."

"I most certainly did not." Chris grinned at Matt as he came back inside and set the fresh basil on the counter. "I'd never have to resort to such crude methods with you. You'd go naked all the time if you could."

Matt shrugged, dropped the scissors on the table, and wrapped his arms around Chris from behind. "Yeah, well, when you're right, you're right." He kissed Chris's neck. "You love it."

Chris leaned back against him. "Yes, I do." He turned his head to collect a quick kiss. "My darling, I wouldn't change a single thing about you. I adore your nudist tendencies."

"I know." Matt bit Chris's ear, then let go of him and rested his elbows on the counter. "Now tell me what you need me to do."

Chapter Two

They spent nearly an hour cutting vegetables for grilling and making salad, bruschetta and stuffed mushrooms. It was almost five and Chris had just started grilling the steaks when the first of the guests arrived. Matt ran to the front door to let them in. Chris smiled as they all trooped into the backyard. Before long, the yard and deck were full of people talking and drinking wine or local microbrew.

Chris was piling sizzling steaks onto a platter when Rick Gonzalez arrived. Catching Rick's eye over the crowd, Chris waved at him. Rick smiled and waved back, then weaved his way through the throng.

"Chris, hi." He flashed a movie-star smile and brushed back the chestnut hair that curled below his shoulders. "How you doing, man?"

Chris wiped his hands on his I'm Too Sexy For My Grill apron. "I'm good, Rick. It's great to see you." He shook Rick's hand. "I'm so glad you could make it."

"Me too." Rick scanned the crowd from his six-foot-four height. "Wow, Matt said this was 'just a few friends.' You guys friends with the whole city or what?"

Chris laughed. "Well, considering that Matt makes at least three new friends every time he leaves the house, I'd say probably so at this point."

"Hey, Chris!"

Chris and Rick both turned toward Matt's voice. He was inside, leaning out the kitchen window.

"What?" Chris called.

"How 'bout some music, huh?"

"That would be nice."

Matt grinned. "Coming right up." He disappeared through the window.

Rick chuckled. "You're letting him pick dinner music?"

"I like to live dangerously. Would you grab those vegetables for me, please?" Chris picked up the platter full of steaks and set it on the buffet table. Rick followed with a pan full of grilled vegetables.

Chris had just piled a second platter with skewers of chicken, peppers and tomatoes when the music blasted from the outdoor speakers. Rick laughed and Chris rolled his eyes.

"Matt," he said when Matt came strolling back outside, "do you really think that 'Up The Bracket' is the best dinner music?"

Matt threw both arms around Chris's neck. "What, you don't like The Libertines now?" He ran one bare foot up Chris's calf and gave him a wide, sunny smile.

"I like them fine." Chris pulled Matt close. "As a matter of fact I'm quite fond of this album. It's just that it seems a bit…exuberant for dinner."

Matt shook his head. "Relax, babe, it's just a cookout." He slid his hands through Chris's hair and kissed him.

One kiss led to another, then another. Soon they were pressed together, kissing like there weren't fifty people watching. They were reminded of their yard full of company when they came up for air and everyone burst into spontaneous applause. Chris waved. Matt stood on a bench and bowed.

"Thank you, thank you very much!" he shouted. "And now that you've had your pre-dinner entertainment, it's chow time. Everybody come and get it."

Matt set out a huge plate of potatoes baked on the grill while Chris went inside to get the bruschetta from the oven. He had the warm bread piled into three big baskets and was trying to balance them all when Rick came in through the screen door.

"Hey," Rick said. "You need some help with that?"

Chris smiled. "Sure, that would be great. Thanks, Rick."

He handed Rick one of the baskets. An electric charge shot up Chris's arm when their fingers brushed. He looked into Rick's dark brown eyes. They were soft and heavy with desire.

"I still think about it, you know." Rick's voice was barely audible over the music and laughter from outside. "That kiss, and what Matt said."

Not quite two months before, Rick had confessed to Chris that he had a crush on him. They'd kissed, a quick, chaste kiss Chris hadn't forgotten either. And Matt not only hadn't minded, but had suggested a threesome. Rick was all for it. The thought of it made Chris's whole body tingle, but he still wasn't sure.

"I still think about it too," Chris admitted. "I want to do it, Rick. But I just don't know what it would do to my relationship with Matt. I love him so much, I can't do anything to jeopardize that."

"It won't."

They both jumped at the sound of Matt's voice. Chris turned to him. The heat in those huge blue eyes surprised him. He bit his lip as Matt walked over to them.

"Matt, I..."

Matt put a hand to Chris's mouth. "Shut up. This isn't gonna break us up, okay? We love each other. We're in this for life, and we both know that. So what's wrong with a little fun, huh?" He glanced up at Rick with an evil gleam in his eyes. "Kiss him for me."

Chris blinked. "What?"

"Kiss him, stupid. I wanna see. Here, gimme those." He snatched the baskets of bruschetta out of their hands and bumped Chris's hip with his. "Go on."

Chris hadn't felt so awkward since high school. He looked up at Rick. "Okay with you, Rick?"

Rick stared down at him with burning eyes. "You know it is."

Chris hesitated only a second before reaching up to brush Rick's hair out of his face. Rick sighed at the touch. Sliding one big hand around the back of Chris's head, Rick bent down and covered Chris's mouth with his.

The touch of Rick's lips started a warm glow deep in Chris's belly. He buried both hands in Rick's hair and opened his mouth, letting Rick's tongue in. Knowing that Matt was watching them made him hot all over. By the time they pulled apart, he was weak and dizzy with desire.

"Goddamn, that's hot," Matt panted. Chris looked over at him. His eyes had darkened to deep sapphire, a sure sign of his arousal.

"You like that?" Chris pulled Matt to him, bread baskets and all. He wound one arm around Matt's waist and the other around Rick's.

"Hell yeah," Matt said. "That was hotter than fuck."

"So, should we...you know?" Rick sounded nervous.

Matt grinned at him. "Why don't you stay after everyone else leaves?" He turned back to Chris. "What about it, babe?"

Chris stared into Matt's eyes. He seemed completely sure.

Chris took a deep breath. "Yes. I'd like that too."

"Great." Matt pressed close and kissed Chris with plenty of tongue. "Mm. Tastes good. Now come on, let's get back outside. I'm starved."

As they walked back onto the deck, Chris felt like he'd fallen into another dimension. The air crackled with sex. When Chris leaned over the table to pile grilled peppers and tomatoes on his plate, Rick managed to grope his ass without anyone else noticing. At least Chris assumed no one else noticed. If they had, whistles and laughter would be the least he could expect. Chris returned the favor by sliding a hand between Rick's legs when they sat side-by-side.

Matt plunked himself down on Chris's right, so that Chris sat between them with a warm thigh pressed against each of his. It was a distracting place to be. He nearly inhaled a piece of steak when he felt two hands, one quite large and one smaller, intertwine over his crotch and gently squeeze.

"Whoa, babe, you should be more careful," Matt said. "You don't have to cram the whole thing in your mouth at once." He blinked innocently while Chris cracked up and almost choked again.

"Matt," Chris gasped when he got his breath back, "you are an evil little demon."

"Yeah, but I'm cute." Matt winked at him and picked up his beer bottle.

Rick watched Matt for a minute. "Don't think cute's the word that comes to mind when you're watching somebody deep throat their beer bottle." He grinned.

Matt pulled the bottle out of his mouth. "You like it, you perv." He tongued the bottle up and down, moaning like a five-dollar whore. Chris laughed.

By the time everyone had gotten their fill and the last crumb of cheesecake was gone, the sun was sinking behind the mountains, painting the sky pink and lavender. Chris leaned against the big oak tree beside the wooden fence and smiled at the whooping crowd of people following Matt in a wild dance around the torch-lit yard. The balmy late summer breeze smelled like honeysuckle and felt soft on his skin.

"Chris!" Rick called. "What're you just standing there for? C'mon!"

Rick pulled him in before he could say a word, and he spent several mind-scrambling minutes trying not to get a raging hard-on with Rick's muscled body pressed to his. Matt sidled up behind him, wrapped his arms around his waist, and started grinding into his backside. Chris gave up at that point and let himself enjoy the pressure of Rick's thigh on his crotch and Matt's body against his back.

An hour or so later, a quiet, sensual mood lay over the darkened yard. Couples lay kissing on the cool grass, small groups sat under the flickering torches and discussed life. Matt had put Rufus Wainwright on the CD player, and he and Chris were slow dancing to "Peach Trees". Chris pressed his cheek to Matt's hair and watched the twinkling fireflies through half-closed eyes. He sighed in contentment.

"This is one of those times, isn't it?" Matt lifted his head from Chris's shoulder and smiled at him.

"Hm?" They kissed, a long slow kiss because it was that sort of night.

"It's one of those perfect moments. If time stopped right here, I wouldn't mind."

"I feel the same way." Chris ran his hands the length of Matt's back, over and over in long, languid strokes. "I love you, sweetheart."

"I love you too, baby. Kiss me again."

Chris obliged, and they lost themselves in each other, swaying to the lazy rhythm of the music.

"Aw, that's so sweet."

Chris turned his head and raised an eyebrow at Rick, who was dancing with the willowy redhead from next door. She had her eyes closed and her cheek pressed to his chest. Her boyfriend sat huddled under a tree with several other people, drinking beer and talking in low tones.

"Trying to steal Deb out from under Jimmy's nose, are you?" Chris teased.

"Yep. I think it's working too."

"Mm. Could be," Deb mumbled. "You know Jimmy doesn't dance. Thank God for gay guys."

"I'm not gay," Rick protested. "I'm bi, I like me a hot sexy woman like you. You want a gay boy, get one of those two."

Deb cracked open one chocolate-colored eye. "What about it, Chris? Want to try a little walk on the straight side?" She smiled and licked her lips suggestively.

"Hands off, woman," Matt warned. "He's mine."

"You wouldn't share with me?"

"Bring Jimmy and it's a deal."

"Matt!" Chris laughed.

"What? He's cute."

"Matt," Rick said, "you're such a slut."

"Yeah, you wish. Now shut up, I'm trying to dance with my man." He burrowed his face into Chris's neck.

Rick laughed and Deb snuggled closer to him. He caught Chris's eye, and the hot anticipation in his gaze mirrored how Chris felt when he thought of what might happen later. They smiled at each other.

Chapter Three

It was after midnight by the time the last of the guests left. Laurie raised an eyebrow and grinned as she hugged Chris goodbye. Chris watched her retreating back nervously. The woman was far more perceptive than he liked sometimes.

Rick offered to stay and help clean up, making sure he said it loud enough for the exiting partygoers to hear.

"Dude, don't worry," Matt said. "Nobody's gonna think anything of it if you stay." He gave Rick a sharp pop on the butt and grinned up at him.

"Yeah, well. Okay, yeah, so I'm a little nervous." Rick laughed. "Stupid, huh?"

"Naw. I bet Chris is more nervous that you. Aren't you, babe?"

Chris nodded as he doused the final torch and headed back up the steps to the deck, where Matt and Rick were picking up trash. "I must admit, I am a little nervous."

"See, I told you." Matt shook his head. "Sad. You guys are so hot for each other, but I bet I'm gonna have to work you both like a porn fluffer before you get going."

"Matt, really..."

Matt laughed. "Hey, I was just kidding, Chris." He wrapped both arms around Chris's waist and kissed the end of his nose. "C'mon, relax, will you? It's nothing to worry about." He flicked his tongue over Chris's lips. "Just sex, baby, that's all. Just a little bit of sin. It's good for you."

Chris smiled. "That's not what I learned in Sunday school."

"There are degrees of sin, Chris." Matt sucked Chris's bottom lip into his mouth for a second. "This is just a little one. If you believe in that sort of thing, that is."

"Matt, my darling, I know you don't believe in sin, raging atheist that you are."

"Look who's talking."

"You're a raging hedonist too."

"It's still not wrong, Chris."

"I agree with you, it's just…I don't know. I'm just nervous. So's Rick."

Rick kept his gaze fixed on his feet and didn't say anything. Matt frowned.

"Look, nobody has to do anything they don't want to here, right? If you guys have changed your minds, that's fine. It's no big deal."

Chris stared hard at Rick. His hair hung thick and shining over one eye and caught on his full lower lip. The lean muscles in his arms made Chris's skin ache.

"No. I haven't changed my mind." Chris reached out and brushed his fingers across Rick's wrist. "Rick?"

Rick moved closer and wound an arm around each of them. "I still want to." His long fingers slid into Chris's hair, and Chris leaned into the caress.

Matt smiled. "Let's go inside now." Taking their hands, he led them into the house.

They followed in silence. Matt snagged an almost full bottle of Shiraz off the kitchen counter and brought it along to the bedroom. Upstairs, Chris sat on the padded window seat and gazed out at the moonlit yard.

"It's a lovely night," he said.

"Sure is." Rick walked over and sat beside Chris.

"Matt, do we have any condoms?" Chris asked. "Not to kill the mood, but frankly, I can't remember the last time we used any."

"I got some last week." Matt shuffled through a pile of CDs on the built-in shelves. "Just in case, you know. But we don't have to use 'em if you don't want. Rick's clean. We shared test results yesterday."

Chris gaped at Matt, then Rick. Rick had the good grace to blush. Matt gave Chris a sweet smile that he knew from long experience to be pure deception.

"Okay," Chris said. "I suppose it's a good thing that you two have already discussed this."

"Hey, we're pretty responsible guys when we feel like it." Matt popped a CD into the portable player and jungle drums sounded through the room.

"What the hell's that?" Rick asked.

Matt shrugged. "Some sort of Polynesian music I downloaded the other day. I kinda like it, it's sexy." Digging some matches out of a drawer, Matt started lighting the candles Chris kept scattered around the room. He took a long swallow of Shiraz, then held the bottle out. "Want some?"

"Yeah, give it here." Rick took the bottle Matt offered, drank, and passed it to Chris.

The urge to tease was strong, and Chris saw no reason to question it. Holding Rick's gaze, he ran his tongue along the rim of the bottle and dipped it briefly inside before drinking. Rick's cheeks flushed pink.

Matt nodded. "Yeah, that's it. Damn, I'm getting hot just watching you guys flirt."

Rick laughed. "If you're so hot, why don't you take some of those clothes off?"

"Good idea." Matt pulled his T-shirt off and tossed it over his shoulder, then shoved his shorts down. He wasn't wearing any underwear.

Chris grinned at him. "That's my little nudist."

"Hey, never say 'little' to a naked guy." Matt stretched like a cat, perfectly comfortable in nothing but skin and body jewelry.

"I see someone's ready for action." Setting the wine bottle on the windowsill, Chris slid his hands up the sides of Matt's hips, not quite touching his swelling cock. Having Rick sitting right beside him, watching him caress Matt's naked body, sent a sharp thrill through him.

"You know it, baby." Matt glanced over at Rick, who was staring at Chris's hands on him. "Touch me, Rick."

Rick's gaze darted up to meet Matt's. Licking his lips, he laid his open palm on Matt's bare hip. Matt closed his eyes.

"Mm. Feels nice." He pushed Rick's hand around to his backside. "Touch me some more, don't be shy."

Rick slid closer, pressing his body in a long line against Chris's. Chris watched, fascinated, as Rick ran one palm over the swell of Matt's butt, down the back of his thigh, up over his hip and around again to the small of his back. The sight of Rick's big hand roaming over Matt's body had Chris harder than steel, his heart racing.

"Rick," Chris said, "come here."

Rick swiveled his head around to look at Chris. They stared into each other's eyes for a heartbeat, then they were at each other like rabid dogs. Before he knew what was happening, Chris was sitting astride Rick's lap and they were grabbing at each other, hands everywhere, mouths locked together. He heard someone moaning and realized with a shock that it was him. He pulled away from Rick's mouth with a huge effort.

"Don't stop. It was just getting good."

Chris turned toward Matt's voice. Matt was sprawled on the edge of the bed, thighs wide apart, leaning back on one hand and stroking his erect cock with the other. Rick followed Chris's gaze and sucked in a sharp breath.

"Lovely, isn't he?" Chris said, half to himself.

Rick nodded, his eyes glued to Matt's crotch. "Too bad he's so shy though."

"Smart-ass," Matt grumbled while Chris nearly fell off Rick's lap laughing. "You guys better get naked and get on this fucking bed right now."

Rick raised his eyebrows at Chris. "He always this bossy?"

"You have no idea." Chuckling, Chris brushed a kiss across Rick's lips. "We'd better do as he says before he has a tantrum."

"Chris, quit teasing and get your hot ass over here." Matt leaned back on his elbows and stared at the two other men with lust-darkened eyes.

"Come on, Rick." Chris stood, pulled Rick to his feet, and led him to the big king-size bed.

Lifting one bare foot, Matt plucked at the hem of Rick's shirt with his toes. "Off."

Rick removed his T-shirt. Matt smiled appreciatively at the smooth, defined muscles in Rick's chest and abdomen. "Nice."

"Indeed." Moving to stand behind Rick, Chris traced the tattoo on Rick's back with his fingertips. He found the sight of Matt's creation etched into Rick's skin incredibly erotic. "Very nice."

Matt snickered. "You should see Rick's face, Chris. You about made him cream his pants."

Rick said nothing to refute Matt's claim. Reaching behind him, he grabbed Chris's wrist. "Come back around here."

Chris obeyed. Taking his time, Rick unbuttoned Chris's shirt and pushed it off his shoulders. It slid to the floor with a whisper of silk and a clink of buttons on wood. Chris's heart was pounding so hard he thought it might burst. The feel of Rick's hands caressing his chest, thumbs catching on his nipples, sent shudders of pleasure rippling through Chris's body.

"Jesus, that's hot." Matt's voice was low and rough. Chris glanced over at him. He was masturbating in long, slow strokes, tugging on the metal ring in the head of his dick. The piercing had only been healed for a week or so, and Chris was still discovering all the ways it could make Matt purr with pleasure.

Sliding his arms around Rick's waist, Chris gently bit one brown nipple. Rick gasped, fingers clutching Chris's shoulders. Out of the corner of his eye, Chris saw Matt stroke himself harder, teeth digging into his lower lip.

"Rick," Matt said breathlessly, "take his pants off."

Rick shot a wide-eyed look at Matt, then turned back to Chris. "Okay?" he asked.

Chris nodded. "Yes. Undress me, Rick."

Rick smiled at him. "I've been wanting to do this for a long time." Leaning down, he kissed Chris's lips, the touch careful and tender.

He flipped open the button on Chris's shorts, then pulled the zipper down, never once looking away from Chris's face. Only when the shorts fell to the floor and his thumbs were hooked through the waistband of Chris's black Calvin Kleins did he look down. Rising to his knees, Matt helped Rick remove Chris's underwear. Chris stepped out of them and stood naked under Rick's heated gaze.

"Isn't he just brutally hot?" Matt licked Chris's side.

Rick nodded. "Beautiful."

Chris's knees almost went when Rick traced a finger up his erect shaft. He grabbed Matt's shoulder for support.

"Here, baby, sit down." Matt tugged on Chris's arm until he plopped onto the edge of the bed. "Now take Rick's pants off."

"Damn, Matt. It's kinda hot the way you order him around." Rick grinned at Chris with a teasing twinkle in his eye.

"Yeah, he likes it." Flipping open the button on Rick's jeans, Matt sank his teeth into the skin just above Rick's waistband. Rick yelped.

"Don't be so rough." Chris laid a gentle kiss on the reddening skin where Matt had bitten and smiled at the tremor that ran through Rick's body. "Be careful where you let him put his mouth, Rick. He likes to bite."

"Yeah, I noticed." Rick laughed and pushed on Matt's shoulders when Matt bit him again. "Ow! Shit, man, you're leaving marks."

Grinning, Matt removed his teeth from Rick's side. "You like it. Chris does too. God, you guys are such pervs. You're corrupting my innocence."

Chris and Rick both burst into laughter, which Matt ignored. He had Rick's zipper down before Rick or Chris noticed.

"Hey!" Rick exclaimed. "Wow, who knew you were so hot for my bod all this time?" He reached down and gave Matt's nipple ring a tug.

Matt stared up at him with the determined air of a man on a mission. "Rick, I'm gonna fucking die if I don't get to see you guys going at it pretty goddamn soon. Take your jeans off."

Rick's eyes turned heavy. He cradled Matt's face in both big hands. "You want to watch me and Chris fucking? What about you? Don't we get to play with you too?"

Chris held his breath and waited. Two months ago, he'd thought Matt wanted to leave him for Rick. He'd been dead wrong, of course, as he'd quickly realized, but it had been a traumatic few hours for all three of them. Now, he was surprised and relieved to find himself hugely aroused by the thought of watching Rick and Matt have sex.

Matt glanced over at Chris and was evidently reassured by whatever he saw in Chris's eyes. Reaching up, he slipped his arms around Rick's neck.

"Yeah," he said, "I wanna play too. C'mere."

Chris watched, pulse racing, as Matt wound both fists into Rick's hair and pulled his face down. The quick wet glints of tongue in the candlelight as they kissed were almost enough to make him come. Grasping Rick's jeans and underwear in both hands, he yanked them down to mid-thigh. Rick's cock sprang free. Chris wrapped a hand around the thick shaft and swirled his tongue over the wide, smooth head.

"Oh fuck," Rick gasped. "Fuck, Chris."

"Mm. Yeah, good idea," Matt mumbled. "Fuck Chris, and let me watch."

"Oh, no." Chris licked the tip of Rick's cock and Rick trembled. "I mean 'yes' to the fucking, 'no' to the watching. This was your idea. I want you involved." He opened his mouth and slid Rick's cock in until the tip hit the back of his throat. The feel of hot flesh filling his mouth sent a jolt of pleasure through him.

"Uh, oh God." Rick's voice was strangled. "Goddamn, Chris. I'm not gonna last if you keep that up." His hands ran over the back of Chris's head and down his neck, his touch warm and gentle.

Reluctantly letting Rick's cock slip out of his mouth, Chris turned to Matt and nuzzled his flat belly. "Do you know what I'd like?"

"What, baby?" Matt leaned against Rick's chest and raked his fingers through Chris's hair.

"I'd like to get it both ways." Chris flicked Matt's pierced nipple with his tongue. "Your cock in my mouth and his in my ass." Rick's body tightened against him and he smiled.

"Oh hell yeah." Matt pulled Chris up into his arms. Chris cupped his face in his palms and they kissed.

"Mm. Damn, Chris, you taste like cock." Matt licked Chris's lips again. "Fuck, that's good. Your cock tastes great, Rick."

"It's so much better firsthand," Chris murmured.

"I bet." Matt shot a devilish grin at Rick, then bent and lapped up the pre-come dripping from Rick's cock.

Chris felt a violent shudder go through Rick's body. "Shit, Matt, shit." Rick groaned. "God, please…"

Chris drew Matt away. "You can have some later. Right now I want this cock inside me." He kissed Matt's lips. Matt lay back on the mattress, propped on his elbows.

Turning to Rick, Chris traced the edge of one sharp hipbone with his fingertips. "Will you fuck me now, Rick?"

"I sure as hell will." Rick kicked off his sandals and tugged his jeans the rest of the way off. Taking hold of Chris's shoulders, he pushed Chris gently down onto the bed. "Turn over. Let me see."

Chris rolled onto his belly. His heart was racing and he felt dizzy with anticipation. "Lube, darling," he said to Matt.

Matt stretched in a way that Chris would've sworn was impossible if he hadn't seen it, and snagged the tube of K-Y out of the bedside drawer. He sat up and ran a hand down Chris's back.

"All fours, babe," he whispered in Chris's ear.

Before Chris could move to obey, strong arms lifted his hips and spread his thighs. Long silky strands of hair tickled his butt, gentle hands pulled his ass cheeks apart, and a warm, wet tongue probed at his hole.

"Ohjesuschrist," he breathed. "Fuck, oh fuck, oh fuck."

Matt chuckled. The sound was coming from the wrong place. Chris turned to look when his lust-addled brain realized that Matt had moved behind him. Matt grinned.

"Just helping out." Matt reached a hand between Chris's legs to stroke his cock.

"Fuck!" Chris cried when Rick's lube-slick finger penetrated him. "Oh God yes, fuck, Rick, yes!" Another finger entered him, teeth nipped at the base of his spine. Matt. His muscles began to relax, his body opening. Rick's hand joined Matt's on Chris's cock, and suddenly he couldn't wait a second longer.

"Fuck me," he gasped. "Rick, Rick now, now, fuck me."

"Damn, it's hot when you talk dirty like that," Matt declared.

"Come over here," Chris ordered, throwing Matt a desperate glance over his shoulder. "I need your cock in my mouth."

Leaning over, Rick kissed Chris's back while Matt scrambled to get in position. "Tell me if I hurt you," Rick whispered. "I don't want to hurt you."

Chris managed a smile. "You won't. Just do it, Rick. Want you inside me."

He felt rather than saw Rick smile before pulling away. Chris heard the squelch of lube being squeezed out. A cool slipperiness on him, then the sweet burn as Rick's cock penetrated him. He sucked in a hissing breath.

Rick stopped and held still. "You okay?"

"Fine," Chris managed. "God, it feels good." He rocked back against Rick and his cock slid in to the hilt. Whimpering, Chris reached for Matt, and Matt obligingly spread his legs. Chris swallowed his dick whole.

"Mm, oh yeah, suck it, baby," Matt growled in his best porn-star voice. He pushed Chris's head down, forcing himself in deeper, just the way Chris liked it.

Rick grasped Chris's hips and started to move, an agonizingly slow grind that turned Chris's brains to soup. He felt every inch of Rick's erection like a brand inside him. Closing his eyes, he gave himself up to the feel of hard cocks filling his mouth and ass and the sharp, musky smell of sex.

Rick leaned over his back, holding himself up on his hands, and traced a wet trail up Chris's spine with his tongue.

"You're so hot and tight inside," Rick whispered, his lips brushing Chris's ear. "I love fucking you." He gave a sharp thrust, hitting the magic spot and sending electricity zinging over Chris's skin. Chris moaned with his mouth full.

"Yeah, Rick, fuck his ass." Matt's voice was husky with lust. He grabbed a handful of Chris's hair, keeping them locked together as he sat up on his knees. "Jesus, Chris, you're so hot like this, getting your mouth and ass fucked at the same time."

Chris hummed deep in his throat, which made Matt gasp and squirm in the most wonderful way. Pulling back a little, Chris grasped the steel ring in Matt's cock between his teeth, making Matt squirm even more. Rick's hair brushed Chris's shoulders as he leaned down and flicked his tongue over the head of Matt's cock.

"Oh! God, God, suck me!" Matt demanded.

Chris moved his head to the side so he and Rick could share. They took turns, one sucking Matt's cock while the other tongued his balls and nibbled at his thighs. Chris could feel Rick moving inside him, filling him and stretching him tight. The sheer wicked thrill of what they were doing made him burn all over. The knowledge of Matt's excitement, and of Rick's, fed his own arousal.

"Oh fucking hell," Matt moaned. "Fuck, gonna come."

Rick raised his head. "Do it, Matt." He played his tongue over Matt's piercing.

Matt's breath hitched, his hips jerked, and hot semen pulsed out of him. Chris and Rick wrapped their lips and tongues together around the head of his cock to catch every tangy drop. When it was all gone, they licked the sticky remains off each other's mouths.

Matt sighed. "Jesus fucking Christ. Wow." He flopped back onto the mattress with a big grin plastered over his face. "You guys are good."

Chris couldn't answer. Rick was pounding into him so hard his body rocked forward with every thrust. Digging his fingers into the mattress, he pushed back against Rick's hips.

Matt bit his lip. "Goddamn, that's hot." He turned onto his stomach, then rose onto hands and knees and leaned over Chris's back. Chris heard the soft wet sounds of kissing. Raising his face, he nuzzled between Matt's legs, licking and biting the insides of his thighs.

"God, Chris," Rick said, his words broken by Matt's persistent kisses. "Gonna come. Mm."

"Yes, fuck, come inside me," Chris gasped.

Rick's fingers clamped onto his hipbones, holding him still. Chris let out a sharp cry when Rick thrust into him, once, twice, three times, plunging deep. He felt Rick's cock swell inside him, and Rick came with a kiss-muffled groan.

Rick's shaft was still imbedded in him when Matt pushed them both over into a tangled heap and dove straight between Chris's legs. His warm wet mouth descended on Chris's cock.

"Matt, baby, yes," Chris sighed. Rick ran a hand through Chris's sweaty hair. Turning his head, Chris captured Rick's mouth with his.

"Hey, Rick," Matt said, "wanna come share some cock with me?"

Rick broke the kiss and drew back. The hunger in his eyes sent waves of heat through Chris's body.

"Hell yeah." Rick gave Chris one more lingering kiss, then pulled out of him and stood. Before Chris could ask him what he was doing, he grabbed Chris's ankles and tugged until his backside hung off the edge of the bed.

"C'mon down here, Matt." Rick sank to his knees on the floor and gestured to Matt, who hopped off the bed to join him. Chris spread his legs wide to make room for them both.

"Go on, Rick," Matt said, rubbing his cheek against Rick's arm. "Suck him."

Chris pushed up on his elbows to watch as Rick bent and kissed the head of his cock, then opened his mouth to probe at the dripping slit with his tongue. He slid Chris's erection past his parted lips and took him deep. Chris clenched a handful of Rick's hair where it brushed his groin.

"Fuck, fuck, that's good." Digging a heel into Rick's shoulder for leverage, Chris thrust his hips up, shoving his cock all the way into Rick's throat. Rick's moans said that he liked it as much as Chris did.

Chris's brain barely registered when Matt ducked down out of sight between his legs. But it registered plenty when his thigh was shoved out of the way and Matt's skillful tongue entered him. The combination of sensations tumbled him to the edge.

"Ah, oh fuck, I'm coming!" he cried.

Rick responded by sucking harder, rasping his tongue over the sensitive underside of Chris's glans and pumping his shaft with his hand. Taking Chris's balls into his mouth, Matt plunged two fingers into Chris's ass, and that was it. Chris came hard, shaking all over.

Chris flopped onto his back and watched Rick and Matt kissing, sharing his semen between them. He felt light and boneless. Matt crawled onto the bed, followed by Rick, and they both wrapped him in their arms. With Matt's familiar warmth against his chest and the exciting newness of Rick's body pressed to his back, he felt safe and warm and utterly content. He sighed happily.

"God, that was amazing." Chris snuggled deeper into Rick's arms and kissed Matt's throat. "I don't think I'll ever again be capable of movement."

Rick's laugh rumbled against Chris's back. "Yeah, I know." He buried his face in Chris's hair. "Chris, you're a great lay."

"Yeah, he's a real tiger in the sack," Matt chimed in.

"I have to be," Chris said. "Since sex with you is pretty much like doing it with a wild animal."

"And you'd know that how exactly?" Matt raised his eyebrows. "Jeez, what a pervo."

"Chris is right. You're crazed, man. A total animal." Rick ducked down behind Chris's back when Matt took a swipe at his head. "Hey, that's a good thing."

Slithering right over Chris's body, Matt pushed Rick onto his back and sat on his stomach. Rick let out an "oof" as the air rushed out of his lungs. Matt leaned on Rick's chest and grinned down at him.

"A good thing, huh?" He plucked at Rick's chest hair.

"Yeah," Rick wheezed. "It's hotter than fuck. Ow! Quit pulling my hairs."

Matt laughed as he rolled off Rick. He sat cross-legged on the bed, looking thoughtful. "You know, I really liked watching you fuck Chris like that. I mean really a lot."

"I could tell." Rick turned shining eyes to Chris. "I liked doing it."

"I know how fantasies can be." Propping himself up on one elbow, Chris stared into Rick's eyes. "They can be impossible to live up to. So was the reality as good as the fantasies?"

Without a word, Rick pulled Chris to him and kissed him. Chris's body was already starting to respond again by the time they broke apart.

"It was even better," Rick whispered.

The mattress moved and Matt's warm, sweaty body pressed against Chris's back. He could feel how happy Matt was to be there. Reaching one arm behind him, he cradled Matt's head against his neck and slid the other arm around to cup Rick's ass. They twined arms and legs together, and he kissed them each in turn.

"I could get used to sin like this."

Sweet Life

Chapter One

"Thank you, sir, have a nice day."

Chris Tucker smiled at the young woman behind the candy shop counter. "You too, thanks." He picked up the small bag and headed outside.

He hummed to himself as he strolled down the busy Asheville street, picturing Matt's face when he saw what Chris had brought him. Chris had passed the candy store on his way to the restaurant where he was head chef, and decided on impulse to bring Matt some of the candy he loved so much. Dark chocolate from The Chocolate Fetish never failed to make Matt smile.

Chris took a deep breath of cool October air. Scents of espresso and cinnamon rolls wafted from one shop, patchouli incense from another. Drumbeats and singing from an impromptu afternoon concert in Pritchard Park floated on the air. Chris crunched red, orange and brown leaves underfoot and thought as he walked.

He and Matt had been together for just over two years. They'd clicked right from the first and rarely had more than minor disagreements. Lately, though, Matt's exuberant personality had been noticeably dampened, and Chris wasn't sure why. Whenever Chris asked if he was okay, Matt would flash his dimpled grin and insist he was fine. Chris wasn't sure he believed that, but he knew how stubborn Matt could be. He'd talk when he was ready, and not a second before.

The waiting room at Dragon's Den was full when Chris walked in. People leaned against the dragon mural on the wall because the chairs and sofa were occupied. The buzz of tattoo needles sounded from the back of the shop.

A woman with long, solid black braids emerged from one of the back rooms. She smiled when she saw Chris.

"Hi, Chris, how are you?"

"I'm fine, Kelly, and you?"

"Great. Looking for Matt?"

"Yes, is he busy?"

She shook her head. "Nope. He just got done with a customer. Let's see." She leaned over the counter to check the appointment book. "Yeah, he's got a few minutes before his next appointment. You can go on back if you want."

"Thanks, Kelly." He walked behind the counter and followed the sound of "OK Computer" toward Matt's tattoo room.

The room was small but bright, with a round window that looked out onto a tiny fenced-in garden. The flowers were dry and shriveled and fallen leaves choked the stone fountain, but the sunny view still lent a peaceful feel to the little room. Pictures lined the pale yellow walls—tattoos Matt had done, Matt's twin sisters, Chris camping it up in a long velvet gown at the Renaissance Fair. A poster of Matt and Chris at the beach with their arms around each other occupied the center position of one wall.

Chris stood in the doorway for a moment, watching Matt clean up inks, needles and other supplies. Matt's long-sleeved purple shirt clung to his body, showing the contours of lean muscle in his arms and back. Threadbare jeans, faded almost white, hugged his slender legs and firm butt. Chris couldn't see Matt's face, since his back was turned, but he knew that face better than his own. Smooth ivory skin, a sweetly sensual mouth, eyes as big and blue as the October sky. Matt ran a hand through his candy-apple red hair and Chris smiled.

"Hello, beautiful," Chris said.

Matt whirled around, then relaxed when he saw Chris. "God, babe, you scared me."

"Sorry." Chris walked over and pulled Matt to him. "How's your day going?"

Matt shrugged. "Okay, I guess." He leaned against Chris's shoulder. "So what're you doing here?"

"I came to see you, of course, what else?" He tilted Matt's chin up and kissed him. Matt gave him a terribly anemic version of his usual thousand-watt smile, and Chris frowned.

"Matt, what's wrong?"

Matt's expression was unusually serious. "You came to see me?"

"Yes, of course. I brought you some dark chocolate from The Chocolate Fetish." He held up the bag.

Matt took it and set it on the counter without a second glance.

"Okay," Chris said, "now I know something's wrong, when you don't even want your favorite candy." He laid his hands on Matt's cheeks. "What is it, love? You haven't been yourself for days."

Matt gave him a strange look. "Did you only come to see me?"

"Well, of course I always enjoy seeing your coworkers, but yes, I came to see you. Why would you ask?"

Matt bit his lip. His brow furrowed. Chris waited.

"I just thought maybe you'd come to see Rick too," Matt admitted after a few silent moments. "I mean, you guys have gotten pretty close, haven't you?"

Rick Gonzalez was one of two body piercers working at Dragon's Den. He was tall, movie-star handsome and bisexual. He'd had a thing for Chris ever since they first met. He'd joined Matt and Chris in bed for the first time the night of their Labor Day cookout. They'd all enjoyed it so much that they'd done it four more times in the seven weeks since. The threesome had been Matt's idea to start with, so Chris was surprised to hear the unfamiliar note of jealousy in his voice.

"Matt, sweetheart, no." Chris kissed Matt's soft lips. "I like Rick a great deal, and I think we all have fun together, in and out of bed. But no one could ever replace you. I love you more than anything else in this world."

"I know." Matt shrugged. "I guess I'm being stupid. I mean I know the whole sex thing was my idea. And if that's all it was it wouldn't bother me any. It just seems like you guys have so much in common, you know? I mean you talk all the time, you hang out all the time, you like the same books and stuff. He's even a pretty good cook. I don't know. I guess I'm feeling kind of left out."

Chris didn't know what to say. He and Rick did have a lot in common, but with Matt he had a connection that went beyond the power of language to explain. Shaking his head, he tried to find the words he wanted.

"Yes, we're similar in a lot of ways and we get along quite well. But at the end of the day, Rick and I are friends. Friends with privileges, yes, but the basis of our relationship is friendship. You, my darling, I love with all my soul. You and only you. And I know that you feel the same way about me."

"I think maybe he's in love with you, Chris," Matt said quietly.

Chris blinked. "Oh, surely not. What in the world makes you think that?"

"He's been acting different lately. All goofy and secretive and guilty. Like he's in love with someone who's not available." He picked up the tiny green dragon statue on the counter, examined it for a moment, then put it down again.

"Well, he admitted to having a crush on me, but that's not the same as being in love. And I'd gotten the feeling that the threesomes had helped him get past that. Don't you think you're misreading it?"

"No, I don't think so." Matt looked down at his purple Keds. "I'm telling you, Chris, he's been different lately. I've got a bad feeling about it."

Chris lifted Matt's chin. "Listen to me. I think you're wrong. Whatever it is going on with Rick, I don't think that's it."

"What if it is?"

Chris was startled to see Matt's eyes well with tears. He kissed both of Matt's eyelids, the tip of his nose, the corner of his mouth.

"If it's true," Chris answered, "then I'm very sorry for him. Because you're the only one for me. I could never love anyone else."

Matt laid his head on Chris's shoulder and slipped both arms around his waist, like a child needing reassurance. Chris held him tight.

"You're the only person I've ever been in love with." Matt's voice was muffled against Chris's neck. "It scares me to think of not having you anymore."

Chris closed his eyes and breathed in the fresh scent of Matt's skin. "Then don't think of it. Because I'll never leave you."

"Never's a long time."

"Matt, look at me," Chris ordered. Matt raised his face and their gazes locked. "I meant what I said. I love you. I will always love you. There's not a man on this planet that could take me away from you."

Matt smiled, showing dimples this time, and the flood of relief left Chris weak in the knees. "I guess I know that. Sorry I'm being so stupid."

"You're not." Chris leaned forward and they shared a deep, lazy kiss.

"I've got a customer due," Matt said several minutes later. He rubbed his cheek against Chris's.

"Mm. All right. Listen, I'll make us a special dinner tonight, okay? Wine and candlelight and soft music, the whole deal."

Matt laughed. "Sounds great."

"What time do you get off work?"

"Early. Ought to be home by eight-thirty."

"Wonderful. I'm only going in to work for a few hours today, so I'll be home by six. See you tonight."

"Okay." Matt pressed close and they kissed again. "Bye, baby. Love you."

"Love you too."

Chris forced himself to let go of Matt and leave. He nearly ran right into Rick, who was coming in the front door of the shop just as he was going out.

"Whoa, hi, Chris." Rick smiled at him. "Is it nice there?"

Chris frowned. "Where?"

"Whatever planet you were on."

"Oh." Chris laughed. "Yes, I suppose my mind wasn't really on where I was going."

"So what were you thinking so hard about?"

Chris gave him a sharp look. There did seem to be something different about him. Rick's cheeks were flushed more than one would expect from the mild breeze outside, and his brown eyes shone. He practically glowed. Chris felt his guts twist.

"Rick, are you feeling okay?"

Rick looked surprised. "Yeah, I'm fine. Why?"

Chris shook his head. "No reason. You just look different."

Something flickered in Rick's eyes and vanished before Chris was sure he saw it. "Well, I'm not any different. Same old Rick."

Chris glanced around the room. A heavily pierced and tattooed couple sat talking on the low sofa. A middle-aged woman in a business suit leaned against the counter, filling out paperwork. No one was paying any attention to him and Rick. "Rick, could we talk for a minute?"

This time the furtive look in Rick's eyes was unmistakable. "Not right now, I've got someone coming in."

"Later, maybe?"

"I don't know, Chris. I'm busy."

"It's important. Please."

Rick stared into Chris's face. His shoulders sagged. "Yeah, okay. I could stop by your place on my way home."

"Good. Matt'll be home around eight-thirty, I'd rather be done with this talk before he gets there."

Rick frowned. "Okay, whatever you say. See you later then."

"Okay." They shook hands and Rick headed to the back of the shop. Chris walked out into the afternoon sun.

Chapter Two

The doorbell of Chris and Matt's Victorian-style house rang at seven forty-five that night. Chris pushed the cherry pie into the oven, then went to answer it. Rick waited on the wide covered porch, looking both miserable and excited.

"Hi, Rick," Chris said. "Please come in."

"Hi." Rick brushed past Chris and stood with shoulders hunched and hands in his jacket pockets.

"Would you like a drink?"

"No, thanks. Listen, Chris, what's this all about?"

Chris sighed. "This is hard for me to say to you, Rick. But I think I have to." He took a deep breath and made himself meet Rick's eyes. "Rick, tell me the truth here. How do you feel? About me, I mean."

Rick didn't hesitate. "I love you, man. You and Matt both. You're the best friends I've ever had. It's not even weird to be fucking both of you. I always thought that would be a freaky thing, but it doesn't feel that way to me. It feels…I don't know. Natural, I guess."

"So you see us basically as friends?"

"Well, yeah. Why, is the sex thing starting to freak you out?"

"No. I just thought…or rather Matt thought, and I thought he might be right… I mean, he said you'd been acting strange, and you did seem different to me…" Chris fumbled for the right words, unsure of how to say it.

Rick's eyes widened. "Oh, hell. You guys thought I *love* love you, didn't you? Like 'in love' love. Oh, shit, no wonder Matt's been so damn moody lately. Shit." He ran both hands through his long dark hair.

"So, you...you don't?" Chris stared hard into Rick's eyes.

"No. Not like that." Rick started to laugh. "You want to know what's going on? 'Cause I'm dying to tell someone."

"Rick, you know you can tell me." Chris took Rick's hand and they sat side-by-side on the sofa. "What is it?"

Rick told him. Chris was so shocked he could barely drink the glass of wine Rick brought him.

• • •

Neither of them heard the front door open at eight-forty. They were listening to "Midnite Vultures" and talking in the kitchen when Matt's voice rang out behind them.

"Well, isn't this just fucking cozy."

Chris jumped, startled, and turned around. Matt's eyes shot blue sparks, but Chris saw the hurt hiding behind the anger. Walking over to Matt, Chris laid a hand on his arm while Rick pretended to check the pie in the oven.

"Matt, Rick came over to talk. He's been helping me cook dinner."

"Yeah, I see that." Matt glared at Rick's back hard enough to drill holes in him. "This was supposed to be just us," Matt whispered. "What's he doing here? I bet he was supposed to be gone before I got home, huh? Guess you lost track of time."

Matt crossed his arms over his chest and scuffed the toe of one sneaker against the floor. A single tear trickled down his cheek. Chris brushed it away with his thumb.

"Sweetheart, I asked Rick about how he felt."

Matt's head shot back up. With a quick glance at Rick, who was leaning against the counter now, Matt grabbed Chris's wrist and yanked him closer.

"You told him?" he hissed in Chris's ear. "What the fuck did you do that for?"

"Because that was the only way to get things out in the open. Honesty can be painful sometimes, but it's the only way to run a relationship. Any sort of relationship."

Matt bit his lip. Releasing his grip on Chris, he rubbed both palms against his thighs. Decision hardened his eyes and he strode over to Rick.

"So what's the deal, Rick? Are you in love with him?"

Rick smiled at him. "No, Matt, I'm not."

"Really?"

"Really."

"Good." Matt flung both arms around Rick's waist and hugged him tight. Lifting Matt right off his feet, Rick kissed him soundly on the lips.

"I love you both," Rick said. "But neither of you is the one I'm in love with."

"Oh, so you *are* in love with somebody, huh?" Matt grinned. "I fucking knew it. So who is it?"

Rick glanced at Chris. Chris laughed. "Go on and tell him, Rick. You won't get a moment's peace until you do."

Matt shot him a dirty look. "God, I hate it when you guys know something I don't know." He poked Rick in the stomach. "Spill."

"Swear you won't tell anyone else?"

Matt drew an invisible X on his chest. "Swear. Now tell."

A blush rose in Rick's cheeks. "Deb."

Matt's jaw dropped. "Deb Woodward? Deb from next door? Deb who has the steady boyfriend? That Deb?"

"Yeah."

"Shit." Matt fell into a chair, still staring open-mouthed at Rick.

"No kidding."

"So how'd it happen?"

Rick's eyes softened. "Well, you know I met her at the Labor Day party. We danced together, remember?"

Matt nodded. "Yeah, I remember."

"We ran into each other a couple of days later at the Fresh Market and got to talking. And we just clicked, you know? I mean at first I didn't think anything about it. I wasn't looking for a steady relationship, and she wasn't available anyhow. But then we started seeing more and more of each other, and it started getting pretty intense. We just figured out how we felt about each other a few days ago."

Chris nudged Rick over so he could take the rice pilaf off the burner. "Tell him about Jimmy before he explodes."

"Shut up," Matt said. "Let him tell the story. I can be patient."

Rick grinned at him. "Since when? Lucky for you I was just getting to that part anyhow."

"So go on." Matt stuck his tongue out at Chris then turned his attention back to Rick.

"Well," Rick continued, "I don't know if you knew this, but Deb and Jimmy had been having problems for a while."

"Yeah." Plucking a daisy from the flower arrangement on the table, Matt twirled it between his fingers for a moment before letting it drop. "She didn't talk much about it, but you could tell she was unhappy."

"It's more than that. She caught him red-handed with another woman. Then he had the nerve to tell her it was her fault because she didn't give him any privacy. They had a huge fight and she broke up with him. That was a week ago. She came to my apartment all upset afterward, and we talked most of the night. And we realized we were in love. So there you go."

Matt shook his head. "I didn't know anything about them breaking up. How come she didn't tell us? Or me, at least. I thought we were pretty good friends."

"She was afraid people would think she and Jimmy broke up because of me and her being together, when that wasn't it at all. She asked me if we could keep our relationship sort of quiet for a little while."

"Yeah, I can see that." A huge smile lit Matt's face. "So. You and Deb. That's way too cool."

"I agree." Chris took the cherry pie out of the oven and set it on the counter. The thick, sweet smell filled the room. "I always thought Jimmy was a nice guy. Looks like I was wrong about that. But I know you, Rick, and you're a great catch. I hope you'll be happy together."

"Thanks, guys," Rick said. "I think we'll probably start seeing each other openly pretty soon. No one's gonna blame her for wanting to move on."

Tilting his head to the side, Matt gave Rick a curious look. "Did you tell her about us?"

"No." Rick picked idly at the chipped place on the edge of the counter. "Wasn't sure how you guys would feel about that."

"It wouldn't bother me." Opening the cabinet, Chris took out two plates. "Deb's a friend, I'd trust her with that knowledge. But I don't know how she would react to knowing you've been sleeping with us. I don't know if that would affect her decision to be with you or not."

"She knows he's bi," Matt pointed out.

"Yes," Chris conceded, "but let's face it, this thing between the three of us is beyond the pale for most people, even the very open-minded ones like Deb."

"I think she'd be surprised, but she'd be okay with it," Rick decided after a thoughtful moment. "In any case, I can't start a new relationship by keeping secrets. I have to tell her. I don't have to mention names if you'd rather I didn't."

"You can. Might as well have the whole thing out there." Matt gazed up at Rick with something like sadness. "This is gonna mean no more threesomes, isn't it?"

"I think so, yeah." Taking Matt's hands, Rick pulled him to his feet. "Still friends, though, right?"

Matt grinned at him. "Hell yeah. C'mere." He buried his hands in Rick's hair and they kissed for a long time.

When the kiss ended, Chris wound an arm around Rick's neck. "My turn," he said and pressed his mouth to Rick's.

"Mm. I'm gonna miss this." Rick wrapped his long arms around Matt and Chris both and hugged them against him. "I should go now. I need to talk to Deb. And I think you guys probably want to be alone."

"Okay." Chris squeezed Rick's hand. "Best of luck, Rick."

"Yeah, man, hope she doesn't give you a hard time," Matt said as he and Chris followed Rick to the front door.

"She won't." Rick smiled. "Love you guys."

"Love you too." Matt opened the door and Rick headed out into the crisp night air. "Bye."

Rick waved over his shoulder. Closing the door, Matt turned back to Chris.

"Guess I was wrong, huh?"

Chris took Matt in his arms. "I'm glad you were wrong."

"Me too." Matt raked his fingers through Chris's hair. "Sorry about how I acted."

"Don't think any more about it."

"How 'bout a quickie before dinner?" Matt caught Chris's bottom lip between his teeth and sucked on it.

"Matt, you have the best ideas."

"I know." Taking Chris's hands, Matt tugged him toward the big throw rug in front of the sofa. "Let's sixty-nine." He dropped to the floor, pulling Chris down with him.

Chris rolled Matt underneath him. "Nothing would make me happier right now than having that delicious cock of yours in my mouth while you're sucking me."

Matt's eyes hazed over. "God, you're making me hot talking that way."

"Good." Chris bent down and licked the end of Matt's nose. "I never get tired of your body." He kissed the corner of Matt's jaw, then his throat, and felt Matt's breathing quicken. "I want to kiss every inch of you." Lifting Matt's shirt, he tongued Matt's nipple ring. Matt trembled underneath him. "I could make love to you forever."

"God, Chris," Matt whispered. "I love you so much."

"I love you too, sweetheart." He captured Matt's mouth in a deep, sweet kiss.

They undressed as fast as they could and fell back into each other's arms. Matt pushed Chris onto his back and straddled him, head to foot. Tugging Matt's hips down, Chris opened his mouth and let Matt's erection slide between his lips and into his throat. Matt's silky-soft mouth engulfed Chris's cock at the same time, and the world fell away.

Chapter Three

Later, they padded naked into the kitchen to heat up their dinner. They spent a pleasant half-hour eating and discussing plans for the upcoming holidays. While Chris washed the few dirty dishes, Matt stood at the window, eating cherry pie with his fingers and gazing out into the night.

"Oh! Chris, c'mere."

Chris laughed at Matt's urgent whisper. "What is it?"

"Just come look."

Chris dried his hands and went to stand behind Matt. Sliding both arms around Matt's waist, he pressed their bodies together and squinted out the window. "Look at what?"

"There." Matt pointed to Deb's house. Following Matt's finger, Chris saw the dim light in the upstairs window, and the shadowy forms silhouetted against the sheer curtains in an intimate embrace.

"Good for them," Chris said. "Now come on, let's give them their privacy."

Matt let Chris lead him away from the window, though he kept looking back over his shoulder. "I hope it all works out for them."

"I think it will." Chris pulled Matt into his arms and kissed him. "Let's not worry about it right now. I'm hungry."

"You just ate, you hog."

"That's not what I meant."

"Oh yeah?"

"Yeah." Sliding his hands down, Chris cupped Matt's bare butt in his palms and squeezed. "All I'm hungry for right now is this sweet little ass."

Matt's blue eyes burned. "Take it, then."

Chris did, pushing Matt face down on the kitchen table and fucking him hard and fast. As his orgasm roared through him, a heartbeat after Matt came on the table, Chris felt a wash of liquid peace. *This is it*, he thought, *this is what it's all about. Being with the person you love.* He leaned over Matt's heaving back and whispered something against his neck.

"What's that, babe?" Matt panted.

"Life," Chris repeated.

"What about life?"

Chris kissed Matt's shoulder, savoring the taste of sweat and sex on his skin. "It's so sweet."

One Red Cord

Chapter One

"Chris!"

"Yes?"

"You seen my shades?"

Chris looked up from the Saturday morning paper which he had spread across the kitchen table. "You mean those wraparound ones?"

"Yeah." Matt hopped into view from the living room, pulling on a purple snow boot. "Not a cloud in the sky this morning, I'm gonna need those to block the glare."

Chris frowned in thought. "Did you look in the car? You wore them to work yesterday, didn't you?"

Matt's face broke into a smile that could outshine the sun. "Hey, yeah! Thanks, babe." He bounded over, gave Chris a quick kiss, then ran out the front door.

Chris chuckled to himself. Matt was an excitable person anyway, but the first big snow of the winter always turned him into a little kid again. The first flakes had barely hit the ground the previous morning before Matt and their next-door neighbor, Deb Woodward, had started making plans to go snowboarding.

The front door banged open and slammed shut again as Matt raced back inside. "You were right, they were in the car." He stuck the sunglasses on top of his hair, newly dyed a shocking neon green, and plopped down on Chris's lap. "I'm going on over to Deb's now. We probably won't be back 'til pretty late, so don't wait up."

"You know I can't go to sleep until you're home." Chris wrapped his arms around Matt and kissed his neck.

"I know. You worry too much."

"It's a dangerous sport, why wouldn't I worry?"

"'Cause I'm damn good, that's why."

"I know, but last year—"

"It's just a chipped tooth. And that was the worst spill I've had since I was fourteen. C'mon, Chris, I wish you wouldn't worry so much. Makes me feel bad for going."

Chris smiled. "Don't feel bad. I want you to have fun. Don't mind me, I just worry because I love you."

"I know." Matt cradled Chris's face in his hands and kissed him. "I love you too, babe. Gotta go."

He jumped up. Chris watched him grab his jacket and knit cap from the hall closet.

"Where are you going this time?" Chris asked.

"Cataloochee. We're gonna do Cat's Cage."

That was difficult terrain, for experts only, and it always scared Chris to think of Matt out there. But he'd come home from Cat's Cage unscathed many times, so Chris swallowed his fear and put on a smile. After all, he reminded himself, Matt was an expert snowboarder.

"Don't forget your gloves," Chris called as Matt started for the front door.

"In my jacket pockets, Mom." Matt hoisted his snowboard under his arm and grinned, practically vibrating with excitement. "Bye, Chris. I'll be extra careful, just for you. Love you, baby."

In a flash, Matt was out the door and gone. Chris smiled. "Love you too, sweetheart."

• • •

By mid-afternoon, Chris had cleaned the whole house and shoveled the snow off the driveway. The phone rang just as he was about to leave for the restaurant. He set his wallet and keys back on the hall table and went to answer it.

"Hello?"

The voice on the other end was faint and panicky. "Chris! Thank God you're there."

"Deb?" Chris put a hand on the wall to steady himself against the sudden rush of fear washing over him. "Deb, what's wrong?"

"It's Matt," she said, her voice thick with tears. "He's hurt bad. They called the helicopter to take him to the hospital, he's on his way now. I left my cell phone in the Jeep so I had to wait 'til I got back to call you. Chris, you gotta go to the hospital right now."

Chris barely heard her. He slid down the wall to sit on the floor, with the phone still glued to his ear.

"How bad?" His own voice sounded far away. "How bad is it?"

Deb didn't answer right away. Chris fought back the panic wanting to consume him. "Deb, please tell me. Please."

"I don't know what's gonna happen, Chris. You gotta go now, okay? Hurry." She let out a strangled sob before cutting the connection.

Chris sat on the floor with the phone beeping in his hand and stared at nothing. He felt ice cold all over. Deb's words echoed in his head. *Matt's hurt bad, you gotta go, hurry, Matt's hurt.* Desperate terror rose like a tide inside him and he started to shake.

"Stop it," he ordered himself. "Matt needs you, just fucking get up and go."

He clenched his teeth and forced himself to his feet. As soon as he was sure his legs would hold him, he grabbed his wallet and keys and ran for the car.

Chapter Two

He made it to the hospital in less than ten minutes in spite of the slushy snow covering the roads. His hands trembled so violently it took him three tries to get his seatbelt undone. He hurried to the emergency room entrance on legs that felt like limp noodles.

Inside, he weaved his way through a standing-room-only crowd of the ill and injured to the triage desk.

"Excuse me," he said.

The harried-looking woman at the desk glanced up at him with a tired smile. "Yes, can I help you?"

"I'm looking for Matthew Gallagher. They brought..." Chris stopped and fought to get the quaver in his voice under control. "They brought him in on the...the helicopter. From Cataloochee."

The woman—Carol Goldsmith, RN, according to her name tag—tapped on the computer keyboard. "Are you a relative?"

"No. No, I...he's my boyfriend, we live together. He doesn't have any family except his sisters, and they're overseas right now." He put a shaking hand on the desk to steady himself. "Please, may I see him?"

"Your name, please?"

"Christopher Tucker."

Pursing her lips, Carol tapped more keys. Chris bit his tongue to keep from screaming.

"Okay, Mr. Tucker," she said at last. "You're listed as emergency contact." After a moment spent fishing through the desk drawer, she drew out a white plastic tag with the word "Visitor" written on it in bold letters. She clipped it to his shirt.

"Go through those double doors," she instructed. "The nurses' station desk is right inside. I'll call back to let them know you're here." She laid a hand on his arm. "Is there anyone I can call for you? Anything you need?"

He managed a wan smile. "No, thank you. May I go back now?"

"Yes. I hope everything turns out okay, Mr. Tucker." She pushed a button on the wall and the double doors swung open.

Walking through those doors felt like entering a war zone. The place hummed with frantic activity. A nurse brushed past him at a dead run, carrying a bag of blood in each gloved hand. She disappeared into a crowd of scrub-clad people gathered around a stretcher. Chris followed her with his eyes. He caught a glimpse of a bare foot with a green and purple lizard tattooed on the ankle, and the room wavered.

Matt.

Matt's foot.

It was Matt lying on that stretcher.

Time slowed and stopped, trapping Chris in an eternal instant of bright, crystalline horror. Eons came and went while he stared wide-eyed at the bit of blood-splattered skin that was all he could see of the man he loved.

"Sir, are you all right?"

The world started moving again with a lurch. He turned and looked into a pair of large, calm gray eyes. The eyes belonged to a small, slender woman with graying hair wound into a long braid down her back.

"I'm Chris Tucker." Chris wished his voice wouldn't shake so much. "I'm here to see Matt Gallagher. He's over there, I, I think he's over there." He pointed a trembling finger toward the stretcher with all the people around it. "Please, I have to see him."

The woman's face was grave. "Mr. Tucker, I'm Dr. Norris. We've been expecting you. The flight nurse said that Matt's friend Deb called you to come over."

"That's right. She, she couldn't tell me how badly he's hurt. Can...can you..." He couldn't continue.

Dr. Norris took his arm and led him around behind the nurses' station and into a small family conference room. She pushed him gently down into a chair.

"Mr. Tucker..."

"Chris."

"Chris. Matt had a very bad fall while snowboarding. His left leg is broken in three places. He has some fractured ribs, which should heal on their own, and a bruised lung. He's also bleeding internally. We're getting ready to take him to surgery right now, to stop the bleeding and stabilize his broken leg."

Chris stared at her, feeling cold and sick. "When can I see him?"

"After surgery."

"Why...why can't I see him now? Please?" Tears rolled down Chris's cheek. He couldn't seem to lift his arms to brush them away.

Dr. Norris sat beside him and took both of his hands in hers. "I'm sorry, Chris. But he wouldn't even know you're there right now. He's already been sedated and had a breathing tube put into his lungs."

Chris drew a shaking breath. "Will someone let me know...let me know when he's out? Out of surgery?"

"Of course." She took a small pager out of her pocket, switched it on, and handed it to him. "We use these to keep in contact with families. You'll get a page when Matt's out of surgery. Just come back to the desk here and tell them you were paged for a conference with the doctor. Someone'll tell you where to meet me."

Chris smiled through his tears. "Thank you, doctor. Where should I wait?"

"You can wait here for a while if you like. Matt's likely to be in the OR for several hours, so you might want to go get something to eat. The nurses can reach you on the pager wherever you are, so don't worry about that."

"Okay."

She gazed solemnly at him. "You should probably call someone, Chris. You shouldn't be alone right now."

He didn't answer. She squeezed his shoulder and went back out into the bustling ER.

Chris followed her, heading toward the place where he'd seen Matt. As he walked into the hallway, a stretcher flew by, surrounded by at least five nurses. Chris caught sight of Matt's face, deathly white, bruised and bloodied. A clear plastic tube was taped in place in his mouth. A nurse rhythmically squeezed a blue bag connected to the end of the tube, causing Matt's chest to rise and fall. Deep purple bruises splotched the bare skin over his ribs. His left leg hung suspended in a traction device with weights attached to it.

In less than a second the stretcher was gone, rattling down the hall to the operating room. But that one glimpse burned itself into Chris's brain, so that he thought he'd never again see anything else. He walked back into the little conference room, curled up in the chair, and sobbed until he had no tears left.

• • •

Four hours later, Chris came dragging back from the cafeteria, carrying a cup of strong, bitter coffee. He was leaning against the window watching the snow fall when Deb walked through the ER doors with Rick. Deb's deep brown eyes were red and swollen and her hand shook in Rick's.

"Chris." She fell into his arms, hugging him tight. "God, Chris, I'm so, so sorry. I'm so sorry."

"I'm glad to see you both." Chris managed a shaky smile. "Are you all right?"

She pulled back, nodding. Rick wrapped his arms around her and she leaned against him. "I'm okay. But Chris, he, he was b-bleeding, the bone was…was sticking out of his leg, and, and he p-passed out, I couldn't wake him up. I was s-so scared he was gonna d-die."

Deb turned and sobbed into Rick's chest. Chris looked up into Rick's dark eyes. They were clouded with fear and worry. "How is he?" Rick asked.

Chris led them to a group of empty chairs in the corner near the window. "He's in surgery right now. His leg was badly broken, and he had some internal bleeding. I didn't get to talk to the doctor long before she had to take Matt to surgery, so that's really all I know right now."

Rick reached out and took Chris's hand. Chris moved closer, and the three of them huddled together to wait.

• • •

Chris lay stretched out on a large, pillow-strewn bed, balmy night air caressing his bare skin. He looked around and saw that the bed stood on a wide, empty beach. The waves whispered and sighed on the sand.

"Chris."

Chris looked up. Matt was leaning over him, naked and beautiful, pale skin pearlescent in the moonlight. Chris reached for him and they kissed. A faint vibration against his hip pulled a low moan from Chris's throat.

"It's my new toy," Matt whispered. "I think you should answer it."

What? *Chris thought, but no words came out.*

"Answer it, Chris. Chris. Chris…"

"Chris!"

Chris woke with a jolt. Rick had a hand on his shoulder. "What?" Chris muttered.

"Your pager's going off," Rick said.

Chris put a hand to the pager clipped to the waistband of his jeans. It was vibrating. He switched it off.

"Matt must be out of surgery." He stood. The desk seemed a thousand miles away. Blindly he reached a hand behind him, and Rick took it.

"Will you come with me?" Chris asked.

Rick rose, pulling Deb with him. "Sure. Let's go." He put one arm around Deb and the other around Chris, and together they headed for the ER nurses' station.

It was only five minutes or so before Dr. Norris entered the conference room, but it felt like five hours to Chris. He stopped pacing when the door opened.

"How is he?" Chris demanded. "Is he all right?"

Dr. Norris smiled. "The surgery went very well. We were able to stop the bleeding, and we were able to get the broken bones in excellent alignment. They should heal quite well. He lost a good bit of blood, but not as much as I'd feared. Of course it's always difficult to predict, but I think he'll do just fine. He's young and healthy, that's in his favor."

Chris fell into a chair, weak with relief. "Thank God." He reached out and squeezed Deb's hand. "When can we see him?"

"He's in the recovery room right now. They'll be transferring him to intensive care shortly. You can see him for a few minutes once he gets there. I'll show you where to go."

"Only a few minutes?" Deb said.

Dr. Norris glanced at her. "His body needs to rest right now, so he'll be on the ventilator at least overnight. Hopefully we can extubate him in the next day or two and let him go to a regular room. But he'll remain sedated most of the time he's on the vent, so he won't know you're there anyway."

Chris nodded. "All right. Thank you, doctor."

Dr. Norris smiled. "Come on, I'll show you where the ICU waiting room is. The nurse will call for you when they get Matt settled."

They'd barely sat down in the waiting room when a young man in blue scrubs walked in and started toward them.

"Are you Chris Tucker?" the young man asked.

Chris leapt to his feet. "Yes, I am."

The man smiled. "I'm Josh, Matt's nurse. You can come back and see him for a minute now."

Chris glanced back at Deb and Rick. Deb was dead white and wide-eyed. "Can they come too? They're very close friends of Matt's."

Josh shook his head. "Sorry, but we can only let one person in at a time. He can have more visitors tomorrow, but right now he needs rest more than anything else."

Deb started to protest. Rick stopped her with a hand on her arm. "It's okay, baby. We'll go see him tomorrow. Chris can give us an update. Right, Chris?"

Rick's tone was calm, but worry filled his eyes.

"Don't worry, Deb," Chris said. "I'll tell Matt you and Rick are here too."

Deb managed a smile. "Okay."

Chris nodded, turned and squared his shoulders. "Okay. Let's go."

Josh warned him that Matt's appearance might be shocking to him. Nothing could have truly prepared him though. Matt's face was greyish-white, scratched and swollen and bruised. The tube in his mouth was now connected to a machine—the ventilator, Josh called it—to breathe for him. A huge black and purple bruise covered the left side of his naked chest. The traction set-up was gone. Chris didn't lift the sheet to look at the broken leg.

The worst thing, though, was the complete absence of Matt's usual buzzing energy. Normally Matt was in almost constant motion, even when he slept, and it unnerved Chris to see him so still and unresponsive.

"Five minutes," Josh told him. "Sorry it can't be longer. You can come in again in four hours."

"Thank you." Chris approached the bed and took Matt's limp hand in his. He barely noticed Josh leaving the room.

"Hi, Matt," Chris whispered. "I know you can't hear me right now. But I just want to tell you that…that I love you, and I'm not going to leave you. They'll only let me visit for a few minutes right now, but I'll be back again later. Rick and Deb are here too, they'll come to see you tomorrow."

Matt didn't move. The machines hummed. Bending down, Chris kissed Matt's forehead. The pallid skin felt cool to the touch. Chris closed his eyes, fighting back tears. He wished he could kiss Matt's lips and feel them moving against his.

"Love you so much, sweetheart," he said. "Please be all right. Please."

He sat there, clutching Matt's hand in his, until Josh told him it was time to leave.

Chapter Three

Matt got out of ICU two days later. The breathing tube was removed without incident, and the drugs keeping Matt asleep were allowed to wear off. Chris was beside himself with impatience when they told him Matt was going to a regular room.

"God, how long does it take to move him?" He stopped pacing a trench in the waiting room floor and gestured in the general direction of the ICU. "It's been at least an hour!"

Rick laughed. "Chris, it's only been twenty minutes. Settle down, will you?"

"I'm sorry," Chris said. "I'm just so anxious to see him."

"You've seen him every four hours since he got here."

"Yes, but he couldn't talk to me. He didn't even know I was there. I just…I want to talk to him. I won't know he's really all right until I talk to him."

He started pacing again. Rick grabbed his wrist and pulled him down into a chair. "Chris, just stop. He must be doing pretty well or they wouldn't be moving him out of ICU."

Chris smiled and pressed Rick's hand between his. "You're right, of course. Sorry."

"Hey, don't worry about it."

Another fifteen minutes passed. Chris was on the verge of resuming his pacing when a nurse walked in from the ICU hallway. "Chris Tucker?"

Chris stood. "Yes, I'm Chris Tucker."

The young woman smiled. "My name's Sandra. I'm Matt's nurse today. Or was. I'm thrilled to meet you. Matt's been talking about you all morning."

"He has?" Chris felt dizzy with relief.

"Yes. Non-stop." She laughed. "He's really anxious to see you."

"I'm anxious to see him too." Chris plucked at the hem of his shirt, unable to keep his hands still. "Is he in his new room now?"

"Yes. Fourth floor, right from the elevator and push the intercom button just outside the double doors. That rings the nurses' station, and they'll let you in. I promised I'd come straight here and tell you where he is. He says to come right over to see him."

Chris let out a breathless little laugh. "I certainly will. Thank you, Sandra."

"You're welcome. Tell Matt I said to behave himself." She turned and started back toward the ICU.

"Okay," Chris said, glancing at Rick. "Let's go."

Rick rose and laid a comforting hand on Chris's shoulder. They headed for the elevators. On the fourth floor, the nurse who let them in pointed them to Matt's room. Chris stood outside the door with his knees shaking.

"You okay?" Rick asked.

Chris nodded. "Yes. I'm just a little scared. I know it's ridiculous, but I can't shake the feeling that he won't be…well, himself. I'm afraid he won't be Matt anymore." He turned to look at Rick. "Does that make any sense?"

"Weirdly enough, it does. My dad had to have brain surgery last year for a tumor, and I remember being scared to death that he wasn't gonna be the same when he woke up from the surgery. I think anybody might feel that way."

"Oh my God, Rick. I had no idea. How is your father now?"

"Oh, he's fine. It wasn't cancer, it was a benign tumor. They got it all out and he's back to his old self now."

"Good." He turned to look at the half-closed door. "Okay. I'm going in now."

"It'll be fine, Chris, don't worry. I'm gonna go down to the lobby, I promised Deb I'd meet her there. We'll come up and see Matt in a little bit. You okay to do this alone?"

"Yes, I'm fine." Chris smiled. "Thanks, Rick."

"That's what friends are for, man." Rick pulled him into a hug. "See you in a little while."

Rick squeezed Chris's hand and started back toward the elevators. Drawing a deep breath, Chris pushed open the door to Matt's room.

Matt's face still sported numerous cuts and bruises, but the dried blood had been washed off and some color had returned to his pale cheeks. A thin plastic tube fed oxygen from a flowmeter in the wall through tiny flexible prongs in Matt's nose. His eyes were closed, his lips slightly parted. One hand was curled under his chin. The hospital gown, which was far too large for him, had slipped off one shoulder, showing more bruises. He looked fragile and battered. Chris blinked back tears as he approached the bed. He sat on the edge of the mattress.

Matt's eyelids fluttered open. For a moment his face was blank with confusion. Then his blue eyes lit up. "Chris. God, baby…I'm so glad…to see you." His voice was weak and scratchy, and he stopped every few words to catch his breath. The sound of it, so unlike Matt's usual clear-voiced chatter, made Chris's heart ache.

Matt held his arms up. Chris bent and hugged him, very carefully.

"I'm glad to see you too, sweetheart," Chris said. "You look much better today."

"Yeah?" Lifting the sheet, Matt took a long look underneath. "Shit. This is better?" He let the sheet drop again and gave Chris a woozy smile. "Looks like it…oughta hurt…a lot." The laughter that began to bubble up abruptly stopped, Matt's face scrunching with pain. "Thank God…for drugs."

Chris ran his fingers through Matt's hair. "Are you in pain, love?"

Matt shrugged. "Leg hurts some... The ribs bother...bother me more. Fucking hurts...to breathe." Grimacing, he rubbed gingerly at the big bruise on his left side. "Fucking stomach...hurts like...like hell...feels like...like they cut...cut me in...in half." Sorrow filled his eyes as he gazed at Chris. "Sorry. Didn't mean to...to get hurt."

"Oh, sweetheart, don't do that." Chris bent and kissed Matt's lips. "Of course you didn't mean to. I'm just so relieved that you're going to be okay."

"There was a rock...under the snow... I ran...ran into it...and fell down...the hill." Matt sank into the pillows, his breathing shallow and ragged.

"Don't try to talk so much, darling, you'll wear yourself out." Resting his forehead against Matt's, Chris stroked his lover's cheek. "You're lucky you weren't killed."

"No shit." Matt tilted his head to kiss Chris. His tongue slipped into Chris's mouth, warm and slick and eager as ever. Chris couldn't help responding, though he tried hard to keep his touch gentle.

Gentle evidently wasn't what Matt had in mind. Grabbing Chris's hand, he shoved it under the sheet between his legs. Chris let out a sharp little cry of surprise, but didn't move his hand.

"Matt, what are you doing?"

"I need you...to touch me," Matt whispered. He pushed up against Chris's hand. Matt's hiss of pain when his leg moved made Chris wince.

"I don't think this is really the time," Chris said. "You're hurting."

Matt stared up at Chris with a strange blend of pain and need. His cock lay flaccid under Chris's palm. "I know. And I don't...don't really feel...like doing...anything... I just..." He looked out the window, shaking his head.

"Just what, love?" Chris moved his hand to Matt's uninjured thigh and squeezed softly. "Tell me."

"I could've...could've died... I remember...the last thing...I thought...before I passed...passed out...was that I...I was gonna...gonna die...and I'd never...never see you...again. I just need...to feel...feel alive...right now...and nothing...makes me feel...more alive...than making…making love…to you." Matt's pain-hazed eyes pleaded with Chris. "Does that make…make sense?"

"Actually, I think I know what you mean." Chris took Matt's hand and rubbed his thumb across the knuckles.

Matt grinned weakly at him. "Besides…orgasm…releases en…endorphins."

"What?" Chris laughed.

"Endorphins. Natural…painkillers. Your brain…releases them…when you…when you come. That's one reason…it feels so…so good. I read that…somewhere."

"Trust you to find a way to make sex a medical necessity."

"Sometimes…science is…is fun." Matt waggled his eyebrows.

Chris laid both hands on Matt's cheeks. "I love you, crazy boy."

Matt smiled. "I know. I love…love you too." He traced a finger over Chris's lips. "Kiss me…Chris, please."

They were still kissing when Rick and Deb walked in. Rick's low chuckle made them both jump.

"Looks like you're not feeling too bad," Rick said as he and Deb approached the bed.

Matt grinned at him. "My private…private nurse…is kissing it…all better." He held his arms up, grimacing. "Stupid ribs. C'mere."

Chris stood and went to lean against the wall. Rick obediently walked over and hugged Matt, holding him like he was made of bone china. He planted a kiss on Matt's forehead, then stepped back again. Matt smiled at Deb.

"Hey there…gorgeous," he said. "Don't I get…get a hug…from you too?"

Tears spilled down Deb's face as she sat next to Matt and kissed his cheek. He squeezed her hand.

"It's okay. I'm all right." He raised her face and thumbed the tears off her cheek.

She stared at him with haunted eyes. "I was so scared, Matt. I was so afraid you were gonna die, and it would be all my fault."

Matt laughed, wheezing a little. "Wouldn't've been...anyone's fault...but mine...if I did. But I didn't. I feel like...I've been beat...with a really...big stick...but I'm gonna...gonna be...okay."

"Why on earth would you think Matt's accident was your fault?" Chris asked.

Matt and Deb glanced at each other and smiled identical wide, knowing smiles. Frowning, Chris turned to Rick. His face was blank, but something in his eyes said he knew exactly what Matt and Deb were grinning about.

Chris crossed his arms and gave Matt his stern face. "All right. What's going on?"

Matt, Deb and Rick exchanged questioning looks. Rick shrugged. "You tell him, Deb."

Deb nodded. She stood and took Rick's hand. "I told Matt something just before we started the run where he had that fall. I was afraid he fell 'cause he was distracted by what I'd said."

"Naw," Matt said. "Just my time...to crash and burn...I guess."

Deb smiled gratefully at him. Chris bit his lip in frustration.

"Go on and tell him, Deb." Rick laughed.

She squeezed his hand. "Okay. Chris, Rick and I are getting married."

Chris stood thunderstruck for a second. Rick and Deb, getting married. His chest tightened. Marriage was something he didn't allow himself to think about. He and Matt loved each other as much as any straight couple out there, but the law didn't care about love. It hurt to know that. Pushing his rising envy to the back of his mind, he scooped Deb up in his arms.

"Oh my God, how wonderful! Congratulations, both of you." He let go of Deb and turned to hug Rick.

Rick lifted him up and kissed him on the mouth. Heat rushed into Chris's face. He, Matt and Rick had been together a few times as a threesome, and Rick's lips on his brought those memories flooding back. He resisted the urge to open his mouth and suck Rick's tongue in. Deb knew about the three of them, but he didn't think she'd appreciate him making out with her intended right in front of her. That part of their lives was in the past. Deb was Rick's future now.

"I'm so happy for you both," Chris said. It was true, in spite of the pain in his heart for the wedding he and Matt could never have. "My goodness, you've only known each other, what, about five months now? Since Labor Day weekend?"

Rick nodded. "Yeah. I know it doesn't seem like long, but we feel like we've known each other forever. When it's right, it's right, you know?"

Chris looked over at Matt. His blue eyes shone with happiness for his friends, but Chris could see his own sorrow echoed in Matt's face. Their gazes locked, and they shared a moment of perfect understanding.

"Yes," Chris said softly. "I know."

Chapter Four

Matt recovered quickly. Three weeks after his accident, his appetite was nearly back to normal, he was able to walk over one hundred feet on his crutches, and he no longer gasped with pain every time he tried to move. Dr. Norris declared he would be able to go home soon.

"God, finally," Matt said when she told him he'd probably be discharged the next day. "I mean everybody here's been great, but man, it'll be so awesome to be home again." He beamed at Chris, who sat in the recliner next to the bed.

Chris took his hand. "That's wonderful. I'll certainly be happy to have you home." He turned a furrowed brow to Dr. Norris. "But how on earth is he to get along? He can't possibly manage the stairs."

"Hey, the physical terrorists started me on steps a couple of days ago," Matt protested. "I'm doing good too. It's slow with the crutches, but my ribs don't hurt so much now so that makes it easier."

Dr. Norris laughed. "Yes, you've been doing remarkably well. You'll need to continue therapy after you go home. I'll write orders for outpatient physical therapy, and you'll be given an initial appointment before you leave here."

Matt made a face. "Oh great, just when I thought I was done."

"You thought no such thing," Dr. Norris said. "I warned you that you'd need to continue therapy for a while."

"Yeah, okay." Matt grinned sheepishly at her. "Can't blame a guy for hoping, though."

She shook her head. "I'll check on you again in the morning, and barring any unforeseen circumstances, I'll discharge you tomorrow. You'll continue to have some pain for quite a while, and it'll likely be several months before you're able to resume all your normal activities, such as snowboarding. But you should do just fine." She stared solemnly at him for a moment. "You're a very lucky young man."

Matt raised Chris's hand to his lips and kissed his knuckles. His blue eyes shone. "I know."

Somehow Chris didn't think he was talking about the accident anymore.

• • •

True to her word, Dr. Norris released Matt from the hospital the next day. Chris brought Matt home with prescriptions for pain medicine, an appointment for physical therapy and three pages of instructions on what to do, what not to do, and when to call the doctor. Chris was grateful they'd written it all down. He thought he'd never remember everything otherwise.

"Well, here we are." Chris turned and smiled at Matt as he pulled the car into the driveway. "Welcome home, sweetheart."

Matt laughed, grabbed Chris by the hair and planted an enthusiastic kiss on his mouth. "Baby, it's fucking great to be back."

Chris came around to help Matt out of the car. He hovered nervously while Matt levered himself up the porch steps with his crutches.

"I wish you'd let me help you," Chris said once Matt was safely up the steps and inside.

"You might have to help me upstairs to the bedroom, but I'll be goddamned if I'm gonna pussy out over four steps to the porch. I did that many at the hospital." With a deep sigh, Matt sank onto the sofa and stretched his leg out on the cushions.

"Fine, tough guy," Chris teased. "I think I'll make some espresso, would you like some?"

"Oh, man, that'd be great. I've been dying for some of your coffee. You've got me spoiled, Mr. Chef."

Chris laughed. "I live to spoil you, princess." He dodged Matt's swipe at his backside, bent and kissed the top of Matt's head, then headed for the kitchen to make the coffee.

"Hey, Chris," Matt called.

"Yes?"

"Do we have any cinnamon rolls?"

Chris smiled. "Yes, we do. I made them last night."

"Cool! Let's have some."

"Matt, you read my mind."

A matter of minutes later, Chris curled up on the sofa next to Matt. They talked about little things while they sipped espresso and ate warm, gooey cinnamon rolls. Eventually the conversation rolled around to Deb and Rick's wedding.

"It's not gonna be a traditional ceremony," Matt said.

"Oh? What sort is it going to be, then?"

"Handfasting."

Chris blinked. "Handfasting?"

"Yep." Matt shoved half a cinnamon roll in his mouth. "Ih Wihuh."

Chris grinned. "Again, in English this time." He leaned over and scooped a trickle of icing off the corner of Matt's mouth with his finger.

Matt chewed and swallowed. "Smart-ass. I said it's Wiccan. The ceremony they're using, I mean. Basically, the happy couple joins hands and the priest or whoever ties their hands together with cords. Different color cords mean different things. Deb says all sorts of religions use handfasting, but they're doing a Wiccan ceremony, since Deb's Wiccan. Gimme that." He snatched Chris's hand and sucked the bit of orange icing off his finger.

"I, um…I thought Deb wasn't part of any of the Asheville covens," Chris said. Matt's tongue circling the tip of his finger made it decidedly difficult to concentrate on the conversation.

"She wasn't until a few weeks ago." Matt turned Chris's hand over and kissed his palm. "But you know she was active in the local coven in Oregon before she moved here. Guess she missed it."

"Yes." Matt licked a wet line up Chris's wrist, making him gasp. "What about…about Rick?" Chris asked. "He's not Wiccan. God, Matt…"

Matt's fingers stroked the inside of Chris's thigh, so lightly Chris could barely feel it through his pants. Matt's smile was pure evil.

"Doesn't matter," Matt said, his voice far too low and seductive for what he was saying. "You don't have to be Wiccan. You don't have to be anything. They'll do handfasting for anybody."

Chris stared thoughtfully at him. "Anybody?"

"Yeah. Deb told me all about it, real interesting." Matt scooted forward, wincing a little as he moved his leg. "Now shut up and kiss me."

The hunger in Matt's eyes sent what little blood remained in Chris's brain racing to regions somewhat lower. He reached for Matt and kissed him.

"I missed you, baby." Matt's words were broken by kisses. "Want you so bad right now."

"Want you too," Chris answered breathlessly. He ran a hand over the brace that covered Matt's left leg from ankle to mid-thigh. "But what do we do about this?"

"Aw, man," Matt grumbled. His brow furrowed in thought. "Guess it's gonna have to be all oral for a while. Dammit."

"This is bad?" Chris nuzzled Matt's throat.

"No." Matt arched his neck so Chris could kiss it. "I love it when you fuck my ass, that's all."

"Me too. But I suppose we can live with the alternative for a few weeks, don't you think?"

"Uh. Uh-huh." Matt's pulse raced beneath Chris's lips. Chris pulled back to look into Matt's face. His blue eyes were clouded with desire.

Matt didn't resist when Chris unbuttoned his shirt and slid it off, then lowered him onto his back. Chris brushed his fingers over the bruises fading on Matt's chest. He trailed tender kisses over Matt's belly, following the line of soft brown hair to where it disappeared into his sweat pants, trying not to touch the healing incision running from the bottom of Matt's ribs all the way to his pubic bone. Hooking his fingers in the waistband of Matt's sweatpants, Chris tugged them off.

He knew Matt didn't have underwear on, because he'd helped him dress. Being busy with other things, he hadn't thought about it at the time. Now, he found Matt's nakedness under the sweats unbearably exciting. He buried his face between Matt's legs and inhaled his scent.

"Fuck, Chris," Matt groaned. "God, suck me now."

Kneeling on the floor beside the couch, Chris took Matt's cock in his hand and looked up into his eyes.

"You have no idea," Chris said, "how much I missed this."

"Yeah, I do." Matt wound his fingers in Chris's hair. "I missed it too. I missed you."

Chris smiled. He opened his mouth and let Matt's erection slide inside.

It had only been three weeks since they'd last made love, but it seemed like years. Having Matt in his mouth again felt like coming home. Matt's taste, his smell, the heat of his body, made the blood sing in Chris's skull. The gentle roll of Matt's hips set the rhythm for his heartbeat. When Matt came, his sharp cry of release and the taste of warm semen sent fierce joy blazing over Chris's skin. He felt tears prick his eyelids and didn't try to stop them.

"God, baby," Matt sighed. "That feels so fucking great." He tugged on Chris's hair. "Now let me do you."

Chris grinned at Matt's flushed cheeks and heavy-lidded eyes. "Are you sure you feel up to it? I don't want to rush you."

Matt gave Chris a don't-be-stupid look. "Chris, the day I don't want to suck you off, you better call the funeral home, 'cause I'll be dead. Now gimme it."

"So impatient." Chris smiled indulgently at Matt as he stripped his clothes off. "Here, lift your head." Matt pushed up on his elbows. Chris tucked a large square pillow under his head.

Matt licked his lips. "God, I've been dying to suck your cock again, Chris."

"Well, here it is, my love. All for you." Chris settled his knees on either side of the pillow under Matt's head and brushed the tip of his cock across Matt's lips. Matt sighed, opened his mouth, and took Chris in.

The feel of Matt's warm, wet mouth after three long weeks of enforced celibacy was nearly enough to make Chris come right away. Holding back required a huge effort. Cradling Matt's head in both hands, Chris started thrusting into his throat. Matt moaned and dug his fingers into Chris's hips.

For all his efforts at delaying the moment, it didn't take more than a few minutes for Chris to come. He pumped what felt like gallons of semen down Matt's throat. Matt swallowed it with practiced ease. When the orgasm peaked and ebbed away, leaving Chris weak and breathless, he sat on the floor and laid his head on the cushions beside Matt's hip. Matt stroked his hair.

"Matt," Chris said when he got his breath back, "have I ever told you how good you are at that? You have quite a talent."

"You know what they say, practice makes perfect."

"Mm."

"Come up here with me."

"What about your leg?"

"It's already here."

Chris laughed. "I meant I don't want to hurt your leg."

"You won't. C'mon, please. I wanna hold you."

"Okay."

Matt pulled his sweats back up and scooted over. Chris climbed up beside him.

Matt squirmed around until he could wrap both arms around Chris and lay his head on his shoulder. "You know what, Chris?"

"What?"

"I love it like this. Just you and me, together." He raised his head and smiled, showing dimples. "That's what really matters, isn't it? That's what's important."

Chris cupped Matt's cheek in one palm. "My darling, sometimes you're very wise."

Matt smiled and snuggled back into Chris's arms.

Ten minutes later, Matt lay sound asleep on Chris's chest. Chris ran his hand up and down Matt's bare back, tracing the curve of spine and hip. As he listened to the soft sound of Matt's breathing, he thought about the day of the accident. He'd come so close to losing the single most important part of his life that day. The shock of it had made him realize that Matt was the bedrock upon which his life was built. The best thing they had was each other, and that should be honored.

"Maybe there's a way," he whispered to himself.

Matt stirred in his arms. "Hm?"

"Nothing, love. Just talking to myself. Go on back to sleep."

"Mm." Matt rolled onto his back, already sleeping again. Chris disentangled himself and put his clothes on. Matt didn't move.

Chris stood looking down at him. Matt had lost weight in the hospital, and his skin was paler than normal. The yellowing bruises stood out in stark contrast on his too-prominent ribs. Dark smudges under his eyes told of sleep lost to the pain he stubbornly denied.

Chris thought of Matt's wicked smile, the intense emotions he couldn't hide even when he bothered to try, his unabashed delight in life. All the little things and big things that made him more vital to Chris than air and water, blood and breath. Chris thought of all those things, and swore to himself that he would show Matt and the world how much this love meant to him. He kissed Matt's forehead and tiptoed into the kitchen.

He dialed the phone. Deb picked up on the third ring.

"Deb? It's Chris, hi… Yes, the doctor discharged him this morning… He's doing fine. He's sleeping right now. Listen, Deb, I wonder if I could ask you something."

They talked for almost an hour. By the time Chris hung up, he knew exactly what to do.

Chapter Five

Two days after coming home, Matt started outpatient physical therapy. Chris stayed with him during his first session, watching him struggle through the exercises meant to strengthen his injured leg. The movements were gentle, and he was not yet allowed to bear weight on the leg, but Chris could see the pain etched into his face.

By the end of the session, Chris felt tense and exhausted just from watching. Matt didn't even argue when Chris made him take two painkillers and lie down on the couch once they got home.

"You okay?" Chris sat beside Matt and stroked his hair.

"Yeah, I'll be fine. It was harder than I thought. Harder than what I had to do in the hospital, anyway."

"You did wonderfully."

"I think you're biased." Matt gave him a tired smile. "But keep telling me that anyway."

"You did wonderfully," Chris repeated. He traced the line of Matt's jaw with his fingers. "Beautifully. Absolutely the best physical therapy session in the history of the world."

Matt laughed. "Yeah, that's the ticket. Keep it coming." He stuck one hand behind his head and grinned in that little-boy way that always made Chris's throat tight.

Chris cradled Matt's face in both hands. "You're wonderful." He leaned down and kissed Matt's forehead. "Beautiful." He kissed the spot where Matt's right cheek dimpled when he smiled. "Perfect."

"You really are gonna spoil me rotten," Matt said when they stopped kissing several minutes later.

"You're already spoiled rotten."

"Rottener, then. Picky." He yawned.

"You're worn out. Why don't you take a nap while I cook dinner?"

"Hm. I'd argue with you, but you're right. I'm beat." He frowned up at Chris. "You sure you don't mind? I feel bad just lying around while you do all the work."

"Matt, you've been through a terrible trauma. It's barely been three weeks, and you've only just gotten out of the hospital. You need to lie around and rest right now." He grinned. "Besides, don't I do all the cooking already?"

"Only 'cause you're the best chef in the whole world and I can't even make microwave popcorn."

"On the contrary, dearest, you make the best microwave popcorn in Asheville." Chris bent and stifled Matt's laugh with a kiss. "Now go to sleep and stop worrying about it. I'll wake you for dinner."

"You take such good care of me, babe." Matt's eyes were already drifting closed. "I love you."

Chris smiled down at Matt. "Love you too." He touched Matt's cheek, then headed for the kitchen.

He put Norah Jones on the portable CD player and started getting dinner together. The familiar comfort of cooking filled him with a warm satisfaction, as always, and he sang softly along with the CD as he worked. Within an hour, the delicious aroma of spicy shrimp etouffee filled the air. Chris opened a bottle of wine, set it on the dining room table, and stared thoughtfully around him.

Evidence of his and Matt's shared history filled every corner of the house. The furniture they'd picked out together, the pictures hanging on the walls, the ceramic tiles they'd laid themselves when they remodeled the kitchen. Chris smiled, remembering that weekend. They'd christened their new floor by making love on it. Chris hadn't noticed until later that Matt had snuck a green tile with a purple lizard on it right in the middle of the tastefully earth-toned floor.

This home belonged to the two of them. They'd made it, together. He'd known the first time he looked into Matt's eyes while they made love that theirs would be a lasting commitment. They'd both known it, and they'd built a life together based on that unspoken promise. Chris smiled to himself as he went to wake Matt.

Matt lay on his side with his broken leg resting on a pillow and one arm curled under his head. Chris sat beside him and kissed his cheek. "Matt, dinner's ready."

Matt opened his eyes and lay blinking up at Chris. He took a deep breath. "Mm. That smells great, baby." He stretched until his head hung over the edge of the couch and gave Chris an upside-down grin.

"Shrimp etouffee," Chris said with a smile. "With garlic toast and brown rice."

Matt sat up and wrapped his arms around Chris's neck. "Can I have you for dessert?"

Chris feigned deep thought while Matt nibbled his ear. "Well, I made lemon chess pie, but I suppose…"

Matt's tongue in his mouth cut him short. "I like lemon chess," Matt mumbled without breaking the kiss. "But I'd like it better if I could lick it off you."

Chris laughed. "Very tempting."

"Let's fuck."

"Right now? What about dinner?"

Matt pulled back. "You know, you're right. I'm starved." He reached for his crutches. "C'mon, let's eat."

Chris helped him to his feet. "You're usually more persistent than this."

"Disappointed?" Matt grinned in that deliciously sinful way he had.

Chris pulled Matt into his arms, crutches and all, and kissed him. "Never."

"I love you."

"I love you too."

"Feed me."

"Your dinner awaits."

Chris led the way into the formal dining room they rarely used. Matt's eyes narrowed. "Okay, what's going on?"

"What do you mean?" Chris gave Matt his best innocent expression as he piled their plates with etouffee.

"We usually eat in the kitchen. And we don't usually have candles and music." He picked up the bottle of wine and examined the label. "And this is one hell of a pricey bottle."

"It's nice to have a change of pace now and then." Chris plucked the wine out of Matt's hand and poured two glasses. "Besides, I think having you home and safe is worth a celebration."

Matt bit into a shrimp and chewed thoughtfully. "Hm. Chris, I know you too well. You're not fooling me."

"Matt…"

"But I know you'll tell me when you're good and damn ready. So I'll quit bugging you."

"Smart boy."

"I know. Pass the bread."

Matt kept his word surprisingly well. Chris watched with amusement as he squirmed his way through dinner, clearly burning with curiosity. They were halfway through dessert when Matt finally broke down.

"Okay. I've been really good, and I can't stand it anymore." Matt set his fork down and slapped both palms on the table. His eyes glinted with determination. "What are you up to, Chris?"

Setting his wineglass down, Chris took Matt's hands in his. "I've been thinking about things lately. Ever since your accident. I was terrified that I was going to lose you that day, Matt. Terrified."

Matt's eyes softened. "I'm sorry, baby."

"Don't be. I hate that you've had to go through all of this, but the whole experience made me realize something."

"What?"

"I've realized that the most important thing in the world to me is you. Us. I mean I knew that all along, yes, but when I saw you in that hospital bed, it suddenly seemed so clear to me. What we have together, Matt, is such a precious thing, and I feel that we should honor that."

"What are you saying, Chris?" Matt's voice was so soft Chris could barely hear it.

Chris took a deep breath. "What I'm saying is...I want to marry you, Matt."

Matt's eyes went wide. His hands trembled. "Wh... but Chris, it's... I mean, we're not..." He stared into Chris's eyes with a mixture of longing and fear.

"I know the law won't recognize it. But that doesn't matter. What matters is that we'll be committing ourselves to each other, in a way that no one can deny or ignore. It may not be a marriage in the eyes of the law, but we'll know what it is. That's what's important." He laid a hand on Matt's cheek. "So what do you say, Matt? Will you marry me?"

Matt sat silent for a moment, his face white with shock under the yellow-green of the fading bruises. He laid his hand over Chris's. "Yes, babe. I'll marry you." Laughing, he threw both arms around Chris's neck. "God, I can't believe this. I never thought I'd be proposed to."

Chris helped Matt slide carefully onto his lap. "And I never thought I'd propose to anyone."

"I love you so much, Chris." Tears glittered in Matt's eyes. He cradled Chris's face in his hands. "So fucking much. I've never been so happy in my life."

"I love you too, my darling. Come here."

Matt's mouth was soft and sweet, his body warm and pliant in Chris's arms. Chris knew every inch of Matt by heart, but his fascination never lessened. Every touch was a revelation, every kiss felt like the first. Every time he looked into Matt's expressive eyes, he knew it was forever. They both knew it.

"Let's go upstairs," Chris whispered.

"You read my mind."

"It's not hard."

"Oh, yes it is."

Chris laughed. "You know what I mean."

"Yeah." Matt pushed up off Chris's lap and hopped over to where his crutches leaned against the wall.

Chris followed him to the stairs. "Leave the crutches here. I'll help you up."

"Okay." Matt left the crutches at the bottom of the steps. Chris got a firm hold on his waist and they began the slow, laborious journey up the stairs.

"Hey, Chris?"

"Yes?"

"How are we gonna get married? I mean since we can't have even a civil union or anything."

"I was thinking of handfasting, like Deb and Rick are doing."

Matt glanced at Chris in surprise. "Hey, pretty smart. I didn't even think of that."

"I spoke with Deb the other day and she told me quite a lot about it."

"Cool." They reached the top of the stairs and made their way to the bedroom.

"So," Matt said as he sank onto the bed, "what colors should we use, you think?"

Chris grinned. "Matt, I believe this is the first time you've ever wanted to talk about something else when we're about to make love."

Matt gave him a sheepish smile. "I know, I'm just really excited about it." He pulled his shirt off and stretched out on the bed.

"Me too." Chris discarded his clothes and lay down naked next to Matt.

"So what colors?" Matt's voice was breathless with arousal.

"Mm." Chris traced a finger over the soft skin of Matt's lower belly. "I was thinking we could have blue, for one."

"What's blue for?" Matt took off his leg brace and threw it on the floor.

"Health, longevity, truth, devotion. Several other things. I think it fits." He leaned over and kissed Matt's lips. "What do you think?"

"I think blue's good." Lifting his hips, Matt shoved his sweat pants down. Chris helped him remove them.

Chris straddled Matt's body and showered tiny kisses over his chest and neck. "What colors would you like? We can have as many as we want."

Matt's breathing was ragged and shallow. He pulled Chris's face down and kissed him deeply. "How 'bout red?"

"Red?" Chris licked behind Matt's ear. "Why red? That's the color for danger."

"Uh. Oh, God." Matt pushed up against Chris's hand between his legs. "It's the color for passion too, right? Lust and passion."

"So it is." Chris took Matt's erection in his hand and stroked him hard. Matt whimpered.

"What about it, babe?" Wrapping his hand around Chris's cock, Matt ran his thumb over the head in a way that turned Chris's bones to water. "One red cord. 'Cause if there's one thing we've got plenty of, it's passion."

Chris gazed down into those huge blue eyes that owned his soul. "Okay, my darling. One red cord. For you."

"For us."

Chris smiled. "For us."

Matt kissed him again, and words ceased to be necessary. They made slow, simmering love, and when Chris came in Matt's mouth, red explosions flared in his mind. He closed his eyes and watched the bright ruby bursts. *That,* he thought, *is such a beautiful color.*

With This Ring

Chapter One

When Chris opened his eyes one fine Saturday morning in mid-June, his first thought was *six more days*.

It had been that way for a couple of months. Every morning and every evening, counting down the weeks and days and hours separating him from the most anticipated event of his life. And now, only six more days remained until he and Matt were married.

Chris grinned up at the sun-splashed ceiling of their bedroom. He stretched carefully, then began the process of extricating himself from Matt's sleeping embrace. Matt had a tendency to wind like a vine around Chris during the night, so that they woke hopelessly tangled together. Chris loved it. Having Matt's beautiful nude body clinging to him all night more than made up for the extra few minutes it took to get out of bed in the morning.

A soft sigh and a sudden tightening of limbs around him told Chris that Matt was beginning to wake. Chuckling, he kissed Matt's sleep-flushed cheek. "Good morning, sunshine."

"Mmph." Matt curled up tighter, clutching at Chris like a child with a favorite toy. "'M sleeping."

"But it's a lovely morning." Chris nibbled at Matt's earlobe. "We could work in the backyard."

"Don't wanna work," Matt mumbled. "Wanna sleep."

"Hm." Chris slid a hand down Matt's back to squeeze one firm butt cheek. "Are you certain?" He traced his fingers up and down the cleft of

Matt's ass, lingering over his tight little hole. "We don't have to work, you know. We could play for a while instead."

Matt wriggled happily against Chris's hand, eyes still closed, a drowsy smile curling his lips. "'K. I'll be the virginal but sexually curious schoolboy and you be the deceptively straight-laced teacher who can no longer contain his burning lust for my untouched young body."

Chris burst out laughing. "I don't know whether to find it amusing or disturbing that you've given this scenario so much thought."

Matt cracked open one brilliant blue eye and grinned. "You *could* find it sexy, you know."

"Could I."

"Mm-hm." Matt pushed back against Chris's fingers, obviously seeking a deeper touch. "Please, Professor Tucker," he said in a high, breathy voice that didn't sound nearly as innocent as it was probably supposed to. "Please put your fingers in my butt, sir. I promise not to tell."

The words turned Chris on in spite of himself. He pressed a fingertip against Matt's hole. "Kinky boy."

Matt didn't deny it. He rolled onto his stomach and arched his ass into the air. "I've been really bad, Professor Tucker, thinking about doing dirty things with you. I deserve a spanking."

With no warning whatsoever, Chris gave Matt's rear a sharp smack. Matt yelped, eyes flying wide, and Chris stifled a laugh.

"I dare say you do deserve to be spanked, Mr. Gallagher," Chris said, trying to keep the amusement out of his voice and sound appropriately stern. "But I can think of better things to do with your delightful posterior." Laying a gentle hand on the posterior in question, he caressed the palm-shaped mark blazing red against the pale skin.

"Goddamn," Matt breathed. He kicked the covers loose from his ankles and got his knees under him, raising his ass higher. "Fuck me."

Chris laughed. "Are you no longer the virginal schoolboy?"

"Don't know, don't fucking care. Just stick your cock in me, right now!"

Chris didn't waste any time arguing. It had only been four months since the snowboarding accident that had broken Matt's leg in three places, cracked several of his ribs, and ruptured his spleen. The doctor had given Matt the go-ahead to engage in the contortions necessary for anal sex less than a month ago. Chris hadn't minded three months of all oral and hand jobs, but he'd still missed fucking Matt almost as much as Matt had missed being fucked. Which was a lot. Now that they were allowed to do it again, they both wanted it frequent and vigorous.

Chris was a little puzzled by the strength of their mutual need. After all, they'd been a couple for over three years, and even though they still wanted each other as much as ever, they hadn't been this desperately horny since their first months together. Matt claimed they were catching up on what they'd had to miss while his leg healed. Chris suspected he was right, but privately thought they were also simply ecstatic Matt was alive.

He knew he was.

A quick grope through the drawer of the bedside table, and he had the lube in hand. He slicked his fingers and plunged two into Matt's body.

"Oh yeah, babe," Matt whispered, rocking his hips. "That's it. Feels good."

"Is your leg all right?" Chris asked, leaning over so he could see Matt's face.

"Fine, it's fine." Matt shot Chris a wild-eyed look over his shoulder. "C'mon, please!"

Chris bit back the urge to say "are you sure?" Matt didn't seem to be in any pain, and Chris knew he had to trust Matt to speak up if he needed to stop or change positions. Matt's initial amusement over Chris's constant worrying was rapidly degenerating into annoyance, and Chris didn't want to turn perfectly good morning sex into an argument.

Removing his fingers from Matt's ass, Chris lubed his erection and pressed the head against Matt's slightly stretched hole. "I'm going to fuck you now, Mr. Gallagher," he said in his best Menacing Authority Figure voice, "and there's nothing you can do about it."

Matt let out a breathless laugh, which became a moan when Chris pushed inside him. "Yessir, Mister Professor Sir," he panted. "I'm…oh God…sexually curious, you know."

"I'd heard." Chris gave a sharp thrust, angling to nail Matt's gland.

"Oooooooh, professor," Matt moaned, writhing in the most wonderful way. "Your big, hard cock feels sooooo good up my ass."

Chris agreed, though he couldn't say it because his voice seemed to have stopped working. Nothing could feel as heavenly as the hot satin grip of Matt's body around his cock. Unable to do anything but make incoherent noises and so turned on he could barely think, Chris decided he'd had enough roleplaying for one morning. He got a firm grip on Matt's hipbones and pounded into him with all his strength. They came more or less at the same time, Chris with a soft groan, Matt wailing like a banshee as he clawed the sheets.

As soon as Chris pulled out, Matt collapsed onto his stomach, a wide, sated grin plastered across his face. "Damn, professor," he purred. "You popped my cherry hard."

Chris lay down next to Matt and hauled him into his arms, spooning against his back. "Where on earth did this student/teacher fantasy come from?"

Matt shrugged. "Dunno. Just sort of popped into my head."

Chris smiled, nuzzling Matt's neck. "You, my love, are full of surprises."

"That's good, right?"

"Indeed, it is."

Matt turned in Chris's embrace, wrapped both arms around his neck, and kissed him. "I like playing with you, baby. It's fun."

"I agree. Though I don't believe I'd ever want to do that with anyone else."

"Good. I want you all to myself."

"You have me, sweetheart. Forever."

Matt smiled, blue eyes shining. "Six days, Chris."

A lump rose in Chris's throat. He laid a hand on Matt's silky cheek. "Six days. I love you."

"I love you too." Matt touched his fingers to Chris's lips. "Kiss me?"

Chris happily obliged. Six days, he thought as Matt's tongue slid over his, couldn't come soon enough.

Chapter Two

Chris and Matt had both taken time off from work the week before their handfasting ceremony, and their days were filled with pleasant hours of planning. The time flew, yet dragged at the same time. By the time the day before the ceremony arrived, Chris was practically vibrating with anticipation. Matt, never the calmest person in the first place, could no longer sit still for more than a few seconds in a row. Chris had begun to wonder if lacing Matt's food with tranquilizers might be called for.

"Tomorrow, Chris!" Matt exclaimed, bounding in from the living room and grabbing Chris's ass in both hands. "God*damn*, I'm so fucking excited!"

Chris turned his head to receive Matt's kiss. "So am I, love. Now go sit down, I'll bring you some coffee."

Matt obediently parked himself at the kitchen table, where he sat bouncing one knee and drumming his fingers on the table. "Just think. This time two days from now, we'll be having breakfast again. Only we'll be married."

Chris poured two cups of coffee. Black for himself, cream and a tiny bit of sugar for Matt. "It's hard to believe, isn't it?"

"Yeah." Matt took the mug Chris handed him. His expression was wistful. "I wish it would be legal though. I think we deserve that."

Chris laid a hand over Matt's. "Yes, my darling. We do."

One corner of Matt's mouth lifted in a crooked smile. "It bugs me sometimes, you know?"

"I know. It bothers me too." Chris squeezed Matt's fingers. "But our handfasting ceremony is going to be beautiful. And we'll belong to each other, even though the law won't recognize it."

Matt cupped Chris's cheek in his free hand. "We always have, baby. This just makes it official."

"You're right, of course." Chris smiled and leaned in until his lips almost touched Matt's. "I can't wait to be officially yours."

Matt made a small sound in the back of his throat. Closing the space between them, he captured Chris's mouth in an eloquent kiss.

They were still kissing, and Matt was making those needy little noises that usually meant he'd be ripping at Chris's clothes any minute, when the phone rang. Chris broke the kiss with some difficulty, leaned back in his chair and snatched the phone from the counter.

"Hello?" he said, trying not to sound as aroused as he felt. Matt's insistence on biting his neck at that moment didn't help.

"Chris? Hey, it's Deb."

Chris smiled at the sound of their next-door neighbor's voice. "Hi Deb, how are you?"

"I'm great, how about you? Getting excited about tomorrow?"

"Very much so, yes. Matt is about to explode, I believe."

Deb laughed. "I can imagine. Speaking of Matt, is he there? I need to talk to him a minute."

"He's right here, hold on." Chris smacked Matt's hand away from his crotch and held the phone toward him. "It's for you. It's Deb."

Matt's eyes lit up. "Thanks, babe." He snatched the phone out of Chris's hand. "Hi, Deb, is it here? Cool. They got the you-know-what, right? Perfect... Yeah... Okay, I'll be over in a sec. Bye."

Chris raised his eyebrows. "What's this all about?"

"Got my Sensual Desire stuff." Hanging up the phone, Matt plopped himself down on Chris's lap. "'Bout time, too. I was afraid it wasn't gonna get here before the wedding."

"Sensual Desire." Chris wrapped both arms around Matt's waist. "That was that party Deb had last month, right? Where they sell the sex products?"

"Yep. I got lots of wild stuff, wait'll you see." Matt framed Chris's face in his hands and kissed him. "Gotta run over to Deb's and get it, I'll be right back."

Matt jumped up and was gone before Chris could say another word. He chuckled as he sipped his coffee, remembering the night Matt had gone to Deb Woodward's Sensual Desire party. Matt—the only male at the event, as it turned out—had come home just before midnight with a massive credit card receipt and an evil grin. He'd refused to tell Chris what he'd bought, claiming it was all for their wedding and honeymoon. Chris had been burning with curiosity ever since. Now, it looked like he might finally find out what Matt had in store for him.

• • •

Forty-five minutes and two more cups of coffee later, Matt still hadn't returned. *Probably talking about the ceremony with Deb,* Chris thought with a smile. Deb and her now-husband, Rick Gonzales, had been married in a Wiccan handfasting ceremony two months previous. They'd been a tremendous help to Matt and Chris in planning their own ceremony.

Figuring Matt would be at Deb and Rick's place for a while longer, Chris stood and headed toward the stairs. He could download his email, then double-check the to-do list for the wedding and start packing for their honeymoon. They were planning a single night at the local bed and breakfast where the wedding was taking place, followed by a two-week trip to Jamaica.

Chris had just turned on his laptop when a firm knock sounded on the front door. He sighed. "Coming," he called, and hurried back downstairs.

Rick stood at the front door, shirtless and grinning, chestnut curls wound into a long braid. "Boy, are you in for an interesting couple of weeks," he said, pushing past Chris and kicking off his battered, grass-stained sneakers.

"Come on in," Chris offered, amused. "Would you like a glass of raspberry tea? I made some last night."

"Sure, that'd be great." Mopping his sweaty brow with a none-too-clean forearm, Rick followed Chris into the kitchen. "I've been working in the yard, I'm about roasted."

"So, Rick." Chris got out the pitcher of tea and scooped ice into a glass. "Would you care to explain your previous remark?"

Rick laughed. "Not really. Matt would kill me for stealing his thunder." He took the glass Chris handed him. "Thanks. Let's just say it'll be a honeymoon to remember."

"I'm sure," Chris said drily, more curious than ever but resigned to waiting. "So what are our other halves doing over there?"

"Plotting, what else?" Rick shook his head, brown eyes bright with laughter. "Those two are as bad as each other."

"True. I tremendously appreciate Deb's help with this, though. And yours. Matt and I would've been lost without you both."

"Hey, we were happy to do it. Especially Deb." Rick leaned his elbows on the table and dropped his voice, though there was no one else around to hear. "I don't think she's completely gotten over Matt's accident. Which sounds weird, I know, but you know how sensitive she is, and she saw the whole thing. She had nightmares for weeks."

"I don't think her reaction is at all unusual. It must have been terrible for her." Chris swallowed, fighting the tightness in his chest that always accompanied the memory of that horrible day. "I'll never forget it as long as I live. Seeing Matt so bruised and bloody, and so damn *still*. I was terrified that I was going to lose him."

Rick's big hand closed over Chris's. "Sorry, man. Didn't mean to bring it all back."

Chris smiled. "No, it's all right. He seems to have made a complete recovery. And the accident was the catalyst for everything that's happening now."

Rick returned Chris's smile. "They do say everything happens for a reason."

"I never did believe that. But you have to wonder."

"Yeah." Rick drained his tea in several long, deep swallows and set the empty glass on the table. "Everything all set for tomorrow?"

"I think so," Chris said, glad for the change of subject. "The Azalea Inn has the rose garden reserved for us from ten 'til two. The ceremony itself will be in the garden proper, weather permitting of course, and the reception will be in the gazebo."

"That huge one, right?"

"That's the one." Chris laughed. "I believe Matt's invited most of the city. It's a good thing the Inn has the space to accommodate us."

"No kidding. Did you get the honeymoon suite?"

"Oh, yes. Private balcony, jacuzzi, champagne, the works."

Rick grinned. "Now I know Matt didn't think of all that."

"No, indeed. But he deserves it."

"You spoil him, you big sap." Rick's eyes twinkled.

"I enjoy spoiling him, and I don't intend to stop anytime soon."

"Good enough."

The front door banged open, making them both jump. "Chris!" Matt yelled. "Where are you, babe?"

"Kitchen," Chris called.

Matt bounced in, carrying a large black bag with a stylized red heart on it. His face sported the grin that invariably meant he was up to something naughty. Which could be good or bad, depending. Chris swallowed.

"Hello, love," he said. "You got your things?"

"*Our* things," Matt corrected, blue eyes glinting with mischief. "I told you, they're for the wedding and the honeymoon. Well, mostly the honeymoon."

"Guess I better get back to work." Rick stood. "Thanks for the tea, Chris. See y'all in the morning. Oh, and Matt? What time do your sisters get in from England? Me and Deb want to meet them."

"Their plane gets in at six tonight. We'll call you when they get here, they won't mind visiting for a while before they have to sleep off the jet lag." Matt threw himself at Rick, hugging him so hard he grunted. "Bye, Rick. See you later."

"Yeah." Rick extricated himself from Matt's grip and arched an eyebrow at him. "Take a Valium or something, huh? Don't want to wear yourself out before you get to Jamaica."

Matt laughed and popped Rick on the butt as he headed for the front door.

Chris waited until Rick had left to ask, "Matt, love, are you going to show me what's in that bag?"

"Some of it."

"Not all of it?"

"Nope. There's two things that're surprises." Sliding his arms around Chris's shoulders from behind his chair, Matt leaned down and licked Chris's ear. "And you better not peek."

"Darling, I promise that I won't spoil your surprise." Chris lifted his face to collect a kiss. "But won't you show me the rest of it?"

"Sure." Matt's lips moved teasingly down Chris's neck, raising goose bumps. "Let's go upstairs, baby. We can try some of it out right now."

"Mmmmm," Chris hummed as Matt sucked at the juncture of his neck and shoulder. "Sounds wonderful."

Matt pulled back, took Chris's hand, and tugged him to his feet. They headed for the bedroom with fingers wound together, Matt's bag of goodies dangling from his other hand.

• • •

Chris had always thought he'd tried most things at least once. And to be perfectly fair, most of the objects in Matt's black bag were not unfamiliar to him. Peppermint-flavored lube, chocolate body paint, anal beads in various sizes, a complicated-looking cock-and-ball harness with a chain to connect to Matt's piercing. There was even a velvet drawstring bag containing a satin blindfold, four cloth restraints, and a small leather whip. All of it seemed playful, fun and extremely Matt. The thing that really threw Chris was the leather case containing ten stainless steel sounds. Although he knew about sounds, it was the first time he'd handled them. They were heavier than he'd have thought, and even the smallest looked huge to him.

Matt shocked him to the core by announcing that he'd tried them before and liked it.

"Do you mean to tell me," Chris said, frowning at the long, thin metal rod in his palm, "that you've actually inserted something like this into your penis, and you *enjoyed* it?"

"Hell yeah." Matt snatched the sound from him and twirled the handle between his fingers. The rosebud-shaped end sparkled in the light. "Feels amazing."

"Good Lord." Chris sat on the edge of the bed, staring at the object in Matt's hand with a kind of horrified fascination. "Sweetheart, I don't know if I can do this."

Matt put the sound back in its box, sat next to Chris, and leaned against his shoulder. "I didn't figure you'd want to use it yourself, babe. It's not your style. But I'd love for you to use it on me."

Chris's breath caught at the sudden mental picture. His cock started to twitch. "I have to admit, I find that quite intriguing." He turned and nuzzled Matt's soft cheek. "Would you mind if we waited until the honeymoon? I'd like some time to get used to the idea."

"No problem." Matt pressed a light kiss to Chris's lips. "Hey, you gave me an idea."

"What is it?" Chris slipped an arm around Matt's waist, urging him closer.

Matt's lips brushed Chris's, tongue flicking out. "Let's wait," he whispered.

"Hm? Wait?" Chris kissed Matt again, deeper this time. "What do you mean?"

"I mean, let's not fuck again until after the wedding." Matt moaned, contradicting his own words by arching into Chris's touch. "It'll be mind-blowing."

Chris drew back, surprised. "You don't want to make love right now? I thought you wanted to play with some of your new products."

"I do. That's kind of the point." Matt's gaze darted down to Chris's mouth, eyes hot and wanting. "I want you so bad I can't stand it. Just like always. But if we make ourselves wait, can you imagine how fucking wild it'll be after the wedding?"

"I see your point." Chris took a deep breath, willing his erection away. "All right. We'll do it. We'll wait until after we're married to make love again."

Matt stared at Chris, his expression tender. "Next time we're together, we'll be married. I can't even explain how that makes me feel, Chris."

Chris smiled and kissed Matt's palm. "Probably the same way it makes me feel, sweetheart."

Matt grinned. "What about we put all that sexual-frustration energy into packing?"

"An excellent idea."

Matt jumped up and started pulling bags from the closet, singing something under his breath. Chris watched him with a smile. *One more day.*

Chapter Three

Friday morning dawned clear and bright. Chris watched with a smile on his face as the sky shaded from black to lavender to bright blue. He'd had a restless night. Matt had been as clingy as ever and twice as fidgety, squirming and mumbling in his sleep. Chris didn't mind, in spite of endless hours spent fighting the need to fuck Matt through the mattress. Nothing could spoil the sheer joy permeating him this morning.

Today, he thought, grinning at the cardinal chirping on the windowsill, *I'm getting married to the most wonderful man in the world.* He laughed out loud at his own sentimentality.

Matt stirred, muttered something unintelligible, and rolled over so his body draped across Chris. Chris nudged him with the hand not trapped under Matt's ribcage.

"Wake up, sleeping beauty," he whispered in Matt's ear.

"Is it today yet?" Matt asked in a sleep-slurred voice.

"Yes, darling, it is." Chris kissed Matt's tousled hair, currently dyed red, pink and pale blue in honor of their chosen handfasting colors. "Today's the day."

Matt lifted his head, rested his arm on Chris's chest and propped his cheek in his hand. A wide, joyful smile lit his face. "God, I can't believe it's finally here. We're getting married today, Chris. In just a few hours."

"I know." Chris reached up to cradle Matt's face in his hands. "I'm so happy, Matt. I love you."

Matt blinked rapidly a few times, leaned down and gave Chris a gentle kiss. "Love you too, babe."

The kisses that followed were predictably heated. Chris let his thigh slip between Matt's legs, pressing against the hardness there, knowing he shouldn't but unable to help himself. Matt whimpered and rocked against him.

"Need to stop," Matt breathed, eyes glazed. "Gonna come if we don't."

"Me too." Chris forced himself to push away, keeping a hand on Matt's hip. "This is even more difficult than I thought it would be."

"It'll be worth it tonight." Matt sat up and wiped a faint dew of sweat from his upper lip. "Let's go downstairs and get breakfast, huh? We can visit with Shannon and Siobhan for a while."

"I'd like that. We didn't get to spend much time with them last night."

The girls had arrived the previous evening bursting with excitement over their brother's wedding, but both were too exhausted from the flight to talk for long. They'd met Deb and Rick, then Chris had fixed them a light dinner and sent them off to rest.

Thinking of the reunion between Matt and his sisters made Chris smile. The girls had always reminded him very much of Matt—same outgoing, energetic personality, same delicately chiseled features, same bright blue eyes. The three of them clearly adored each other, and the twins had accepted Chris into the fold from the first moment they'd met three years before. Chris was glad to hear they were renting an apartment together in Asheville for the summer. He looked forward to spending some time with them.

Shannon and Siobhan were already huddled at the kitchen table when Chris and Matt got there. Siobhan grinned at them. "Hi, guys. We made coffee."

"And sausage," Shannon added. "Oh, and biscuits. Hope that's okay?"

"Of course. Our home is yours." Chris took a deep breath. His stomach rumbled. "It smells delicious. But you didn't have to cook. I would have gladly made breakfast for you both."

"But it's your wedding day!" Shannon protested.

"Yeah, we couldn't let you cook today." Siobhan glanced at her sister, and they turned identical wide-eyed gazes to their brother. "Matt, make him sit down."

"And you too," Shannon continued. "We want to wait on you guys."

Matt laughed and tugged on Shannon's long strawberry blonde ponytail as he sat in the chair next to her. "Better do what they say, Chris. There's no fighting the Twin Power."

Siobhan leapt to her feet, laid both dainty hands on Chris's shoulders and steered him firmly toward the table. "Sit. How do you take your coffee?"

"Black," Matt answered, yawning.

The girls sighed at the same time. "God, that's adorable," Shannon said, hopping up to help her sister get coffee and food.

"It just melts me that they know all those little things about each other," Siobhan added.

"So sweet."

"I know! It's too cute."

"Why is it so much cuter when gay guys do that?"

"I don't know, but it is."

"Yeah."

The twins leaned their heads together, smiling in that moony-eyed way Chris had seen more than once from his female friends when they found something romantic.

"You guys are weird," Matt said, grinning at his sisters as they handed him and Chris each a steaming mug of coffee.

"But you love us," the girls chorused. They looked at each other and burst into laughter.

Matt shook his head. "See, Chris, now you know why I'm so fucked up. Can you imagine growing up with those two?"

Chris laughed. "Your sisters are as delightful as you are, and I suspect that you know it quite well."

Matt shrugged. "Maybe."

Shannon wrapped an arm around Matt's shoulders. "Seriously, Matt, Siobhan and I are incredibly happy for you both."

"You'll just have to forgive us for being all girly about it," Siobhan added, setting a plate of biscuits and bacon in front of Chris and another in front of Matt.

"No sweat, sis." Matt took his sister's hand and kissed it. "I love you guys, you know?"

"We know." Siobhan threw her arms wide. "Group hug, c'mon."

Chris held back at first, watching with a smile as the three siblings became a giggling knot of limbs. Then each of the twins snagged one of his arms and pulled him in, and just like that he had a second family.

He decided he liked it.

• • •

After breakfast, the girls shooed Chris and Matt off to finish packing and get ready to go to the Inn while they cleaned up the kitchen. The necessity for separate showers didn't need to be voiced. Chris let Matt have the first turn, busying himself with packing last-minute items to drive out the mental image of Matt in the shower. Matt's wet, soapy, naked body, the water snaking down his chest and belly, running in rivulets from his prick and the hand caressing it, the piercing sparkling silver, moving just a little with the pulse of Matt's heartbeat through the rapidly hardening flesh...

Chris shook off the enticing vision, wishing he could also get rid of the urge to strip and join Matt in the shower. "Just a few more hours," he muttered. "You can do this. You're an adult, for God's sake. Control yourself."

When Matt emerged from the bathroom, suspiciously flushed and bright-eyed, Chris pulled him close and kissed him, opening Matt's silky lips with his tongue. Matt's damp skin smelled of soap and the soft, musky cologne he wore for special occasions. He sighed and wrapped his arms around Chris's neck. The thin towel clinging to Matt's hips seemed to emphasize his hardness rather than hide it. It was all Chris could do to keep from ripping the towel away, dropping to his knees, and sucking Matt off right then and there. He was quite proud of himself for stopping with a kiss.

"Only a few more hours," Matt whispered against Chris's lips. "God, I've never wanted anything this much."

"I was just thinking the same thing." Chris kissed Matt again, a chaste brush of lips, then pushed him gently away. "Let me get showered, and we can go."

"Okay. I just have a couple more things to pack and I'm done." Smiling, Matt squeezed Chris's hand and started toward the closet.

Chris took two steps toward the bathroom, stopped, and turned around. "We have the cords and rings, right? And the chalices?"

"In the bag there on the dresser." Matt took the garment bag containing their wedding clothes out of the closet and laid it on the bed. "Deb's got the birdseed. We're checking into the room soon as we get there, right?"

"Yes. I thought it would be nice to go ahead and get settled. We can change over there."

"Cool." Hanging onto his towel with one hand, Matt bent to open the bottom dresser drawer. "Now get out of here and go take your shower. You can't see me naked until after the wedding."

Chris laughed. "Be sure that you pack the new bottle of lube. We're going to need it."

Matt grinned. "You know it, babe."

Chris smiled as he entered the bathroom and shut the door behind him. The steamy air still smelled like Matt's shampoo. Chris closed his eyes and took a deep breath, stroking the fourth finger of his left hand. That spot would soon be occupied by a silver band with a tiny diamond embedded in it. Its mate would circle Matt's ring finger.

The knowledge sent a thrill of happiness through him. Laughing with his joy, he turned on the water and started undressing.

Chapter Four

"Whoa, this place is something else." Matt dropped his bag in the middle of the king-sized bed and bounded over to the big bay window. "Look, Chris, we can see the garden from here."

"I know. I asked for a garden-view room." Chris set down his suitcase and the garment bag, then wandered over and put his arms around Matt from behind. "Do you like it?"

"I love it," Matt said, grinning at Chris over his shoulder. "You're the best."

"You inspire me." Chris pressed a kiss to Matt's lips. "We have a little while before we have to get dressed, what would you like to do?"

"You can probably guess, but we already promised not to do that."

"So we did."

Matt turned in Chris's arms, sliding his fingers through Chris's hair. "It's been tough, but I'm glad we did it. It's gonna be so amazing to make love with you and know that we're married."

Chris's throat threatened to close with the emotion welling up inside him. *Seems to happen a lot lately,* he thought. Laying a hand on Matt's cheek, he bent to kiss the warm, sweet lips he loved so much. Matt opened to him with a little needy whimper.

"Aw, look, they're kissing."

"How *cute* is that?"

At the sound of female voices, Chris reluctantly broke the contact. He turned around. The twins stood shoulder to shoulder in the doorway, strikingly pretty in long, pale green summer dresses.

"Hello Shannon, Siobhan," he said, wishing his voice didn't sound so husky. "What can we do for you?"

"Should've closed the door," Matt muttered as he drew away from Chris, their hands still linked.

"We just came to see what you were doing." Shannon pointed toward the stairs with her thumb. "Deb sent us."

Siobhan grinned at them. "She said you'd get carried away if somebody didn't interrupt you."

Matt and Chris looked at each other and smiled. "She's right, you know," Chris said. "Why don't we go ahead and change, then have a quick look around the garden to make sure everything's ready before the guests arrive?"

"Okay." Matt squeezed his hand. "Mind if I use the bathroom to change?"

Chris raised his eyebrows. "Not at all. Does this have to do with keeping me from seeing you naked?"

"It's just 'til after the reception's over, babe." Matt leaned over and kissed him before letting go of his hand. "Then we can come up here and you can see all my junk." Grabbing his crotch, Matt thrust his hips forward in a way that did nothing at all to dampen Chris's raging libido.

"Ew!" Shannon exclaimed. "Too much information."

"Yeah," Siobhan chimed in. "Don't talk about your junk in front of your sisters."

"This from the girls who thought it was cute that me and Chris were kissing." Matt stalked forward, grabbed a gauze-clad feminine arm in each hand, and steered his siblings into the hall. "You won't hear about my junk if you go away, will you?"

Chris grinned as Matt shut the door on the protesting twins. "You don't see your sisters for months, and this is how you talk to them?"

"They don't mind." Matt dug his dress clothes out of the garment bag and slung them over his arm. "I'm gonna get my finery on now, what about you?"

"I'll dress out here." Chris reached out, brushing his fingers across the back of Matt's hand. "Another hour, my love."

Matt smiled, eyes shining. "I know, baby." He leaned over and grabbed his overnight bag off the bed, kissing Chris's cheek on the way. "Now let's get busy, I'm awfully anxious to marry you."

Chris ran a finger down Matt's cheek. "So am I."

Fifteen minutes later, Chris and Matt left their room and headed downstairs hand in hand. Chris couldn't keep his eyes off his lover. Matt wore soft gray dress slacks and a vivid blue silk shirt. His cheeks were flushed, his eyes bright and a little wild. In spite of his somewhat stiff gait, which Chris attributed to a combination of nervousness and unfamiliar attire, Chris thought Matt had never looked so stunning.

"You look so fucking hot," Matt said, echoing Chris's thoughts. "I love it when you wear green. It matches your eyes."

Chris smiled and squeezed Matt's hand. "Thank you, darling. I was just thinking the same thing about you."

"You gave Deb the cords and stuff, right?"

"I did, yes. She was taking it out to the garden to finish setting up."

"Cool." Matt pressed his body to Chris's, one arm around his waist and the other still clutching his hand. "Kiss me."

Chris did, kneading Matt's ass with his free hand. Matt moaned and rubbed his crotch against Chris's hip. Something about the movement seemed a bit desperate. It excited Chris tremendously.

"My goodness," Chris murmured. "You *are* anxious, aren't you, darling?"

"God, you have no idea." Matt drew a shaky breath. "Let's go before I rip your clothes off and sit on your cock right here."

Closing his eyes, Chris fought to get himself under control. "All right," he managed after a moment, opening his eyes again. "I'm ready."

Matt's gaze locked with Chris's. The near-telepathic understanding they shared sometimes passed between them. Hands wound together, they went out the back door of the Inn and into the garden.

• • •

"Okay, guys," Deb whispered. "Everyone's here, Saffron's all set. You ready to do this?"

Chris, Matt and Deb stood in the shade of a tall hedge, listening to the murmur of the guests gathered in the large courtyard beyond. The scents of roses and stargazer lilies perfumed the warm summer air. It was the perfect setting in which to get married.

Matt grinned. "Yeah. More than fucking ready."

Chris rubbed his thumb over the back of Matt's hand. "I've been ready for this for months."

"Great. You guys know what to do, right?"

"We've practiced a million times. Relax." Matt patted her cheek. "Thanks. For everything."

Deb twisted her wedding ring around her finger, dark brown gaze darting between Chris and Matt. She opened her mouth as if to speak, then threw herself at them, an arm around each of their necks.

"I love you two so, so much," she said, her voice shaking. "I'm so happy for you."

Chris rubbed little circles on her back. "Thank you, Deb. We love you too."

"Sure do." Lifting Deb's chin, Matt kissed her forehead. "Now pull yourself together, woman, you're gonna get raccoon eyes."

Deb laughed, letting go of Matt and Chris to wipe her eyes. "Yeah, okay." She smoothed a hand down the front of her pale yellow dress. The sunlight glinted in her red hair. "How do I look? Is my mascara all smeared now?"

"No." Matt smiled at her. "You look beautiful."

Deb took each of their hands and just held on. She didn't say anything, but the look in her eyes told Chris exactly how she felt. After a moment, she let go, turned away, and hurried through the opening in the hedge. A couple of minutes later, the sounds of conversation died away. A woman's voice said something Chris couldn't quite make out. When the lilting sounds of guitar and flute began, playing the song they'd chosen as a processional, Chris knew it was time. He turned to Matt, and their gazes met.

"Here we go," Matt said, very quietly.

"Yes."

Chris laced his fingers through Matt's. Together, they walked through the honeysuckle-laced arch in the hedge and into the sunny garden.

A crowd of people were gathered in a semicircle around the edges of a huge circular courtyard paved in stone. Behind the guests, beds of roses sent a sweet fragrance into the air. On the stone table at the far side of the courtyard, three silver chalices glinted in the sunlight. Three colored cords—red, pink and pale blue—lay beside them. Saffron, the Wiccan priestess who would be performing the ceremony, waited to one side. The musicians stood behind the table, in a shallow bay in the tall green bushes.

"Look, Chris," Matt whispered as they walked with measured steps toward the altar, and the green-clad woman standing beside it. "Isn't it beautiful?"

Chris pressed Matt's fingers with his. "Almost as beautiful as you."

The worshipful look in Matt's eyes made the sentimental words seem just right. Chris smiled, Matt smiled back, then they were standing before the stone table, with fifty-some odd friends and family members behind them and the symbols of their new life before them.

Saffron moved to stand between them and the table. She smiled, eyes sparkling. "Matt and Chris, why have you come here today?"

Exchanging a brief glance, they said in unison, "To be made one before our friends and family."

"Then take your chalices, and speak your oaths." Saffron stood aside, sweeping her arm toward the table in a gesture of invitation.

Chris stepped forward, with Matt close to his side. His heartbeat hammered in his ears. Reluctantly, he let go of Matt's hand so they could each pick up their chalice. The silver goblets were simply designed, with tiny vines engraved along the rims. Green ribbons held their wedding rings in place around the base of each chalice.

Matt leaned close, his shoulder brushing Chris's as he picked up his chalice. "You go first," he whispered, and flashed his most mischievous grin.

Chris bit the insides of his cheeks. Trust Matt to make him want to laugh in the midst of a solemn moment. He lifted his chalice and turned toward Matt.

"I, Chris, take you, Matt, to my hand and to my heart at the rising of the sun and the setting of the stars." Chris took a deep breath once the words were out, mentally congratulating himself on keeping his emotions in check.

Matt held his chalice in both hands. His thumbs rubbed nervously at the silver, his eyes fixed on Chris's face. "I, Matt," he began, his voice soft but steady, "take you, Chris, to my hand and to my heart at the rising of the sun and the setting of the stars."

Saffron came forward, laying a hand on each of their arms. "Drink now from the chalice of union."

Chris and Matt stepped toward the table and poured the wine from their individual goblets into a third, larger one. Chris took Matt's hand and laid it on the union chalice. "You first this time," Chris murmured.

Matt let out a soft laugh. He lifted the chalice to his mouth and took a sip, licking the red wine off his lips much more suggestively than was strictly necessary. He held the goblet out to Chris with a smile. Shaking his head, Chris accepted the cup and drank from it.

Saffron took the chalice from Chris and set it back on the table. "Take now the rings that are the symbol of your union, and make your promises to one another."

Chris untied the ribbon binding Matt's wedding ring to the chalice, held Matt's hand in his, and slipped the ring onto the end of his finger. Matt's hand trembled, and Chris could see the rapid pulse fluttering in his throat. On impulse, Chris lifted Matt's hand and kissed it. Matt gave him a shaky smile.

"I give you this ring," Chris said, "as a symbol of my love and my promise. I will stand beside you through all of your joys and sorrows. I will give you all of myself, always. I will love you with everything that I am, until the day I die. My darling, you are the one I've waited for my whole life, even before I knew that I was waiting. As you walk your path in life, I ask that you walk beside me."

Matt swallowed, tears spilling down his cheeks. "I will."

Chris pushed the ring fully onto Matt's finger, caressing Matt's palm before letting go. Wetness trickled down his own face, yet he'd never felt happier.

Matt removed Chris's ring from the base of the goblet, glancing back and forth between Chris and the chalice, as if reluctant to look away from Chris's face. Chris held Matt's gaze as Matt clasped his hand and began to speak.

"I give you this ring as a symbol of my love and my promise. That I'll always be there for you, no matter what happens. That I'll always surprise you, but I'll never let you down. That I'll always love you, forever." Matt's cheek dimpled with his sunny smile, but his eyes held a seriousness of purpose Chris rarely saw. "Chris, you are my whole world. You're my everything, and I promise I'll always be yours. As you walk your path in life, I ask that you walk beside me."

It required two tries before Chris could speak, his voice rough with emotion. "I will."

As Matt slid the ring onto Chris's finger, something inside Chris clicked into place. The sun shone brighter than ever, the colors of the flowers seemed more vivid, their fragrance sweeter. Looking into Matt's shining eyes, he saw a perfect understanding. They smiled at each other.

Saffron lifted the cords from the table, then stepped toward the center of the courtyard, beckoning Chris and Matt to follow. She stopped, and they faced her.

"Join hands," she instructed.

Chris took Matt's hand and laced their fingers together. Saffron lifted their joined hands and held the pink cord up before her.

"With this cord," she said in a strong, clear voice, "I bind you, to bless your union with honor, happiness and true partnership."

As she spoke, she wound the cord around their wrists. She tied it in a loose half-knot, then held up the blue one.

"With this cord I bind you, to bless your union with understanding and patience."

The blue cord was tied, and the red cord held up. "With this cord I bind you, to bless your union with the fire of passion."

Chris wondered if he imagined the knowing laughter rippling through the crowd, only half-suppressed. *Probably not.* They'd never made a secret of their powerful physical attraction.

"Will Chris's parents and Matt's sisters please come forward," Saffron said.

Chris's heart swelled to see the love and pride on his parents' faces. His mother smiled, the green eyes so like his own crinkling at the corners. His father steered her toward Chris and Matt, one big arm across her shoulders.

Saffron smiled. "Madeline and Frank, will you give your blessings to this union?"

Madeline started to speak, and evidently couldn't. She nodded. Her husband patted her hair. "We will," he answered in his big, booming voice. "Got you a good one there, son. I always said so."

Chris felt his cheeks color. His father had never gotten the hang of practiced speeches, or of social subtleties, but his love and support of his son had never wavered, and Chris adored him for it.

Chris's mother leaned toward them. "I agree," she whispered, her voice shaking. "I love you both."

"Love you too, Mom." Chris kissed his mother's cheek and let his father lead her away so Matt's sisters could come forward.

"Shannon and Siobhan," Saffron said. "Since your parents are gone, Matt asks that you give your blessings to this union. Will you do so?"

"We will," the twins chorused, smiling through their tears.

Saffron went back to the table, picked up the union chalice, and turned to address the crowd. "All of you present here today, bear witness to this. That Chris and Matt have drunk from the cup of union. That they have made their promises each to the other, and given rings to seal those promises. That they have set hand in hand and been bound together before you all. They are now one in heart and spirit, each still his own man but joyfully committed to walk the path of life together. Drink now from the cup and share in their happiness."

Moving with care, Chris and Matt took the large silver goblet in their bound hands. They carried it to each guest in turn, starting with their own families and then working around the circle. By the time they set the cup back on the stone table, it was almost empty and the sun had risen to noon.

Smiling, Saffron held their joined hands between hers. "May the blessings of air, fire, water and earth grace your life together. Go now, and be happy."

There was a rustle behind them as the crowd formed into two long lines leading back to the arch in the hedge. Matt and Chris turned together. Deb nodded at them from the end of the line, and they started walking between the rows of people. Laughter, cheering and congratulations followed them down the line as the guests peppered them with birdseed. Chris laughed right along with them, and with his husband.

Husband, Chris repeated to himself, rolling the unfamiliar word around in his mind. It felt good, he decided, to be able to say it.

At the end of the corridor of people, Deb and Rick hugged them both, then they passed under the fragrant green arch and it was over.

Matt flung his free arm around Chris's neck, hugging him close. "We're married, Chris," he whispered, his breath warm against Chris's ear. "We're really married."

"I know." Chris held Matt tight, burying his face in the curve of Matt's neck. "It's wonderful, isn't it?"

"Fuck, yeah." Matt drew back, one hand sifting through Chris's hair. "I love you so much."

Chris blinked, still fighting happy tears. "I love you too, sweetheart."

Matt smiled and leaned toward him, and they kissed, a long, deep, unhurried kiss that said it all. They didn't stop until Deb informed them that if they wanted any of their own wedding cake, they'd better break it up and get to the gazebo for the reception.

Chris had to wonder how any food could be better than Matt's kiss. But he went anyway.

Chapter Five

The reception kept them both so busy that Chris didn't have time to wish he and Matt could be alone. He was grateful for that. Chatting with everyone was expected, and of course he wanted to share his happiness with his family and friends. The wide smile never left his face, and Matt never left his side. They made the social rounds hand-in-hand, exchanging heated glances and furtive touches.

At two-fifteen, Chris shook hands with Laurie as she and her husband left, then looked around in surprise when he realized no one else was waiting to say goodbye.

"Is that it?" Matt muttered in his ear.

"It seems so." Only Chris's parents, the twins and Deb and Rick were left, the six of them talking as they nibbled the remains of the buffet lunch.

"Good." Matt took a deep breath and let it out, shoulders sagging. "It was great, but man, I'm totally ready to go now."

"So am I." Chris swept Matt into his arms and kissed him. "It was a lovely ceremony, wasn't it? And a wonderful reception."

"Yeah." Matt nuzzled Chris's cheek. "I loved it. The whole thing. But right now, I need to be alone with you."

Desire flared through Chris's body. He slid a hand through Matt's hair and kissed him again, harder this time. Matt sighed and opened for him, palms caressing Chris's back and squeezing his ass. The kiss went deep. Matt shifted until he was straddling Chris's thigh. He rocked almost imperceptibly, rubbing his rapidly hardening cock against Chris's leg and making those needy little sounds Chris adored.

Chris started when a hand landed on his shoulder. Matt squeaked and jumped back.

"Good God, Rick." Chris grinned up at the man standing beside him. "You scared us half to death."

Rick laughed. "Sorry. But you guys were getting sort of carried away. Maybe you better go on up to your room before you give everybody an eyeful."

"It's just you and Deb left. And the twins. And Chris's parents." Matt looked over at the group still standing beside the table. Shannon and Siobhan giggled behind their hands. Madeline stared at the ground, blushing. Frank had his back turned, picking at the remains of the cheese squares. "Okay, I get your point."

Chris took Matt's hand again and they wandered toward the buffet table. "Rick, I think I speak for Matt as well as myself when I say how much it means to me that you and Deb were able to share this day with us. Thank you."

"Wouldn't have missed it." Rick stopped, wrapped one long arm around Chris's shoulders and the other around Matt's, and hugged them both hard. "Love you guys, you know?"

"We love you too." Matt turned his head and bit Rick's shoulder. Rick squealed, and Matt chuckled. "You always did like it when I bit you."

Chris glanced in alarm at his parents and the twins. Deb already knew that Rick had joined Matt and Chris in bed more than once before he started seeing her, but the others had no idea. Chris wanted to keep it that way.

"Chris," Rick muttered as they drew close to the rest of the group, "spank him for me later, will you?"

"Absolutely." Chris let go of Matt's hand to sweep his mother into a hug. "Mom, thank you so much for supporting Matt and me today. I love you."

"I love you too, honey." Madeline patted Chris's cheek. "Your father and I will always support you, you know that."

"Yes, I do." Releasing his mother so she could hug Matt, Chris turned and let himself be enveloped in his father's arms. "Thanks, Dad," he murmured, cheek pressed to his father's chest just like when he was small. "I know it hasn't always been easy for you and Mom, having a gay son. Your love and support have made all the difference in my life. I just want you to know that."

Frank took hold of Chris's shoulders and pushed him back enough to look him in the eye. "Hell, son. You're my boy. You never made your mom and me anything but proud, ever. Any man who'd turn his back on a son like you just because he's gay isn't any sort of a man." Frank clapped Chris on the back. "Me and your mom have to get going now. You boys have a safe trip tomorrow."

"We will." Matt held out his hand to Frank, who shook it vigorously. "Thanks, Frank. You and Madeline are the best."

After a final flurry of hugs and I-love-yous with Deb, Shannon and Siobhan, Chris and Matt headed down the meandering garden path to the Inn arm in arm.

"Know what?" Matt said as they strolled past a bed of yellow roses.

"What?"

"Our families are great."

"Yes, they are. And our friends."

"We're pretty lucky."

"Agreed." Chris slid his hand down to squeeze Matt's backside. "I feel very lucky indeed right now."

Matt let out a moan that seemed disproportionate to what Chris was doing, which was kneading one firm buttock in his fingers. "Let's hurry. I don't know how much longer my legs'll hold me up."

Chris obediently picked up the pace. Part of him was amused to realize he was walking as stiffly as Matt, and that their mutually aroused state must be obvious to anyone who bothered to look. The rest of him was too turned on to care.

It took a few tries before Chris could get the door to their room unlocked, because Matt was kissing and groping him with single-minded determination. Finally, on the fourth attempt, the lock turned. Matt opened the door and they stumbled inside, mouths fused together.

Matt cursed under his breath as he worked his way through the buttons on Chris's shirt. "Damn, why the fuck can't they make silk shirts with Velcro?"

Chris laughed. "You could market that idea."

"Maybe later, when my brain's working again." Matt got the last button undone and shoved the shirt off Chris's shoulders. "Need you so bad right now."

By way of agreement, Chris let his shirt slide to the floor and swiftly divested Matt of his. Their mouths met in a fierce kiss as Chris worked Matt's dress pants open and pushed them down enough to free his erection. Chris tugged at the steel ring in the head of Matt's cock.

Matt whimpered, his body trembling in Chris's arms. "Chris, please…"

"Yes, love."

Chris dropped to his knees and took Matt into his mouth, the way he'd been dying to do ever since they made their pact of pre-marriage celibacy. *It was only one day*, Chris reminded himself as he pulled back and flicked Matt's piercing with his tongue. *We'd never survive real celibacy.*

"Ooooooh, oh God, baby yes!" Matt's fingers clenched in Chris's hair. "So good."

Chris hummed, making Matt shudder and sob his name. He wanted to drown in the taste of Matt's skin, the smell of his need. Matt obviously wasn't going to last long, but Chris didn't care. They had plenty of time for the long, slow, mind-melting lovemaking they both wanted for their wedding day. A quickie to take the edge off first was probably a good thing.

It only took a few minutes for Chris to bring Matt to the edge. When he felt Matt tense with approaching orgasm, Chris relaxed his throat and slid Matt's cock all the way in, squeezing his muscles around it. Matt stilled, made a soft sound, and came hard, shaking all over. Chris swallowed the warm fresh semen like it was nectar.

"Fuck, I needed that," Matt sighed. "Babe, I swear you could suck a golf ball through a straw."

Laughing, Chris rose to his feet, one hand still cupping Matt's balls. "Thank you. I think."

"You know that's good, dumb-ass." Matt pressed closed. "Kiss me."

Chris happily complied, letting Matt taste himself on Chris's tongue. Matt moaned. He backed them toward the bed without breaking the kiss, undoing the button of Chris's pants at the same time. Matt sat down hard when the backs of his knees hit the mattress. He gasped, eyes hazing over.

Chris frowned. "Are you all right, love? Is it your leg?"

Matt licked his lips. "Uh. No. Leg's fine."

"Then what is it?" Chris touched Matt's cheek. The tantalizing proximity of Matt's mouth to his prick made it damn hard to think, but he had to know if Matt was in pain.

Matt flashed an evil grin that put Chris's mind at ease. "You'll see in a minute. Right now, I wanna suck your cock. So gimme."

Chris didn't waste any more time talking. He unzipped and let his slacks fall around his ankles. Matt yanked his underwear down just enough to get it out of the way and went for Chris's cock like a starving man. It felt amazing. Chris let himself sink into the pure bliss of Matt's warm, wet mouth around his prick, those talented artist's fingers rolling his balls and caressing his thighs.

The world went white and silent around him when his orgasm hit. It seemed like he came forever, pumping his release endlessly into Matt's willing throat. When the intense pleasure receded, he pushed Matt onto his back and collapsed on the bed beside him. Matt went right into his arms, giving him a deep, lazy kiss before cuddling against his chest.

"That," Chris said when he could talk again, "was absolutely the most incredible blowjob in the history of the world."

Matt laughed. "You're easy."

"Only with you, my darling." Chris rested his cheek against Matt's hair. "I suppose we should really finish undressing at some point."

"Mm." Matt plucked at Chris's nipple. "Good thing we had a midday wedding. I think it's gonna take the rest of the afternoon and a big chunk of the night before we're done."

"Perhaps. Though I think you might be overestimating my stamina."

"Nuh-huh. I've seen you go all night before."

Chris patted Matt's butt, laughing when his lover hummed and pushed against his hand. "I shall do my very best to please you, sweetheart."

"You always please me, babe." Matt lifted his head and grinned, eyes sparkling. "Hey, you know this time tomorrow, we'll be on our way to Jamaica."

"Yes, I know." Chris trailed his fingers up and down the arm Matt had tucked around his middle. "I'm looking forward to this trip a great deal."

"Me too. Two weeks of nothing but fucking, drinking and lying in the sun. Doesn't get any better than that."

Chris chuckled. "I'd have to agree with that."

They lay in comfortable silence for a while, listening to the sounds of muted conversation drifting up from the garden below their window. A bird trilled from a nearby tree. Sprawled across the four-poster bed with his pants tangled around his feet and Matt snuggled against his side, Chris thought he'd never felt so content.

Chris wasn't sure how long they lay dozing in each other's arms. By the time Matt's hand wandered down between Chris's legs, the wide square of sunlight shining on the wall opposite the bed had shifted upward. Chris guessed that it was about three o'clock. Then Matt's teeth closed around his nipple and turned his mind to other things.

"Want you to fuck me now, babe," Matt mumbled against Chris's chest. "Nice and slow."

"Hmmm, yes." Chris opened his thighs so Matt could stroke the sensitive place behind his balls. His cock twitched and began to fill. "I want that. Want to spend hours inside you."

Matt's cheeks went pink, his swollen lips parting. "God, Chris. Gets me so turned on when you say stuff like that."

"It turns me on just to look at you like this." Chris managed to toe his shoes off, then kicked until his slacks finally fell to the floor. "Get your pants off, love, and bend over for me."

Matt's eyes went dark with lust. He scrambled to obey, drawing his legs up to his chest to pull his pants, shoes and socks off. That task accomplished, he got on his hands and knees and reached down to take off the socks that still half-clung to Chris's feet.

"Why are you bothering with that?" Chris asked, amused.

"You know I can't stand fucking with socks on," Matt answered, and bit Chris's toe. "Too porno."

"True." Chris jerked his foot away from Matt's determined tongue and rose to his knees, laughing. "I certainly hope the lube is nearby, because..."

Chris trailed off, staring in disbelief at the clear crystal lying snug between Matt's buttocks, sparkling in the sunlight. Matt turned and grinned over his shoulder. "Surprise."

Chris swallowed. "What...where...? Good God, Matt."

Matt laughed. "I bought it from Sensual Desire. Jeweled butt plug. I got the fake diamond 'cause diamond's your birthstone, and my ass belongs to you."

Chris ran his fingers over the round crystal. "And you've...you've worn this all day?"

"Naw, I just put it in when we changed clothes before the ceremony." Matt let out a moan when Chris gave the plug a slight twist. "Oh, wow. Do that again."

Chris twisted again, fiercely aroused by the way Matt arched his ass up and spread his thighs. "Tell me what it feels like."

"Feels…oh fuck…" Matt laid his chest on the mattress, fingers kneading the sheets like a cat as Chris manipulated the plug inside him. "Feels heavy. And warm. I can feel it in me every time I move."

Chris pulled the plug out of Matt's ass. He leaned down and licked at Matt's loosened hole, smiling when he realized that Matt had used the peppermint lube to insert the toy. "I like this, Matt. I like that you're slicked and stretched and ready for me."

Matt moaned and rocked back against Chris's face. "Yeah, babe. Stick your cock right in."

Straightening up again, Chris held Matt's cheeks apart, staring at his pulsating hole. "You look so decadent like this."

Matt let out a frustrated whimper. "Chris, c'mon, please!"

As usual, the begging did it. Chris guided his cock to Matt's entrance and slammed in as hard as he could. Matt sucked in a sharp breath, the muscles in his back tensing. Holding still with great effort, Chris ran both palms up Matt's spine. Matt trembled under Chris's touch.

Chris leaned over and licked Matt's neck. "I love being inside you," he whispered. "I love seeing you bent over and spread like this." He gave a sharp thrust and was rewarded by strong muscles clamping his prick like a vise. "I love how hot and tight your ass feels around my cock." He pulled out and shoved in again, changing the angle to hit Matt's gland. "I love the thought of you walking around with that plug inside you, making you so wide open for me."

Matt's hips were moving now, blindly looking for friction. Breathless, needy noises emerged from his lips in a constant stream. Chris smiled. He loved that after three years, he could still reduce Matt to a quivering bundle of sensation, shameless and wanton in his lust.

Chris set up a slow, steady rhythm, making sure Matt could feel every inch of his cock on every stroke. He watched his prick as it plunged in and out of Matt's body, watched that sweet hole stretch to accommodate his girth, and thought it was one of the hottest things he'd ever seen.

Chris kept going until his body was wet with sweat and Matt was moaning and shaking all over. When he sensed Matt getting close, he pulled out and rolled Matt onto his back. Those blue eyes stared up at him, wide and bright with need. Matt slung his legs over Chris's shoulders, locking his ankles behind Chris's neck.

"So close, baby," Matt whispered. "Fuck me. Make me come."

Chris's cock found Matt's hole, and he slid back in, the silky heat making his breath come short. "Matt... Oh, God, I'm almost there..."

Matt arched and cried out when Chris hit his prostate. As his orgasm coiled inside him, Chris took hold of Matt's erection and pumped hard. A few thrusts later, Chris's vision went red with the force of his release. Matt came seconds after Chris, his cock pulsing in Chris's hand.

"Oh yeah." Matt let his legs fall to the mattress. "That's what I'm talking about."

Chris laughed breathlessly as he pulled out and lay down beside Matt. "My darling, sex between us is always incredible."

"Sure is, babe." Matt rolled onto his side and wound himself around Chris. "I love you."

"Love you too, sweetheart."

Their mouths met in an unhurried kiss. Chris stroked Matt's back, fingers trailing up and down the sweat-dewed skin. He felt as lazy and content as a cat in the sunshine. His body sated—however temporarily—and his love in his arms, Chris couldn't think of a single thing lacking in his life.

Eventually, their kisses became deeper, their touches more urgent. Chris felt the need rising in him again, when Matt abruptly broke away.

Chris stared at him in surprise as he wriggled to the edge of the bed and began rifling through his bag, which sat open on the floor. "Matt? What are you doing?"

"It's time for the other surprise." Matt straightened up and scooted back to his spot beside Chris, holding something that looked like an oversized ring box. "Gotta do this before we start getting too turned on."

Chris sat up, his curiosity aroused as much by the anticipatory glint in Matt's eyes as by the intriguing box. "What is it?"

Matt grinned. "Rings."

"But we already exchanged rings. What on earth…" Chris stopped, eyes going wide as a sudden thought struck him. "Oh dear lord, you didn't."

"I did."

Matt opened the box. Two thick metal cock rings lay nestled against the black velvet, their smooth silver curves shining in the afternoon sunlight. Chris picked one up. It felt solid and heavy in his palm.

"What possessed you to get these?" Chris wondered.

"I don't know. I saw them in the catalogue, you know, and it just felt right." Matt bit his lip. "I can probably send them back if you don't like them."

Matt looked more uncertain than Chris had ever seen him. Setting the cock ring back in its box, Chris pulled Matt close and kissed him. He didn't let go until the unhappy tension ran out of Matt's body.

"Don't return them," Chris whispered, stroking Matt's hair. "I love them."

Matt drew back, giving Chris a sharp stare. "You mean it?"

"Yes." Chris cupped Matt's balls in his hand. "Let's put them on each other."

Matt flashed the smile Chris would do anything for. "I wanna do you first, okay?"

"Absolutely."

Chris opened his thighs when Matt nudged him. With infinite care, Matt slid one of the rings down Chris's half-hard shaft and pulled his balls through. The metal warmed quickly with the heat of Chris's skin. It surprised him how good it felt to have that pressure against the base of his cock and balls.

"So, whatcha think?" Matt asked, tugging at Chris's stiffening prick.

"It feels wonderful." Chris ran his fingers over the silvery ring, fascinated by the cool, smooth texture of it. "Let me put yours on now."

"Hell, yeah." Matt leaned back on his elbows, legs spread wide. "Ring me, baby."

Chris lifted the second ring out of the box and crawled between Matt's legs. He sat up on his knees. Every movement seemed magnified by the heavy metal constricting his genitals. He was hard as steel already, his cock jumping with the force of his pulse.

Taking Matt's cock in one hand, Chris slipped the ring on Matt's swelling shaft. "With this ring," he said as he tugged Matt's balls through, "I thee wed."

Matt's laugh was husky with rising desire. Grabbing Chris's hair in both hands, he tugged him down for a rough, lustful kiss. Chris lay between Matt's legs and ground their metal-clad erections together.

"I didn't expect this," Chris said when they broke apart. "But I like it."

Matt smiled, one hand caressing Chris's cheek. "I did promise to always surprise you."

Chris laughed. "You did indeed, sweetheart."

Matt's eyes shone with a tender light as Chris bent to kiss him. Chris stroked his left hand firmly along Matt's erection. The ring on his finger clinked against the one around Matt's cock. The sound made Chris smile.

They both knew which were the real wedding rings.

Under The Breadfruit Tree

Chapter One

"Oh God," Chris breathed, his fingers curling in Matt's hair. "So close…"

Matt hummed around Chris's cock, blue eyes burning with that look, the one that still set Chris on fire after more than three years. He came with a violent shudder and a barely restrained cry. The feel of Matt's throat working as he swallowed was beyond description, drawing Chris's orgasm out for endless blissful seconds.

Licking his lips, Matt stood and wound his arms around Chris's neck as Chris tucked his still-twitching cock back into his swim trunks. "Good?"

"Always." Chris managed a weak smile. "We really shouldn't be doing this in public."

"Yeah, I know. But I can't help it." Matt grinned. "This damn tree makes me horny."

Chris laughed. Most things made Matt horny, but Chris had to agree with this one. The breadfruit tree, with its heavy round fruit hanging in pairs from the lush green branches, looked borderline obscene. According to the bartender Matt had befriended at the beach bar, the tree secreted a milky white fluid when cut, which amused Matt no end.

They'd found the tree their first day at the resort, while exploring the grounds. Tucked into the far back corner of the property and surrounded by jasmine and bougainvillea, the tree's low-hanging branches formed an irresistible private grotto. Matt had pushed Chris against the trunk and sucked him off in the humid green dimness. Chris had gladly returned the favor, and a daily routine was born.

The ever-present danger of discovery just made it more exciting.

Chris kissed Matt's swollen lips, tasting the salty-bitter remains of his own semen. "Shall we go to the beach now?"

"You know it, babe."

Matt grabbed Chris's hand and started dragging him down the flagstone path. Chris let himself be led, content to do whatever Matt wanted.

They'd been at Moonflower Cove for only four days, but it already felt like a second home. Within minutes of their arrival at the artsy little resort on Jamaica's South coast, Chris had felt himself relaxing like never before. It was impossible to feel stressed or worried here. He and Matt had settled into a lazy, unstructured rhythm, swimming or sailing or just basking in the sun. The turquoise sea and the fragrant tropical breeze were nothing short of a balm to the soul.

The fierce heat hit like a physical blow as they emerged from the shaded pathway onto the beach. Chris took his sunglasses from their perch atop his head and put them on, then followed Matt to a pair of beach chairs at the edge of the water.

"I'm going to the bar," Matt said, dropping his plastic beach bag on the sand beside one of the chairs. "You want anything?"

"I'll have whatever you're having, thank you." Chris stretched out on the other chair with a happy sigh.

Matt raised an eyebrow at him. "Didn't you forget something?"

Chris started to say no, then realized what Matt was talking about. "Sorry, darling," he said, lifting his hips to wriggle out of his swim trunks. "I don't know why I have such trouble remembering that clothes aren't allowed on the nude beach."

"No big deal." Matt shoved his shorts down and kicked them out of the way. "I don't mind reminding you."

"Neither do I." Chris ran a finger down Matt's bare thigh. "I like the fact that you enjoy getting me naked."

"Good, because I like you walking around bare." Matt bent and kissed Chris's lips. "Back in a sec."

Chris watched Matt walk toward the bar. The way Matt's delectable ass moved never failed to mesmerize him. He wasn't the only one, judging by the number of heads turning in Matt's wake. Seeing that appreciative look in the eyes of others made Chris feel embarrassingly smug. *Sorry, ladies,* he thought gleefully when two lovely young women licked their lips as Matt passed by. *He's all mine.*

Matt, as always, seemed utterly oblivious to the admiring stares aimed his way. He leaned against the polished wood bar, swirling a bare toe through the sand as he placed his order. He stood talking and laughing with the bartender for a while then started back with a frosty plastic cup in each hand.

"I got Dirty Bananas." Matt handed Chris his drink then flopped down into his chair. "Hope that's okay."

Chris took a sip of the cold, thick liquid, savoring the taste of Kahlua and fresh bananas. "It's delicious. Thank you, love."

"You're welcome." Matt grinned at him. "Everybody's staring at you."

Chris looked down the line of his body. Nothing seemed amiss. "Why? I don't see anything wrong."

Matt laughed. "They're looking at you 'cause you're fucking gorgeous, stupid."

Chris's cheeks heated. "Oh, surely not. You're the one that turns head. Quite literally. Several people nearly broke their necks watching you walk to the bar."

Matt shook his head. "Never saw anybody as clueless as you about their own hotness." Setting his drink on the tiny plastic table between the chairs, Matt sat on Chris's lap. "I want a kiss."

Chris happily obliged him. Before long he'd forgotten all about informing Matt that *he* was the clueless one. He figured they could both live with being hot and not knowing it.

"Good grief, don't you two ever stop?"

Matt bit Chris's bottom lip, then turned to grin at the young man who'd spoken. "No. Now shut up so we can make out some more."

Chris pushed Matt away, laughing at his exaggerated pout. "How are you, Isaac? Is David joining you?"

"I'm good, thanks." Isaac stripped off his dark red swim trunks and stretched out naked on the next lounge chair over, about ten feet away. His copper skin glowed in the sun. "David'll be along later. He's in the weight room."

Matt wrinkled his nose. "He's working out? On vacation?"

"Mm-hm. Got to keep that killer bod somehow." Isaac gave Matt a long, slow look, straight white teeth gleaming in a wide smile. "I'd love to know how you do it without ever lifting a finger."

"Chris works my ass hard," Matt said, straight-faced. "'Sides," he continued as Chris groaned and Isaac cackled, "I'm not nearly as ripped as David."

"Matt, my boy," Isaac said, laying his lounge chair flat and sliding his sunglasses on, "with that face? You don't need great big he-man muscles."

Matt hopped off Chris's lap and settled into his own lounge chair. "I'm telling David you insulted his muscles."

"Go right ahead. Maybe he'll punish me."

Laughing, Matt leaned back in his chair and shut his eyes. Chris looked from one to the other with a smile. They'd met Isaac and David their first night at Moonflower Cove. Being the only two gay couples staying at the resort, they'd naturally gravitated together. The place had a reputation for being the most gay-friendly on the island, but they were still in the minority and it was nice to have another couple to talk to.

Chris had not failed to notice the low-key flirting between Matt and Isaac. It didn't worry him. He'd never questioned Matt's love or his fidelity, not after that disastrous time last summer when he'd thought Matt and Rick had something going on. Isaac seemed just as devoted to David as Matt was to Chris. Matt and Isaac were simply two of kind—friendly, outgoing people who charmed everyone around them with their flirtatious ways. Chris wouldn't have changed a thing about either of them.

Plus, there was no denying the mental image of Matt and Isaac together was the stuff of wet dreams. Matt's paleness against Isaac's darkness, blue eyes and brown burning with lust, Isaac's long black hair falling like a shadow across Matt's back as that thick dark cock plunged into Matt's ass...

A splatter of something cold and wet on his chest shocked Chris out of his thoughts. He blinked at Matt, who'd just shot a strawful of Dirty Banana on him.

"What was that for?" Chris asked, wiping the liquid off with the corner of his towel.

Matt leaned closer, grinning. "Whatever you were thinking of just now," he whispered in Chris's ear, "it's, um...making you visibly happy."

Chris looked down and was mortified to see that the hot ache in his groin was exactly what he thought it was. Thankfully the realization that he was getting an erection on a nude beach went a long way toward solving the problem.

"Dear God," he muttered. "Thank you for telling me."

Matt eyed Chris's wilting cock with open disappointment. "Wish I hadn't now."

"Well, I'm glad you did. I'd rather save it for later, when we're alone."

"So what were you thinking about?" Matt sat up and drew his legs under him, giving Chris a curious look.

The temptation to lie was strong. Chris knew if he owned up to what he'd been picturing, Matt would tease him with it for weeks. Possibly years. But there was no choice, really. He couldn't tell Matt a deliberate lie.

Propping himself up on one elbow, Chris leaned toward Matt. "I was just thinking," he said, his voice low, "of you and Isaac."

"What do you... Ooooooooh." The puzzled look on Matt's face vanished, replaced by the wicked dimpled grin Chris loved and had learned to be wary of. "You were thinking of me and him fucking, weren't you?"

213

"Yes, I was." Chris smiled. "You were quite pretty together, there in my mind."

"I bet." Matt laid his lounger flat and stretched out on his stomach, his face set in a smug smirk. "I'm never letting you forget that, babe. Just so's you know."

"I expected as much." Chris reached over and smacked Matt's bare butt. "Would you like for me to put some sunblock on you? You're still a bit pink from yesterday."

"Yeah, okay. Thanks."

Matt moaned and wriggled suggestively as Chris rubbed the sunblock onto his back. Chris thought he sounded like a porn star. Isaac lifted his sunglasses and stared at Matt's ass, then raised his smoky gaze to meet Chris's. The heat there sent a jolt through Chris's belly. Isaac slid his sunglasses back down, but not before Chris saw the anticipatory gleam in those dark eyes.

Isaac had overheard him and Matt talking, Chris was sure of it. He couldn't decide if that frightened him, or turned him on. Or both.

• • •

Several more Dirty Bananas and one impromptu game of beach volleyball later, Chris was still thinking of it. He couldn't seem to get the image of Matt and Isaac together out of his head. He watched the two of them roughhousing in the clear blue water and kept picturing them kissing and touching one another. David, stretched out beside Chris on the wooden float anchored in the shallows, seemed to be having the same problem, judging by the look in his dark gray eyes.

The four of them elected to have burgers and fries at the swim-up pool bar rather than eat at the resort's restaurant. When the sun began to sink toward the Western horizon, Matt and Chris said goodbye to their new friends and started back toward their bungalow.

Matt slipped an arm around Chris's waist as they walked. "Isaac wants me, you know."

"I know." Chris tightened his arm around Matt's shoulders. "Did he tell you that?"

"No. But I can tell."

Chris licked his suddenly dry lips. "Do you want him?"

Matt shrugged. "Kind of. He's awfully hot."

"Oh. I see." Chris didn't know what to say. Parts of him sat up and begged at the thought, but at the same time, he wasn't sure he wanted the reality.

"Hey." Matt stopped walking and framed Chris's face in his hands. "I'm not gonna do it, Chris. I mean sure, Isaac may be gorgeous, but so are you. And I love you. I married you." Matt leaned forward and pressed a gentle kiss to Chris's lips. "I don't need anyone else."

Chris felt a wash of relief, tinged with a contradictory hint of regret for the scene he'd never witness. "I'm glad. Even though the two of you *would* be orgasmically stunning together."

Matt laughed, thumbs caressing Chris's jaw. "You really do want to watch, don't you, you perv?"

"I must admit that I find the idea quite intriguing," Chris said, sliding his hands down to cup Matt's ass. "But it thrills me more than I can say to know that you are exclusively mine."

"Always yours, baby." Matt stroked the backs of his fingers over Chris's cheek. The silver wedding ring felt cool against Chris's skin. "I love you so much, Chris."

Chris smiled, leaning in to Matt's touch. "And I love you, my darling."

The kiss that followed was tender yet passionate. The perfect kiss for a midsummer tropical evening.

"Let's go inside now," Matt whispered when they broke apart. "Need you to make love to me."

"Yes." After one more lingering kiss, Chris pulled away and took Matt's hand. "Come on."

Back in their secluded little cabin, they showered off the remains of salt, sand and sunscreen, then made love in the fiery glow of the sunset. Afterward, watching the sky darken outside and holding Matt in his arms, Chris no longer saw the image of Matt and Isaac behind his eyelids. Snuggling Matt closer to his side, he sighed in perfect contentment.

Chapter Two

"You're really wearing that?"

"Uh-huh."

"To the beach."

"Yup."

"The *nude* beach."

Matt laughed. "Yes. C'mon, relax, will you? It'll be fun."

Chris glanced down at the black leather harness encasing Matt's genitals. He could barely look at the thing without getting a hard-on. The way it cradled Matt's balls, the sturdy straps lifting his cock in a lewd display. And the chain. The thin silver chain that connected Matt's piercing to the underside of the harness. It was too hot for words. Chris knew he couldn't be on the same beach with that all day without the whole resort knowing exactly how much it excited him.

"I just don't think..." Chris stopped, his gaze flicking between Matt's face and his crotch. "I don't think I can—"

"So it turns you on, is what you're saying," Matt interrupted, eyes sparkling. "And you don't want to have a hard-on where everybody can see it."

"Yes, exactly," Chris said with some relief. "Please take it off. We can play with it tonight, if you like. I know I'd like to."

Matt stared thoughtfully at him, one hand fingering the silver chain. Chris bit his lip and looked away.

"I don't think so," Matt said finally. "I'm keeping it on."

Chris swallowed. "Please, love."

Matt grinned, the evil grin that meant he was up to no good, and Chris knew he was doomed. "Nope. I declare this to be Kink Day. I'm wearing this harness all day, and you're just gonna have to deal with it."

"Oh no," Chris groaned, trying not to let his secret delight show. "Why must you punish me like this?"

"Don't worry, babe." Matt pressed his nude body against Chris's. The leather of the harness rubbed on Chris's thigh, warm and supple and just a little rough. "Tonight? I'll let you tie me up and play with the sounds."

That stopped Chris's protests cold. Matt had talked him into using the sounds on their second night at Moonflower Cove. To his everlasting surprise, Chris had found the sight of the slim metal rods disappearing into Matt's cock incredibly erotic. He took a couple of shallow breaths and tried to find his voice.

"All right," he managed. "You have a deal."

Matt chuckled. "Figured you'd go for that." He bit Chris's chin and then stepped back. "Let's head out before all the best beach chairs are gone."

Chris watched Matt pull on the ragged cut-offs he always wore on the short walk to the beach. The threadbare denim seemed to accentuate rather than hide the obscene bulge between Matt's legs. "I've a feeling that this is going to be a long day."

"You know it. Hours and hours of staring at my cock and balls all strapped up is gonna make you sooooo hard for me." Matt ran his tongue slowly across his upper lip, eyes half-closed as he rubbed his crotch.

"Oh, my love, you're going to pay for this later," Chris declared. He tried to look stern. The urge to laugh wasn't helping.

"I'm counting on it, babe." Matt waggled his eyebrows, and this time Chris gave in and laughed.

• • •

Later that day, as they left the beach to get ready for dinner, Chris thanked his lucky stars that he and Matt had slept until almost noon and therefore hadn't left their cabin until after one o'clock. They'd been out on the beach for about four hours, but it felt more like four days. Chris had spent most of that time huddled in a lounge chair under a palm tree, knees drawn up to hide his erection, pretending to read a book while watching Matt frolic in the water.

"Good lord," Chris groaned as he pulled his baggy swim trunks up over his achingly hard cock. "I cannot believe you made me sit there and watch you flaunting your genitalia in that damn harness."

"Thought you were reading, babe." Matt squirmed his soaking wet self back into the tight cut-offs, blue eyes wide with feigned innocence.

"You know very well," Chris said through gritted teeth, "that I wasn't reading."

Matt grinned. "Hey, at least you don't have to be naked for dinner."

Chris snatched the beach bag out of Matt's hand and held it in front of his own crotch. "Thank God for small favors. Are you taking that evil device off before we eat?"

"Yep."

"Good."

"I decided to wear my wedding ring instead."

Chris gave him a puzzled look as they started down the path to their bungalow. "Your wedding ring? It's on your finger now. You haven't taken it off since the wedding."

"Not *that* ring," Matt said, bumping his hip against Chris's.

Chris let out a shaky sigh when he realized Matt was talking about the metal cock ring. "Oh dear."

"What 'oh dear'? You're gonna wear yours too."

"Matt, please. How can I enjoy my dinner if all I can think of is how hard I am, and how hard *you* are, and how desperately I want to fuck you?" Chris heard the whine in his voice but he didn't care.

"You can't," Matt admitted cheerfully. "Neither can I. But just think how awesome the sex'll be later."

"Yes, well..." Chris tried to think of a reasonable argument and couldn't. "But, Matt, why? We have incredible sex all the time, why do we need to torture ourselves first?"

"Because," Matt clarified, opening the door of the cabin, "it's Kink Day. I told you that."

"You have a one-track mind," Chris said, though it wasn't a complaint.

Without warning, Matt shoved Chris against the wall and kissed him hard. "You're always so in control," he breathed against Chris's mouth. "Tonight, I want you to be so horny for me that you can't control it. I want you to sit there during dinner with that metal ring around your cock and that metal plug up your ass and not be able to think about *anything* but fucking me. We'll come back here, and you'll fuck my mouth hard and fast, right here on the floor because you can't wait a second longer. Then, you'll tie me to the bed and do all the things I know you want to do to me. Use all those toys on me. You can even whip me, if you want, for keeping you hard all day."

The picture Matt painted had Chris throbbing in his shorts, but one thing bothered him. "Plug? You want me to wear that jeweled butt plug?"

Matt nodded. His eyes gleamed with something dark and feral. "Will you? For me?"

A wicked thought struck Chris. It went straight from his fevered brain to his mouth, and he wondered how stupid he was being. "If you'll agree to let me tie you to the breadfruit tree instead of the bed."

Matt's eyebrows shot up. "Did you just say what I think you said?"

"Yes indeed." Feeling more confident now, Chris shoved Matt's shorts down and grabbed his butt cheeks in both hands, spreading him open. "Just picture it, Matt. You naked and bound for my pleasure, right out in the open.

Anyone could come by. Anyone could see me inserting those sounds into your cock, whipping you and playing with your ass. Anyone."

Chris could tell Matt got the point about exactly who might wander by. Matt's cheeks went pink, his lips parting in a soft moan. "Fuck, Chris."

"No, darling." Chris abruptly plunged two fingers into Matt's unprepared hole. "You're the one who'll be getting fucked."

"Oh God," Matt groaned, arching into the intrusion. "Yeah. Do it, Chris. I want it."

It was all Chris could do to keep from coming right then and there, just from the raw lust in Matt's voice. He bent and sucked at the curve of Matt's throat. Matt's skin tasted of salt and heat. Chris could smell his desire.

"Chris…" Matt moaned.

Chris understood everything that one breathless plea asked for. Pulling his fingers from Matt's body, he spun Matt around to face the wall, dropped to his knees and yanked the cut-offs down to Matt's ankles. Matt let out a sharp cry when Chris spread his buttocks and went to work on his hole. Matt leaned forward, hands braced on the wall, muttering broken obscenities under his breath as Chris opened him with tongue and fingers.

It wasn't until Chris was standing again, swim trunks puddled on the floor at his feet and his cock poised at Matt's entrance, that he realized the lube was on the other side of the room. He groaned in frustration.

"Lube," he gasped. "Let me go—"

"No!" Matt shot a desperate look at Chris over his shoulder. "Just use spit."

"But—"

"Please, Chris, please! Can't wait, 'm gonna come!"

Chris, teetering on the edge himself, didn't argue any more. He spit into his palm, slicked his cock and shoved inside.

"Oh fuck!" Matt cried. His fingers clawed at the wall. "God*damn*…fuck…"

Chris held still with a huge effort. Matt was impossibly tight, his body shaking like a leaf. "I'm hurting you," Chris murmured, one hand caressing Matt's belly. "I'll stop."

Matt shook his head. "No, no please. Doesn't hurt so much." He pressed backward, forcing Chris deeper inside him. A soft whimper escaped his lips. "Oh God. Fuck me, please!"

Chris tried to be gentle. But Matt's obvious need to have it hard and rough undid him. One hand on the wall beside Matt's and the other around Matt's hips, he slammed into Matt with all his strength. Matt met him blow for blow, grunting and cursing, sweat running in rivers down his back.

Chris slid the hand on Matt's hips down his groin and was shocked at the feel of leather straps digging into the flesh there. He'd forgotten all about the harness. Matt's erect prick strained the chain to its limit. Chris ran his fingers up to where the silver chain pulled hard on the ring piercing the head of Matt's cock. Matt whimpered and pushed into his hand, and that did it. Chris came buried to the root in Matt's ass. Matt wasn't far behind, spurting all over Chris's hand, his insides rippling around Chris's prick.

"Fuck," Matt gasped, and collapsed to the floor, taking Chris with him.

Chris rolled onto his back and hauled Matt into his arms. Matt kicked the shorts off his feet and snuggled into Chris's embrace, his heart pounding against Chris's chest.

"Are you all right?" Chris asked, concerned.

"Yeah, I'm fine." Matt wound himself tighter around Chris, face buried in his neck. "That was fucking amazing."

Chris ran a hand over Matt's ass, stroking his opening with a gentle touch. "You're certain I didn't do any damage? It was so rough."

"Babe, I'm fine, stop worrying." Matt kissed Chris's throat. "I wanted it rough, in case you couldn't tell."

"Yes, I noticed." Chris rubbed his cheek on Matt's damp hair. "I'm sorry to be a pest. I simply can't stand the thought of hurting you, love."

"I know." Matt raised his head to look into Chris's eyes, one hand on Chris's cheek. "That's why I wanted to try the toys with you, and the bondage and all. Because I know I'm safe with you. I know you'd never do anything to hurt me."

Staring into Matt's trusting eyes, Chris felt a surge of protectiveness. He clutched Matt close, both hands caressing his bare back. "I love you, sweetheart," Chris whispered.

"Love you," Matt echoed, his voice muffled in Chris's neck.

Chris lay there on the hard floor of the cabin, afternoon sunshine in his eyes and his love in his arms, and knew he was the luckiest man on earth.

Chapter Three

Two and a half hours later, sitting gingerly on the edge of his chair and sweating his way through the longest dinner of his life, Chris had almost changed his mind about being lucky.

Almost.

Knowing what lay in store for him after dinner was the only thing keeping Chris from dragging Matt outside and fucking him senseless. If he tried to leave before Matt was ready, he'd be lucky to be allowed a hand job, never mind real sex.

"You okay, babe? You're kind of flushed." Matt smiled sweetly. "Is the wasabi too hot?"

Chris shot him a deadly glare. "No," he growled. "It's fine. I just… Uh…"

"Hey, buddy, you really don't look so good." David, who was sitting to Chris's left, laid a massive hand on his shoulder. "Maybe you should go lie down."

Chris caught the half-playful, half-serious warning in Matt's eyes and shook his head. "No no, I'm fine, really. I think I got a bit too much sun this afternoon."

Isaac gave him a thoughtful look from across the table. "Could be. You look a little sunburned."

"Don't worry," Matt said, patting Chris's thigh. "I'll take care of you, babe. Long as you let me stay for dessert."

Matt slid his hand higher, fingertips just brushing Chris's tight and hypersensitive balls. Chris nearly came out of his chair. Matt blew him a kiss before turning his attention back to his blackened shrimp.

Smug bastard, Chris thought, staring at his own half-eaten sushi and wishing he could fuck Matt right across the table.

Between the heavy steel ring constricting his cock and balls and the pressure of the butt plug inside him, Chris could barely string together a coherent sentence. It wasn't his first experience with cock rings and butt plugs, but it was his first experience with metal toys. That solid weight made all the difference. He felt as if every ounce of blood in his body had been shunted to his privates, leaving his mind barren of intelligent thought and utterly focused on the sensations between his legs.

Chris managed to make it through another fifteen minutes until everyone else had finished their dinner. The waitress gave Chris an odd look when she brought the desserts. When his rather anemic smile was met by a concerned frown from the young woman, Chris gave up. He leaned toward Matt.

"Matt," he whispered. "Let's go now, please. I can't take this anymore."

"Hm." Matt scooped up a spoonful of mango ice cream. "I'm not done, babe. Wanna eat my dessert."

Chris bit back a moan when Matt held the spoon to his mouth and rubbed the ice cream against his lips. "Please, Matt."

Matt shot him a sidelong look full of evil intent. "I finish my dessert," he muttered under his breath, "or no sounds."

Chris sighed. Matt had him, and he knew it. "Very well. We'll wait."

"Hey." Isaac grinned. "Didn't your mother ever teach you that whispering at the table is rude?"

"Sorry," Chris said. He wished it didn't sound so abrupt, but the blatantly sexy way Matt ate his ice cream was rapidly eroding Chris's ability to speak.

"We were just clearing something up." Matt swiped his tongue along the concavity of his spoon in a way that had Chris squirming in his seat. "Sorry 'bout that."

Isaac's eyebrows went up. "No problem. There's some conversations that really need to be private, huh?"

"Oh, hell yeah," David chortled. "I think maybe this is one of those *really* private ones, don't you, Isaac?"

"Sure enough." Isaac's dark eyes glittered. "You know, Matt, if you guys need to, um…get out of here, it's okay. We'll understand."

"That's awfully nice of you. But," Matt continued before Chris could get his hopes up, "I really, really want to finish this ice cream. It's so good." He lapped up another spoonful and let out a soft little moan that did nothing for Chris's deteriorating composure. "Mmmm. It's practically orgasmic."

"Oh God," Chris breathed. He closed his eyes and drew several slow, deep breaths. A single touch, he thought, might shatter him.

"Hey," David muttered in Chris's ear. "When you get him alone? Be sure to fuck him 'til he screams for mercy. He deserves it."

Chris opened his eyes and turned to look at David. The man wore a teasing smile, but his gray eyes were hot with lust. Chris's insides twisted. For a blazing second he pictured himself crushed against that big, solid body, and he liked it. A lot. Then he thought of all the things he wanted to do with Matt later and the mental image of David's arms around him went away.

"David," Chris said, "I plan to do that and more."

David's gaze darted to Matt, then back to Chris. "Hope you don't mind my saying so, but I'd pay to be a fly on the wall."

Chris glanced at Matt. He was flirting with Isaac again, the two of them talking in low tones and wearing smiles that spoke volumes. "I'd pay to watch the two of them together."

"Good lord," David murmured. "That? Would be too fucking hot."

Chris fixed his eyes on David's face. It made him feel much more in control of himself. "Do you and Isaac ever…play around? With other couples, I mean."

David grinned at him. "We have. But truthfully, it's not our scene anymore. Tell you what, though, if we were still into that? We'd be all over the two of you."

Chris laughed. "I understand. Matt and I are exclusive as well, for quite a while now."

"So what'd he make you do?" David asked, watching Matt slurp up the last of his ice cream.

"You don't want to know," Chris muttered. An idea struck him and he went with it, too turned on to care whether it was particularly smart or not. "Listen, David, if you really want to watch, wait about fifteen minutes after Matt and I leave, then come to the breadfruit tree."

David gave him a puzzled look. "What, that tree with the big green balls? How come?"

"Just come. I promise you quite a show."

David didn't have time to answer, but Chris thought the look in his eyes was answer enough.

"Hey babe," Matt said, scooting closer and slinging an arm around Chris's shoulders. "Ready to go?"

"Dear God, yes." Chris jumped to his feet so fast his blood-deprived brain nearly shut down. He stood there swaying like a tree in a stiff wind while the room spun around him.

"Whoa, Chris, slow down." Matt laughed, standing and winding an arm around Chris's waist. "Won't do either of us any good if you pass out now."

"Can I pass out later?" Chris leaned against Matt.

Matt gave him an amused look. "If you have to. Now come on, it's time for *your* dessert."

About time, too. Chris mustered a smile for David and Isaac as he edged toward the door. "Goodnight. I'm glad you could join us for dinner."

"Me too," Isaac said, exchanging an indecipherable look with Matt. "Later, guys."

David's face broke into a mischievous grin. "See you soon."

The way David's gaze lingered on his crotch made Chris feel hot all over. He linked his arm through Matt's, holding on for dear life. He didn't have to voice his need to hurry. He knew Matt could feel it.

They had to stop at the bungalow to get the lube, sounds and other toys. The moment the door shut behind them Chris pushed Matt to his knees. He had his fly open a second later, the tip of his cock just brushing Matt's lips.

"Suck me," Chris ordered, his voice hoarse with pent-up tension.

Matt stared up at him, blue eyes blazing. Without a word, he opened his mouth and gulped Chris down. Chris gasped as the world dissolved into a haze of pure pleasure. He fisted both hands in Matt's hair and pounded into Matt's throat as hard as he could, knowing Matt wanted it that way.

It didn't last long. Before many minutes had passed, Chris came with a harsh cry. He leaned against the wall, trembling with the aftershocks of his orgasm. The wet warmth retreated from his cock and then Matt was pressed against him, kissing him softly, arms loose around his neck.

"Mmmm," Matt purred, flicking his tongue over Chris's lips. "Love how you fuck my mouth, baby."

Chris laughed weakly. "My darling, I love you more than life itself, but you are truly evil. I didn't think I would survive dinner."

"I had faith in you, babe." Matt smiled, one hand stroking Chris's hair. "I didn't come. I wanted to save it for you."

Chris's cock, still half tumescent, twitched in anticipation. He slid both hands down to squeeze Matt's butt. "You might regret that in a little while. I plan on making you pay for dinner."

"Promise?"

"Oh yes."

Matt's eyes gleamed with a primitive light. "Get the equipment and let's go."

"Very well." Chris smacked Matt's rear, then slipped out of Matt's arms and went to collect the things they would need. "Oh, Matt?"

"Yeah, babe?" Matt leaned against the wall, his erection tenting his trousers.

Chris grinned. "From now on, I'm giving the orders tonight. Are we clear?"

Matt's cheeks flushed. He licked his swollen lips. "Yeah."

"Good." Chris crooked a finger. "Come here."

Chris dug through the outside pocket of his carryon bag for the present he'd bought Matt. When he straightened up again, Matt was standing beside him. Matt's eyes went wide when he saw what Chris held.

"Shit," Matt whispered. "Where'd you get that?"

"I bought it the other day, from a local leather vendor who was displaying her wares at the gift shop. You were windsurfing with Isaac." Chris buckled the supple black leather collar around Matt's neck, making sure it was snug but not too tight. "Oh, that's lovely."

Matt ran his fingertips over the collar. "Fuck. All you need's a leash."

"Funny you should mention that." Chris reached back into his bag and pulled out a long strip of leather with a buckle on one end and a wrist loop on the other. "She was selling those as well."

Matt's mouth dropped open. He stood still and silent while Chris buckled the leash to one of the D-rings set at intervals in the collar. To outside eyes, it may have seemed as though Matt was afraid, but Chris knew better. He'd learned long ago to recognize Matt's varying degrees of arousal. The stunned silence, combined with the inferno in Matt's eyes, told Chris that Matt would be putty in his hands, incoherent with lust and noisily responsive to his every touch.

Chris couldn't help laughing with sheer delight at the thought.

It was only a couple minute's work to gather the lube and assorted toys. Chris piled everything in a plastic bag, took hold of Matt's leash and gave it a tug. "Come along, love. Let's play."

Matt followed, docile as a puppy. Only his ragged breathing hinted at the excitement Chris knew he felt.

When they reached the breadfruit tree, Chris led Matt around to the back, out of sight of the walkway. With the tree's wide trunk on one side and a corner of the tall, vine-covered wooden fence on the other, they were in their own hidden world. The broad leaves rustled overhead and the air was sweet with the perfumes of jasmine and moonflower. With the light of the full moon flitting through the dense greenery, the place felt magical. It was the perfect spot in which to indulge one's fantasies.

Chris wrapped an arm around Matt's waist and tenderly kissed his lips. "Undress, darling."

Matt did as he was told, watching Chris's face the whole time. In a few seconds he stood there naked, his clothes discarded in a heap on the ground, bare skin glowing in the fitful moonlight. Chris raked his gaze up and down Matt's body. Matt's prick was stiff and dripping, his balls flushed dark from the pressure of the cock ring. The collar and leash added a whole new level of sinfulness to the picture.

"You look..." Chris shook his head, trying to find the right words. "I can't explain. Amazing. Beautiful."

Matt stared back at him with an intensity Chris had rarely seen in him before. "Please, Chris. Can't wait."

The naked desperation in Matt's voice sent a wave of heat roaring through Chris's body. He ran a finger down Matt's chest, loving the way Matt's skin jumped at his touch. "Kneel."

Matt dropped obediently to his knees, wide eyes fixed on Chris's face. Chris swallowed. The sight of Matt bare and collared, kneeling at his feet, sent his pulse racing. Leaving the button of his trousers fastened, he unzipped his fly and pulled his cock and balls out through the opening. Matt's lips parted with a soft sigh.

"Hold your hands out," Chris said, pulling the cloth restraints out of the bag.

Matt raised his hands in front of his face. His palm brushed Chris's cock, which Chris strongly suspected was deliberate. He chuckled as he wrapped the Velcro cuffs around Matt's wrists, letting the long straps trail the ground. "No more touching me until I say so."

A tiny smile lifted the corners of Matt's mouth. "Please?"

"No." Chris returned Matt's smile. "Don't make me whip you."

The expression on Matt's face told Chris quite clearly that his "threat" had worked. He grinned and yanked Matt's hands over his head.

Matt held perfectly still as Chris tied the restraint straps to a low-hanging branch, but Chris felt his tension in the faint tremors running through his arms. As Chris stepped back to admire his handiwork, a movement in the shadows caught his eye. He glanced to his left just in time to see moonlight glinting off two figures half-hidden behind a branch of the breadfruit tree. The taller and broader of the two stood behind his partner, muscular arms holding the smaller man in a loving embrace.

David and Isaac had come to watch.

The knowledge that he and Matt had an audience had Chris hard as steel between one breath and the next. With one quick glance at David and Isaac, Chris sank to his knees in front of Matt.

"Sounds now?" Matt asked hopefully.

"In a moment." Chris rummaged through the bag of toys until he found the lube and the tremendous purple jelly butt plug they'd had for more than two years but rarely used. "First, I want to make sure that you feel what I've been feeling all night. Turn around and bend over."

Matt gulped and hurried to obey, shuffling on his knees to face the tree. He managed to lean forward a little and brace his elbows on the tree trunk. It looked awkward as hell, but Chris resisted the urge to untie Matt's hands. Part of the attraction of this whole scenario for Matt, he knew, was the loss of control.

For Chris too, if he was honest with himself. He loved having Matt's body so completely in his hands, taking his natural protectiveness toward his lover to a previously unexperienced extreme.

Chris bent to kiss the back of Matt's neck. "I'm going to put this toy up your ass now, love," he murmured, just loud enough for David and Isaac to hear. "It's going to stay there inside you while I play with your cock."

He flipped open the bottle of lube, slicked his fingers and shoved two of them into Matt's hole. Matt's whole body went tight. He let out a long, shuddering breath. Chris twisted his fingers, finding Matt's gland easily and making him cry out. He kept doing it until the tight ring of muscles began to relax.

"Are you ready, Matt?" Chris pulled his fingers out and poured a generous amount of lube on the butt plug. "Because I'm quite anxious to see this giant plug stretching your ass wide open."

"Fuck yeah." Matt's thighs shifted as far apart as was possible in his precarious position. "Stick it in me, baby, please!"

"Mm." Chris pressed the tip of the plug against Matt's entrance. "You're going to feel this…" he pushed harder, forcing the toy halfway in, "every time your insides tighten…" another shove, and the plug was fully seated deep in Matt's ass, "while I'm putting those sounds in your cock."

"Oh God," Matt whispered. His hands clenched into fists, the muscles of his back and thighs rippling. "So fucking good."

Chris laid his cheek against Matt's hair, sliding his hand between Matt's legs. He loved the way Matt shook and moaned. He gave Matt's balls a sharp tug before sitting back on his heels.

"Turn around," Chris said.

Matt did it, his movements slow and stiff. Chris had no sympathy. He himself had been moving like that all evening. He flexed his buttocks, making the metal toy shift inside him.

When Matt was facing him again, stretched in a long line from bound hands to parted knees, Chris took out the clean towel he'd brought and spread it on the ground. The case with the sounding equipment in it came next. Chris set it on the towel and opened it, making sure Matt could see.

"Where shall I start?" Chris asked, taking the little plastic syringe from the kit and filling it from the tube of surgical lubricant that came with the kit. "The smallest? Or do you think you can take a larger one to begin with?"

Matt licked his lips, staring at the sounds with wide, hot eyes. "Bigger. Third one up."

"Whatever you want, love." Very carefully, Chris pressed the blunt end of the syringe into Matt's slit and pumped his cock full of lube. Matt moaned, hips rocking forward.

Matt's gaze followed Chris's hands as he put the syringe back in the case and picked up the third smallest sound. They'd only gotten to the fourth one in the case the last time. Chris told himself not to worry, that Matt would tell him if it got to be too much.

So this is what domination and submission is all about. Trust, on both sides of the restraints.

It was something he'd never understood before. He smiled.

Taking Matt's cock in one hand, he gently squeezed the tip until the tiny slit opened. "Deep breath, darling."

Matt obeyed. Holding his own breath, Chris eased the rosebud-shaped tip of the sound into Matt's cock. Gravity took over, and the metal rod dropped slowly inside.

"Ooooooooh, oh God, oh *God!*" Matt cried as the sound disappeared bit by bit inside his shaft.

Chris gave him a sharp look. "Matt?"

"'S okay," Matt gasped. "Fuck. Do it again."

Chris nodded. His heart thudded against his ribs. *Trust*, he reminded himself. *You must trust him.*

Chris tugged on the sound's handle until only the tip was inside Matt, then let it drop again. Matt's head lolled back, his moans and curses loud in the night. Another moan echoed Matt's. Chris glanced toward where he knew their two-man audience stood. A bar of moonlight illuminated David's hand caressing Isaac's erection.

He could've sworn he saw David grin at him. He returned the smile.

"Bigger one, baby, please," Matt begged.

Chris pulled the sound out, taking care to keep the movement slow and even. Matt whimpered and bit his lip.

"Here we go, sweet." Chris picked up the next largest rod.

The tapered tip went right in, smooth as silk. Chris let it sink in until it met resistance, then pulled it out and did it again. Matt panted and twitched. The effort it took for him to hold still was crystal clear in his tight, tense muscles.

Chris leaned forward and kissed Matt's trembling lips after removing the sound from Matt's cock. "Relax, baby," he whispered, stroking Matt's hair. "You're too tense. I'm afraid I'll hurt you."

Matt swallowed audibly. "'M fine. Please, Chris."

Chris planted a soft kiss on Matt's damp forehead. "Okay. Next one, then. Deep breaths, love, okay?"

Matt nodded. He drew several long, shaking breaths before Chris felt the tension in Matt's body begin to ease. Keeping one hand on Matt's thigh, Chris reached for the next sound. It looked big enough to worry Chris a little, but he keep his thoughts to himself for Matt's sake.

A long, keening cry spilled from Matt's lips when Chris carefully inserted the metal rod. Matt grasped at the strips of cloth binding his hands to the branch above, twisting them between his fingers. "Fuck, fuck, fuck," he chanted in a hoarse whisper. "Oh God, oh fuck…"

Chris stared hard at Matt's face, trying to read his expression. He saw no pain there, no fear. What blazed in those wide, unfocused eyes was a dark hunger that made Chris's exposed cock throb.

"Does it feel good?" Chris let the sound slide further in. "Do you like having that hard metal inside your cock?"

"Ooooooooh, fuck yeah." Matt gasped and arched when Chris partly removed the sound and then let it drop back in. "'S good."

Chris repeated the procedure, giving the rod an experimental twist that had Matt's hips thrusting against empty air. "Can you feel that plug inside you?"

"Feel it," Matt panted. "So fucking big."

Chris hooked a finger through the ring piercing Matt's cock and gave it a tug. "You should see yourself, Matt. On your knees, tied naked to a tree, with a collar around your neck, a plug up your ass, and a metal rod inside your cock. You look positively decadent."

Faint moans and whispers from the shadows seemed to agree with Chris's assessment. He glanced over. Two pairs of burning eyes were fixed on Matt's cock. Isaac's head lolled against David's solid shoulder as David's big hand worked his cock. Chris could see David's hips moving as he rubbed himself against Isaac's ass. Chris grinned and turned back to Matt.

"Can you take another?" he asked, carefully removing the sound and setting it back in the case. He held up the next largest one. "This one will surely stretch you beyond your limits."

It was a challenge as much as a legitimate worry, and Chris knew that Matt knew it. Matt's lips curled into a feral grin. "Gimme it."

Chris pumped more lube into Matt's cock first and slicked the sound itself for good measure. The second the metal tip pushed past Matt's slit, Chris knew that was it. Matt was going to come as soon as he took it out. The way Matt's body writhed, the increasingly desperate sounds he made, said so clear as day. Sweating with the effort of holding back his own orgasm, Chris let the sound drop deep into Matt's prick and held it still. He leaned forward and pressed his lips to Matt's in a gentle kiss.

"Wait for me," he whispered, nuzzling Matt's hot cheek. "Don't come until you're in my mouth."

Matt whimpered, his cock pulsing in Chris's hand. "Hurry," he breathed, the word almost too soft to hear.

Chris drew back and looked Matt up and down. He thought he'd never seen anything so obscenely beautiful, or so tempting. He shifted his knees further apart, hissing as the heavy plug inside him nudged his prostate. The need to come washed over him like a tide. Chris closed his eyes and breathed, deep and steady. After a few frantic seconds, the feeling faded enough for him to get control of himself again.

No way was he coming anywhere but inside Matt.

"Taking it out now," Chris said with some difficulty. His brain felt fuzzy and slow. "Wait for me."

Matt didn't answer, didn't respond at all. One look in those lust-hazed blue eyes told Chris he only had seconds in which to act. Matt was gone, lost in a world of sensation, operating on pure blind instinct. Knowing he had put that look in Matt's eyes gave Chris a strange feeling inside, powerful and tender. Made him feel like the king of the world.

It took every ounce of Chris's concentration to keep his hand steady and his movements careful as he removed the sound from Matt's slit. Once it was out, he tossed it haphazardly into its case, leaned down and swallowed Matt's cock whole.

Not a moment too soon. Matt came almost immediately, moaning low and rough, hips snapping as he fucked Chris's mouth. Chris swallowed the hot, salty semen, grimacing at the oddly blank taste of sterile lube mixed with it.

Chris kept Matt's prick in his mouth, sucking softly, reluctant to let go in spite of the insistent need drawing his balls up tight. Finally, when he felt Matt sag in his bonds, Chris let Matt's softening cock slip from his mouth and sat up.

Matt licked his lips. "Un…untie…"

Chris reached up and untied Matt's hands, smiling at the dazed look on Matt's face. "Bend over, love. Need to fuck you."

Matt blinked, flashed a loopy grin, turned around and fell forward, chest pressed to the ground. "Fuck me."

It was all Chris could do to remove the butt plug carefully instead of just ripping it out. Matt had said he wanted Chris to lose control, but Chris didn't think he'd meant it quite that way. He tugged steadily at the base of the toy and it popped out. Setting it aside, he spread Matt open and plunged his cock into that soft, welcoming heat.

Now I can lose control. Getting a firm grip on Matt's hips, Chris let himself go, slamming into Matt so hard he felt the vibrations in his skull.

God, it felt good. So damn good to just give in and let himself take what he wanted, knowing his lover wanted it too. Matt's body rippled around his cock, hot and tight and so fucking alive. The humid air rang with Matt's cries, and his own, and a faint echo which he knew was Isaac and David finding their own release as they watched him fuck Matt into oblivion.

He came in a matter of minutes, stars exploding behind his eyes as his orgasm tore through him like a hurricane. He pulled out before he was finished, just to watch the last of his spunk splatter onto Matt's quivering and well-fucked ass.

"Fucking hell, Chris," Matt muttered, cheek pressed to the dirt. "You animal."

"Mm." Chris sat down a little too hard and yelped when the movement forced the butt plug further inside him. He held Matt's buttocks apart and stared, fascinated, as his own come trickled out of Matt's open hole. "You did say you wanted me to lose control."

Matt laughed. "You staring at my asshole, Chris?"

"Perhaps." Chris leaned forward and stuck his tongue in, humming at the taste of himself blended with Matt. "Is there anything wrong with that?"

"Not from where I'm sitting." Matt wriggled against Chris's face. "I like having your tongue up my ass almost as much as your cock."

Laughing, Chris bit one firm cheek hard enough to leave a mark before pulling away. He turned to look at Isaac and David. The two had moved behind Chris enough that Chris knew they had a perfect view of Matt's exposed hole. The knowledge made his cock twitch lazily, but he knew he wasn't getting it up again tonight. What he'd just experienced had been so intense that it drained him completely. He grinned at them, and David grinned back. Isaac just blinked at him, obviously too dazed to do anything else.

"Are you ready to go now, love?" Chris patted Matt's rear.

"Mm." Matt rolled onto his side, a wide grin plastered to his face. "Babe, I swear, you fucked me stupid. Don't think I can stand up."

"I see that." Chris rose to his knees. "Just rest for a moment while I put these things away."

"'K." Matt stretched like a cat, smearing his nude body with bits of dirt and crumbled leaves. "Gotta clean the sounds with alcohol."

"We'll do that when we get back." Chris closed the leather case and put it in the bag along with the purple jelly butt plug. He crawled over Matt's body and leaned down, lips brushing Matt's ear. "We had an audience, you know."

Matt chuckled. "So David and Isaac showed up, huh? I wondered if they would."

Chris blinked, surprised. "What? How did you know?"

"I told Isaac where we'd be, and about when." Matt shrugged. "He wanted to watch. Figured you wouldn't mind."

Chris burst out laughing. "You were right about that. I didn't mind at all. In fact, I told David the same thing."

Matt gaped at him. "No fucking way."

"Oh, yes, I did."

For a second, Matt was silent. Then he threw his head back and howled with laughter.

"Oh, shit," Matt gasped when they both wound down a little. "We're a pair, huh?"

"We certainly are." Chris took Matt's left hand in his, their wedding rings clinking together. "Sometimes I truly believe that we share one mind."

Matt shifted until he could wind his arms around Chris's neck. The straps of the restraints still wrapped around his wrists tickled Chris's back. "Love you, babe," Matt murmured, and kissed him.

Chris buried his face in Matt's hair, soaking up the scent of sex and sweat and earth. "I love you too, darling. So much."

Matt kissed his way to Chris's ear. "Are they still here?"

Chris lifted his head and looked, not bothering to be subtle. "No, they've gone."

"Too bad." Matt pushed on Chris's chest. "Let me up, I'm getting a cramp."

"Why too bad? Were you hoping they'd join in?" Chris sat up, wincing as the plug jostled his insides. "Good lord. I have to get this thing out of me."

Matt looked blank for a moment, then grinned. "Oh, yeah. I forgot."

"I didn't." Standing on wobbly legs, Chris flipped open the button on his trousers and let them drop around his ankles. "Take it out for me, love?"

"Sure thing." Matt rose to his knees, looking quite pleased with the prospect of removing the toy from Chris's ass. "Turn around."

Chris obediently shuffled around to face away from Matt and bent over, resting his hands on his knees. He let out a sigh of relief when Matt pulled the metal toy out of him. "Thank you, Matt. Goodness, it certainly... Oh!"

Whatever Chris had planned to say flew right out of his head when Matt's tongue touched his stretched and sensitive hole. He groaned, arching his back to open himself more. Matt hummed and licked, his wet tongue soothing Chris's over-stimulated skin.

"That feels so good," Chris moaned. "Unfortunately, I don't think I have the energy left for another round."

"Mmmmmm," Matt purred, giving him one last lick and a light smack on the butt. "Me neither. Just couldn't resist a little tongue fuck, with your hole all stretched out like that."

Chris straightened up and turned around just in time to get an armful of naked, sticky, happy Matt. Standing there in the fragrant tropical night with his ass throbbing, his pants around his ankles, and his love snuggled against his chest, Chris thought life couldn't get any better.

Chapter Four

Chris woke the next morning just as the sun peeked over the horizon. He stretched, taking stock of his body. Other than a vague soreness in his anus and slightly stiff knees he felt wonderful. Invigorated.

He figured he had the previous evening's episode under the breadfruit tree to thank for that. He and Matt hadn't taken time for anything other than brushing their teeth and cleaning the sounds before falling exhausted into bed. They'd been sound asleep well before midnight, which was a first for them on this vacation, and Chris had slept like the dead. He'd never felt more well rested in his life.

Matt, as usual, was wound like an octopus around Chris, snuffling against his neck. Chris rubbed his cheek against Matt's tousled hair. "Matt, love? Are you awake?"

No answer. Not that he'd expected one. Chris smiled, patted Matt's bare butt and started untangling himself.

A matter of minutes later, Chris crept out the door of the cabin and headed toward the open-air breakfast buffet. He'd let Matt sleep, he figured, and bring him breakfast in bed.

He drew a deep breath of clean, salt-scented air as he strolled down the pathway between the palms, enjoying the peaceful beauty. In another week he and Matt would have to leave this idyllic place, go back to their home and their jobs and their mundane, everyday lives. The thought may have been depressing to some people, but Chris couldn't be anything but happy about it.

As wonderful as their time at Moonflower Cove was, his and Matt's life back home was even better.

David was sitting at one of the umbrella-covered tables, wolfing down eggs, bacon and fried plantain. He waved Chris over.

"Good morning," Chris said, smiling as he sat in the other chair.

"Hey." David took a big gulp of coffee. "Quite a show last night."

Chris laughed. "I did promise you one."

"And boy, was it ever." David shook his head. "Tell you what, Isaac 'bout wore me out after we got back to our room."

Chris arched an amused brow at David's wide grin and sparkling eyes. "Yet I notice that you're the one up at dawn, while Isaac is nowhere to be seen."

David shrugged, popping the last bite of plantain into his mouth. "I slept like a damn rock. Woke up at four and figured I'd go on ahead and get my lifting done."

"Isaac's still sleeping?"

"Mm-hm. Wore himself out even more than me." David drained his coffee cup, sat back and stretched. "What about Matt? He still snoozing too?"

"Yes. I thought I'd bring him breakfast in bed."

"Good idea. He's got to be annihilated today."

"I'll have you know that the whole thing was his idea."

"Figured so." David grinned. "But you, my friend, are a Dom waiting to happen."

Chris didn't know what to say to that, since he'd been mulling over that very thing. It was an aspect of himself he'd never encountered before, and he wasn't sure he was comfortable with it.

"Hey," David said, brow furrowed. "I didn't mean to freak you out, man."

"You didn't, David. I was thinking the same thing, actually. That I do seem to have dominant tendencies. I'm not particularly comfortable with that part of myself just yet. Though if Matt has his way, I expect that I'll have to learn to be."

David laughed. "Yeah, I bet you will." He stood, brushing crumbs off his lap. "Okay, I'm off. Isaac'll be up any time now."

Chris stood as well. "See you both on the beach later?"

"Sure thing." David clapped Chris on the shoulder. "Tell Matt I hope his cock's recovered from all that mistreatment."

David strode away with a wave over his shoulder. Chris wandered toward the buffet, chuckling under his breath.

Half an hour later, Chris stood in front of the bungalow, trying to balance a Styrofoam take-out box and a pot of coffee while opening the door. It took a precarious few seconds, but he managed. He set his burden down on the small table by the window, shut the door again and sat on the side of the bed.

Matt was still asleep, curled around Chris's pillow in the absence of the real thing. Chris leaned down and kissed Matt's sleep-flushed cheek. "Wake up, love."

Matt mumbled something about bananas and suntan oil and rolled onto his stomach. Chris stifled a laugh. He stroked a palm down Matt's bare back and over the curve of his ass. Matt, predictably, moaned in his sleep and spread his legs.

"Matt, darling," Chris said, smiling. "I've brought you breakfast, don't you want some?"

"Mmph." Matt pushed his backside up against Chris's hand. "Wadjaga?"

Chris laughed. "Excuse me?"

Yawning, Matt turned onto his back and cranked his eyelids to half-mast. "Said whatcha got?"

"Coffee, pineapple, scrambled eggs, bacon and fried breadfruit."

Matt giggled. "Breadfruit."

"I thought it was appropriate, considering."

"Mm-hm." Matt stretched luxuriously, then sat up. "Bring it here?"

"Certainly, my love."

Chris got up to fetch the Styrofoam tray with Matt's breakfast in it. He set it on Matt's lap, along with a napkin and a plastic fork, then went to get the coffeepot. Matt watched him as he retrieved a mug from the tiny kitchenette and poured a cup. After he'd placed Matt's coffee on the bedside table, Chris found himself wrapped in Matt's enthusiastic embrace, being kissed quite thoroughly. He sank into it with a happy sigh, hands mapping the familiar contours of Matt's body.

"Thank you," Matt whispered, stroking Chris's cheek.

"You're welcome." Chris kissed Matt's nose and pulled back to let him eat. "You know how I like to pamper you."

"It's not just the breakfast and stuff. It's everything you do for me, all the time." Matt's eyes shone with a tender light that warmed Chris right through. "You always take care of me, Chris. Always. Like last night. I don't think I'd want to be tied up with anybody else, but with you? I knew it would be amazing. I felt so safe, you know? Because I knew you'd take care of me. I knew you'd make sure that nothing we did hurt me."

"Matt, love." Chris took Matt's hand and kissed his knuckles. "You've given me everything I could possibly want, by consenting to share your life with me. I will never stop taking care of you."

"I know." Matt laid a warm hand on Chris's cheek, callused thumb caressing his jaw. His smile was bright and joyful. "We sound like one of those romance novels."

Chris laughed. "Maybe so. But I don't care. Every word of it is true." He kissed Matt one more time, then stood. "Finish your breakfast and we'll go to the beach."

"Cool." Matt reached for his coffee and took a sip. "Think I'll wear that harness again."

"Not a chance," Chris said serenely as he gathered towels and sunblock. "I'd like to be able to get out of my chair today, thank you."

"Oh, come on." Matt leered at Chris over his coffee cup. "I kinda like what it did to you yesterday."

Chris tried to give Matt a stern look. Matt widened his eyes and smiled that childlike smile of his that meant his thoughts were worlds away from anything remotely innocent. Chris sighed. "Very well. Wear your harness."

Matt cackled and settled back to finish his breakfast. "Hey, you never did use the whip last night."

The whip. Chris's groin twitched in spite of himself. "No, I didn't." Chris glanced at Matt, half afraid to see that wicked spark in his eyes. "Why? What are you thinking?"

"Thinking we could break that in tonight." Matt bit into a strip of bacon, chewed and swallowed. "Go back out to our tree, you know?"

The idea was hard to resist. Not that Chris put much effort into it. "All right," he said, snatching a piece of pineapple from Matt's tray. "Whatever shall we do back home without that tree?"

"Guess we'll just have to find other things to tie me to." Matt set the container of food on the bedside table, grabbed Chris's wrist and pulled him to the bed. "Let's fuck."

Chris laughed as Matt shoved him onto his back and straddled him. "What about your breakfast?"

"Sex first," Matt insisted, unbuttoning Chris's shirt. "Food later."

Try as he might, Chris couldn't find a thing wrong with Matt's plan. He slid a hand through Matt's hair. Matt bent to kiss him and the world went away for a while.

"Will you miss it?" Chris asked rather suddenly a few minutes later.

Matt, shuddering as he impaled himself on Chris's cock, gaped at him. "Huh?"

"The…oh *God* you're tight…the breadfruit…uh…tree?" Chris clamped his fingers onto Matt's waist, holding him in place astride Chris's hips. "I will. Miss it." He thrust hard, nailing Matt's gland and making him squeal. "The tree."

"Oh fuck," Matt whispered. "Harder, yeah. Uh. Tree? No."

"Why…" Chris slammed into Matt again, "not?"

"'Cause," Matt panted, "we don't…oh *fuck* right there, yeah…don't need it." He rocked his hips in a way that utterly destroyed Chris's power of speech. "Babe, please, shut up and fuck me."

Chris dug his heels into the mattress and did what Matt wanted, pounding up into him so hard the force of it nearly dislodged the iron grip of Matt's thighs. He didn't need to ask why Matt wouldn't miss their tree, because he thought he knew.

Matt was right. They didn't need the tree to make their time together special. Everywhere they went they took their own magic place with them, in their heads and hearts and their joined bodies. It was a marvelous feeling.

Coming deep inside Matt just as Matt shot all over his chest, Chris had a vision of their future together. Months and years and decades of a sweet passion that never dimmed.

Living each moment as if they were under the breadfruit tree. There might be better life philosophies, but Chris couldn't think of one.

Holding Matt close to his chest, Chris shut his eyes and smiled.

About the Author

Ally Blue used to be a good girl. Really. Married for twenty years, two lovely children, house, dogs, picket fence, the whole deal. Then one day she discovered slash fan fiction. She wrote her first fan fiction story a couple of months later and has since slid merrily into the abyss. She has had several short stories published in the erotic e-zine Ruthie's Club, and is a regular contributor to the original slash e-zine Forbidden Fruit.

To learn more about Ally Blue please visit http://www.allyblue.com. Send an email to Ally at ally@allyblue.com or join her Yahoo! group to join in the fun with other readers as well as Ally!

http://groups.yahoo.com/group/loveisblue/

When Sam Raintree goes to work for Bay City Paranormal Investigations, he expects his quiet life to change—but he doesn't expect to put his life and sanity on the line, or to fall for a man he can never have.

Oleander House

Book one in the Bay City Paranormal Investigation series

(c) 2006 Ally Blue

Available October 3, 2006 at Samhain Publishing.

Sam Raintree has never been normal. All his life, he's experienced things he can't explain. Things that have colored his view of the world and of himself. So taking a job as a paranormal investigator seems like a perfect fit. His new co-workers, he figures, don't have to know he's gay.

When Sam arrives at Oleander House, the site of his first assignment with Bay City Paranormal Investigations, nothing is what he expected. The repetitive yet exciting work, the unusual and violent history of the house, the intensely erotic and terrifying dreams which plague his sleep. But the most unexpected thing is Dr. Bo Broussard, the group's leader.

From the moment they meet, Sam is strongly attracted to his intelligent, alluring boss. It doesn't take Sam long to figure out that although Bo has led a heterosexual life, he is very much in the closet, and wants Sam as badly as Sam wants him.

As the investigation of Oleander House progresses and paranormal events in the house escalate, Sam and Bo circle warily around their mutual attraction, until a single night of bloodshed and revelation changes their lives forever.

Enjoy this excerpt from Oleander House:

One turkey-and-Swiss sandwich and a plate of pasta salad later, Sam and Bo gathered their equipment and headed out back to explore the old outdoor kitchen. The heat smacked Sam in the face like a damp, sticky hand the minute he left the relative coolness of the back porch. Insects droned in the pines that clustered behind the outbuildings.

"Jesus, David wasn't just kidding about it being hot out here." Sam squinted up at the deep blue sky. The sun's disc seemed to waver in the heat-shimmer. "Is it always like this down here?"

"In the summer? Pretty much, yeah." Bo gave him a sidelong smile. "The upside is that the winters are relatively mild most years."

"You mean there's no snow?"

"Rarely."

"Good. Fucking hate snow."

Bo gave him a startled look, then burst out laughing. Sam laughed too. It felt good. He had to remind himself that it didn't mean anything. Just two guys having a laugh.

The outdoor kitchen, a long, low brick building with massive chimneys on each end, was dim inside and wonderfully cool. Grimy windows broke the sunlight into a soft haze that failed to illuminate more than a few feet of the earth floor. Here and there, broken panes let in a single ray of fierce molten gold, all the brighter for the otherwise unrelieved gloom.

Sam switched on his flashlight and swept the beam around the room. Dust and cobwebs lay thick on every surface. In the far corner, something squeaked and scuttled across the floor.

"Mice," Bo said unnecessarily, as he turned the EMF detector on.

Switching the flashlight to his left hand, Sam thumbed on the video camera and started the tape rolling. "Why's it such a mess in here? Didn't Mr. Gentry open the outbuildings for tours?"

"No. He had plans to at some point, but as you can see, they'd need a lot of work before it would be safe to let the public in. He hadn't gotten that far yet when he had to close the house."

"Hm." Sam panned around the room, stopping when Bo's face came into frame. "What're you getting on the EMF?"

"It's a little lower than it is in the house. I've got one point two right now, pretty steady." Bo glanced at the thermometer he held in his other hand. "Temp's seventy-two degrees."

"And that's nice and cool compared to outside. Damn."

"Yep. It's probably pushing a hundred out there." Bo started walking slowly around the perimeter of the room, eyes fixed on the EMF detector. "Are you feeling anything, Sam?"

Nothing you want to know about. Sam licked his dry lips and tried not to stare at Bo's ass. "Not like last night. I assume that's what you meant."

Bo glanced at Sam, the corners of his mouth turning up in a slight smile. His dark eyes flicked down and back up, glittering in the gloom, and suddenly Sam couldn't breath. If he'd gotten that look in a bar, he'd have turned on the charm and bought the man a drink.

He squashed the bright flare of hope before it could burn out of control. *It's your imagination, idiot,* he scolded himself. *This isn't a pick-up joint, and Bo isn't gay.*

"Hm. That's odd."

Sam swallowed and forced himself to focus. Bo was turning in a small, slow circle, frowning at the EMF detector. "What's odd?"

For a moment, Bo didn't answer. Then he sighed and looked up. "The EMF spiked for just a second. But it's gone back down now. Did you get anything on the camera?"

"No. And before you ask, I didn't feel anything unusual either."

Bo grinned. "You're already reading my mind, Sam. That's scary."

Sam laughed. "I've been working on my psychic powers."

"Oh, really?" Bo took a step closer, smiling into the camera. "So what am I thinking now?"

Sam gulped, keeping the camera up to hide his reaction. If he didn't know better, he'd have sworn Bo was flirting with him. But that, he knew, was impossible. *Maybe that's just how he is with everyone,* Sam told himself. *You don't know him at all, really. Don't start reading into things.*

"Let's see," Sam said, lowering the camera and hoping Bo couldn't see him blushing in the dimness. "You're thinking that we should note exactly where the EMF spike occurred, and after we finish sweeping the room, we should see if we can make it spike again. Then, we should search this room and the surrounding area outside to see if there's anything electronic that could've caused it. That right?"

Bo smiled. "Close enough. Let's get to work."

Can two men from different worlds cut the ties binding them to heartaches past and present, and make a life together?

Willow Bend
(c) 2006 Ally Blue

Now available in both digital and paperback at Samhain Publishing.

For Paul Gordon, the little town of Willow Bend, South Carolina is the perfect place to start over. A place where he can move on after his lover's death, alone and anonymous.

Cory Saunders is just trying to survive. Between working two jobs and caring for his ailing mother, it's all he can do to keep his head above water.

When Paul and Cory meet, their mutual attraction is undeniable. When the intense physical attraction starts to blossom into something deeper, neither wants to admit to what's happening. Cory doesn't have time for a relationship, and Paul isn't sure he's ready for one. But sometimes, what you thought you couldn't have turns out to be exactly what you need.

Enjoy this excerpt from Willow Bend::

Paul drove all the way to Savannah to buy condoms. It made him cringe to think of the unspoken questions he'd have to face if he bought them at Willow Bend's only drug store. So now here he stood, in the bland brightness of a big chain pharmacy on the outskirts of Savannah, feeling a bit foolish as he stared at the bewildering variety available to him.

He hadn't bought them in years. He almost didn't think of it. Then an offhand remark on the radio made him remember the first time he and Jay made love, how the latex taste had made him gag, how Jay had laughed until tears streamed down his face. Paul stopped right in the middle of mopping the kitchen floor to go get the necessary supplies before Cory got there. Because he was determined to need them.

"Flavored. Definitely." He plucked a box of mint flavored.

The memory of Cory's erection against his brought a rush of heat to his face. He glanced around, mortified by the bulge forming in his jeans, but there was no one to see. One at a time in the condom section seemed to be an unwritten rule. He grabbed a bottle of lube and hurried to the checkout counter. The gum-snapping young clerk rang him up and bagged his purchases without batting an eye, but he was still relieved to reach the privacy of his truck.

He glanced at his watch. Eleven-thirty. More than three hours until Cory was supposed to arrive. Plenty of time to finish the little bit of cleaning he had left and take a shower. He hummed along with the radio as he drove, pleased with himself for handling this so well. It wasn't until he'd parked the truck in the barn and headed back to the house that the reality of it hit him.

He was about to have his first date in over seven years, with someone other than Jay. And this date would most likely end in the bedroom.

He sat down in the middle of the kitchen floor, shaking. Squeezing his eyes shut, he tried desperately to summon Jay in his mind. He could still see Jay's smile clear as anything, could remember how he'd taken his coffee, all his little habits. But he couldn't quite recall Jay's taste, his scent, the feel of his skin, the sound of his laughter. Jay was fading from him, becoming a memory lovingly kept, but no longer sharp and immediate. The thought terrified him.

No use dwelling, Pauly, Jay's ghost admonished him, cheerful as ever. *Gotta move on. A life spent moping is no sort of life at all.*

Paul smiled, tears leaking down his cheeks. "Right, as usual, Jay-Jay."

He sat there and cried for a little while, letting himself feel the grief of losing Jay, mixed with the terror and excitement of starting something new. Crying felt good. Cleansing. When the tears trickled to a halt, Paul felt stronger. He pushed himself up off the floor and went to get ready for Cory.

• • •

The rattle of bicycle wheels on gravel announced Cory's arrival a few minutes before three. Paul took a deep breath, smoothed his shirt, and walked out on the porch to greet him.

"Hi!" Cory swung himself gracefully off the bike before it had stopped and leaned it against the porch steps. His green gaze raked appreciatively down Paul's body. "You look hot."

Paul smiled. "Thanks. So do you." *That must be the understatement of the century.* Cory looked absolutely gorgeous in a tight white T-shirt and dark green cargo shorts that matched his eyes. His cheeks were flushed and his chestnut curls wildly windblown from the ride over.

Cory bounded up the steps. Paul had a moment of panic, wondering if it were okay to kiss him. He didn't have long to wonder. Cory walked up to him, buried both hands in his hair and pressed their mouths together. Paul sank right into it, pulling Cory close, running both palms over the curves of his ass as they kissed.

"Mm. Hi." Paul nipped Cory's bottom lip, smiling.

"Hi." Cory pressed even closer, kissed Paul's neck. "I've been looking forward to this all week."

"Me too. Come on inside." Paul pulled back, took both Cory's hands in his and tugged him toward the door.

They walked inside hand in hand. Cory grinned, eyes sparkling. "You know, last time I was in here I was ten. I was over here playing with the Thompsons' granddaughter, Jenny. Mrs. Thompson chased us out after we made worm soup in the kitchen."

Paul laughed. "I don't blame her. Worm soup?"

"We didn't eat it."

"You just used her good pots to make it in, huh?"

"Kind of." Cory squeezed Paul's hand. "How about giving me the tour? Just to refresh my memory."

"Sure." Paul swept his free hand in a wide arc. "This is the living room."

"Lovely."

"Thank you. And this," he continued as they strolled down the hallway, "is the hall."

"So it is."

"And here we have the kitchen."

"Very nice." Cory gave him a wicked smile. "No worm soup?"

"Fresh out, sorry." Paul pulled Cory into his arms, unable to resist. "Only two rooms left."

"Yeah." Cory molded himself to Paul's body, soft lips brushing his. "Let's skip the bathroom, huh?"

Paul swallowed. "Oh. Well, that only leaves—"

"I know," Cory interrupted. He ran his tongue slowly over Paul's lips. "Take me to bed, Paul."

Paul's breath caught. "Yes."

He led Cory into the bedroom. His heart thudded painfully against his ribcage and his hands shook. He glanced at the dresser, and his stomach dropped into his feet when he realized he'd forgotten to remove Jay's picture.

"Paul?" Cory laid both hands on Paul's cheeks. "Are you okay?"

"Yeah, I'll be fine." Paul managed a weak smile. "Sorry, it's just…it's been a while."

"Hey, it's okay if you don't want to."

"No, I do. I do. It's just…" Paul stopped, not knowing how to explain.

Cory followed Paul's gaze. He went still when he saw Jay's picture, then turned back to Paul, hurt stamped all over his face.

"Paul, who's he? Are you with somebody?"

Paul sighed. "Not anymore. Jay died over a year ago."

Cory's eyes went wide. "In that wreck."

"Yeah."

"God, Paul. I'm so sorry." Cory stroked his cheek. "Hey, why don't we head on over to the picnic, huh?"

"Probably should." Paul leaned his forehead against Cory's, fingers raking through the tangled curls. "Please tell me I haven't fucked this up already."

"Not hardly. We're coming back here to watch the fireworks, remember?" Cory pulled Paul's face to his and gave him a long, deep kiss. "I'm gonna get you in the sack before the night's out."

"Yeah," Paul whispered, lips brushing Cory's. "I think you will."

Samhain Publishing, Ltd.

It's all about the story…

Action/Adventure
Fantasy
Historical
Horror
Mainstream
Mystery/Suspense
Non-Fiction
Paranormal
Red Hots!
Romance
Science Fiction
Western
Young Adult

http://www.samhainpublishing.com

Printed in the United States
111552LV00013B/52/A